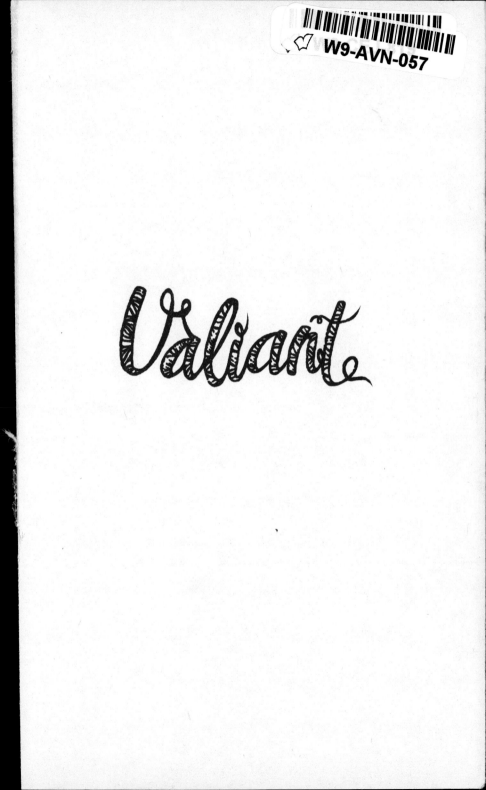

Valiant

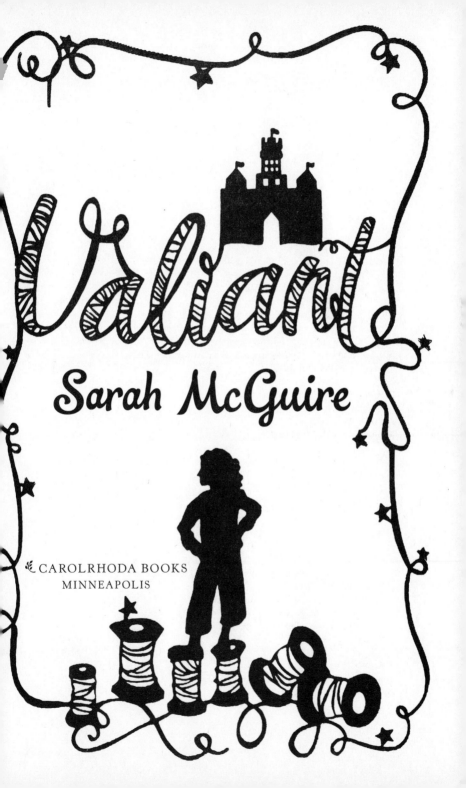

Valiant

Sarah McGuire

❧ CAROLRHODA BOOKS

MINNEAPOLIS

First published by Egmont Publishing in 2015

Carolrhoda Books
A division of Lerner Publishing Group, Inc.
241 First Avenue North
Minneapolis, MN 55401 USA

For reading levels and more information, look up this title at www.lernerbooks.com.

Library of Congress Cataloging-in-Publication Data

McGuire, Sarah
      Valiant / by Sarah McGuire.
            pages cm
      Summary: A reimagined "Brave Little Tailor" about a clever young girl
   who saves her kingdom
      ISBN 978-1-60684-552-3 (hardcover)
      ISBN 978-1-60684-553-0 (ebook)
      [1. Fairy tales. 2. Tailors—Fiction.] I. Title.
   PZ8.M17625Val 2015
   [Fic]—dc23   2014034325

Manufactured in the United States of America
2-46099-20842-5/29/2018

For Mom and Dad,
two of the bravest people I know

Valiant

Chapter 1

The city lay against the far horizon, dark as a lump of coal in the morning light.

I wanted nothing more than to turn around, right there in the middle of the road, with frost-twisted fields stretching away in every direction. If I had my way, I would have left Father and the merchant caravan taking us to Reggen.

I would have walked the full month back to Danavir. I'd go back to Mama's grave and sit beside it. I'd tell her that Father had found a city without a tailors' guild and that he could sew any way he wished—and that I'd never sew for him again. And then I'd sing to her: silly ditties or the lullabies she'd taught me.

It was only right. She'd sung me to sleep as a child.

But I kept walking toward Reggen, while the wagons, all seventeen of them, groaned and creaked as if they were men too old to be out in the morning frost.

When Father joined me, he didn't say anything; just nodded toward the city. I was glad for his silence. I'd heard his complaints, like a chorus, every day of this trip. Even the sight of Reggen hadn't cheered him. I'd only walked the stiffness out of my legs when he began:

"It's a new beginning, Saville. You'll see. *They* will see," he said, the bitterness in his voice sharp as shears. "How dare they tell me that I have to sew their way, or not at all? I'll make a name for myself in Reggen. I'll sew for the king himself!" Father laid his hand against the wagon, the one that held his bolts of cloth. He would have stroked the wood but for the splinters.

"I'd have liked to sew for his brother, Torren. He wouldn't have needed me to sew him clothes that gave him a figure worthy of the throne!" Father rubbed his hands together. "But I like a challenge. And Reggen's new runt of a king . . . *He* will be a challenge. They say even his sister, the princess, would make a better king."

I looked down, concentrating on the sounds of the wagon—one wheel groaning with every revolution—a creaking, wooden pulse. Even so, Father's voice rose above it.

I had sewn for Father after his apprentices left him, sewn late into the night so that he would fulfill his orders. I had watched my betrothed walk away because he wouldn't ally himself with a tailor who defied the guild. I had been dragged to Reggen, a city free of guilds.

But I would not listen to Father this entire trip.

When he paused to draw breath, I began to sing. It was an old traveling song, the kind that has more verses than a rich widow has suitors. Before Father could complain, the merchants near me picked up the song. Our voices rolled out into the silent fields around us. I pulled the sharp morning air deep inside me and sang till my blood danced to the rhythm; till my throat grew hoarse; till Father walked away.

After two hours, Reggen grew larger, its walls distinct. The sight wore against me, like a stone in my boot. We were traveling through tilled fields, dark and stubbly, with black, frostbitten stalks. A half mile ahead, a road joined ours, and another merchant caravan with it. Gregor, our caravan's leader, called out, and one of their dark, cloaked figures called back. They were friends, then.

I jumped when Father appeared and fiercely gripped my elbow. "Don't tell them, Saville," he hissed. "Don't breathe a word of it, you hear me?"

I yanked my arm away from him. "Tell them what?"

"Tell them about . . ." His eyes flicked to the wagon.

The fabric. The silks and brocades in colors so rich and rare that Father could name any price for them. I couldn't look at the bolts without remembering how Father had set himself against the guild and lost everything in his fight. Even when the fabric was all we had left, when we were preparing to join the caravan, he refused to sell even a few yards to buy extra food. He'd guarded it during the journey, convinced our fellow travelers would steal it if they could. Never mind that they were wealthy merchants in their own right.

I'd heard of farmers who burned old fields to prepare for

the new planting. These bolts of fabric were Father's seeds for the future—and he had burned our life in Danavir to make way for them.

"I won't tell them, Father." It was an easy promise to make. I didn't think his cloth was worth homespun compared to what I had packed beside it.

And then the other caravan was upon us. I listened to the snatches of news, the stories they told of thieves and favorite inns, and when they thought the mountain passes would be free of snow.

I walked behind two men from the new group. They were young, a few years older than me. Amid the shouting, they almost whispered.

"Soren says two villages were wiped away," said one. His coat was of finespun wool—dark gray—and cut to fit him. His tailor was a good one. I noticed the grim set of the man's mouth when he turned to speak to his companion.

"It was just a raiding party," replied the other, whose clothes were more weather-beaten. He smiled indulgently, as if used to humoring his friend.

"Not the usual type," said Fine Coat. "Soren said trees were torn out of the ground, the homesteads trampled, all live-stock gone."

"As I said—a raiding party."

"With houses crushed as though they'd been stepped on? With human bones scattered among the wreckage?"

Smiling One laughed at his friend. "You're exaggerating

again. Houses can't be stepped on! And wild animals scaveng-ing after the raiding party would explain the bones."

"Soren says the bones were cooked."

"Charred?"

"I mean cooked. They were boiled."

A prickle of fear rose up my back and I put a hand on the jolting wagon beside me. I'd heard my share of tales over the past month—stories meant to coax a shudder from an eager audience. But Fine Coat didn't look as if he enjoyed his tale. His distaste made the story seem as real as the road we traveled.

I didn't want to hear any more. But before I could walk away, something seized my hand, tugging me to the wagon.

Too frightened to shriek, I looked down.

Sky above. A man lay inside the wagon on a bed of straw. Cuts covered his face, and he wore terror like a mask. His grip on my hand grew tighter.

"I knew it was you," he whispered.

Who did he think I was?

I glanced at Fine Coat and his smiling friend a few paces ahead. They hadn't heard anything over the creaking of the wagon.

"They didn't hurt you?" he asked. He was such a young man—and his fear made him look even younger. "I saw it pick you up, just like you were a doll and . . . and . . . how would I tell Ma? I promised to keep you safe. I'm sorry. So sorry."

I longed to pull away but he reminded me so much of Mama in those last days.

"I'm—" I licked my lips, not sure what to say. Then I did what I'd done with Mama—I told him what he needed to hear. "I'm safe, I promise. You don't have to tell Ma anything."

He stared away over my shoulder, watching things I couldn't see. "Didn't think there were monsters like that, didn't believe. . . . I'd have taken us away—"

"Shhhhh." I put my free hand over his. "There aren't any monsters. We're safe."

But he didn't hear me. "We weren't cowards! We tried to stop the man, the one man. But . . . swords didn't do anything. That's why I rode for help. I didn't want to leave you!"

"What are you *doing*?" demanded Fine Coat. When had he come so close?

I'd have stepped back if the young man in the wagon hadn't clutched my hand so tightly. "He took my hand," I whispered. "He thinks I'm his sister."

Fine Coat peered down at the man, who'd closed his eyes. His grip on my hand loosened and his arm fell limp by his side.

"He spoke to you?" asked Fine Coat. Oh, he was angry.

I didn't care. "Yes. If you can call it that."

"What did he say?"

I raised my eyebrows. How did this man manage to make a simple request sound so rude?

Smiling One put a hand on his friend's shoulder. "You'll pardon Galen, miss. This man has barely spoken the entire journey. We don't even know his name. It's important you tell us what he said."

I reached into the wagon and pulled a bit of blanket up to cover the man's arm. The morning was still cold. "He said he was sorry. That he was glad to see me again after the"—I hesitated, not wanting to use the word—"*monsters* had found me."

Fine Coat glanced at his friend. "What else? Was there more?"

"He said they'd tried to stop someone but failed, so he'd ridden to find help. That's all." I shook my head. "It must have been a brutal raiding party."

Smiling One couldn't hide his surprise. "You heard us?"

I nodded.

Fine Coat studied me, eyes dark with concern. It wasn't concern for me. "You shouldn't have bothered him," he said. "And you shouldn't have been eavesdropping."

I crossed my arms. "You shouldn't have been talking so loud I could hear you."

Smiling One laughed. His friend glared at him, opened his mouth as if to speak, then clamped it shut.

"Don't worry," I said. "I won't repeat your story."

Why would I? The thought of boiled bones itched inside me. I wished the wind gusting over the fields could reach into me and sweep it away.

Fine Coat glanced at the man in the wagon, who was now sleeping.

"Tell me if he speaks again," he told Smiling One. Then he walked ahead, toward Father and our wagon, with only a backward glance.

Good. I wanted him and his stories as far away from me as possible.

Smiling One fell into step beside me. "I am Lynden. And you are . . . ?"

"I am Saville Gramton," I said, glad for his company after the sick man's fears and Fine Coat's rudeness. "My father and I are traveling to Reggen."

He nodded to Father who walked farther ahead. "Is he a merchant?"

"No," I said. "A tailor."

Lynden raised his brows in surprise. "A tailor! He doesn't look like any tailor I know. Still, it's a pleasure to meet his lovely daughter."

It was my turn to be surprised. I had Father's square jaw, and though I sometimes thought my eyes were pretty, my lashes and brows were as wheat colored as my hair. They made my face look pale all over. And I was covered in grime after four weeks of walking.

"Tell me," I said, "how long have you been traveling?"

"Over a month. Galen left Reggen to visit villages near the Steeps, and I have been his guide. Why do you ask?"

"You'd have to be on the road at least two months to give a compliment like that and *mean* it."

He smiled, dimples showing. "I still say you're lovely."

"Then you're too easily pleased." I glanced at the man sleeping in the wagon beside us. "Or trying to distract me."

"Perhaps I want you to distract *me*. It hasn't been a cheerful trip." Lynden smiled again. "But I will not try to compliment you again. What should we talk of?"

"Tell me about Reggen," I said, looking ahead. "Tell me about the Guardians."

"You know about the Guardians?"

I gestured at the caravan. "I've traveled with these men for a month. How could I not know about the Guardians? They're the only part of Reggen I want to see."

Reggen, I'd been told, was built between towering cliffs and a curve in the Kriva River. The Guardians were two great reliefs carved into the cliffs, one on either side of the city.

Lynden peered ahead. "You'll see them soon, when the sun shines on the cliffs. Believe me, a hundred merchants could tell you of the great Guardians, but the first time you see them . . ." He shook his head. "They're old, old as the city's foundation stones. Some say giants cut and laid the foundation as a gift to Reggen's first king, then carved themselves into the cliff behind the city as a reminder of their service—and of their existence." He grinned, as if daring me to be scared.

I raised an eyebrow. There were things that could scare me, but storybook monsters were not among them. "*I* heard that the architect who raised the city walls carved the Guardians. He was a humble man, I'm sure, to carve himself twice, each image as tall as fifty men."

"The Guardians only stand as tall as forty men," corrected Lynden. "So perhaps the architect was not so arrogant."

He laughed and I laughed, and the tightness in my shoulders eased.

Father turned to glare at us.

"I've angered your father," said Lynden.

"It doesn't take much. Talking with me would be enough."

"I've been watching him. All the tailors I know are skinny, hollow-chested men—nothing like your father. He reminds me of a badger I met when I was a child." Lynden laughed. "I think he'd hit someone; I really do."

Lynden was right. Once, when Father returned from a meeting with the guild, I'd told him I didn't care about coats that made a man look like more than a man. Or whether he found an indigo velvet for a customer. He'd struck me with a half-closed fist. He'd wanted it to hurt. I'd flinched—I couldn't help it—but I didn't duck away and I didn't cry out. To my delight, Father bruised one of his fingers and couldn't hold a needle properly for a week.

He never touched me again, and I never mentioned tailoring or the guild.

A year had passed and I still remembered the way my vision had danced. But I laughed as hard as Lynden at his description of my badger father. I made sure of it.

I was laughing still when the wagon wheel broke.

It sounded like a crack of lightning. The wagon lurched forward and then rocked back as the wheel near Father collapsed. He stumbled and I knew he'd be pinned beneath it. Before I could shout a warning, I saw a flash of movement:

Fine Coat yanked Father away just as the corner of the wagon dropped to the ground. Trunks tumbled out, end over end.

It didn't seem real: everything too fast and too slow at the same time. But I felt the impact of the trunks falling. They beat the ground like a drum.

The horse reared up, straining in its harness, scattering more trunks behind it—Father's trunks. Several broke open, spilling their contents along the trail.

There was a sound like broken bells and a shower of silver notes.

I barely heard Father's cries over my own. I gathered my skirts and ran past Father, who lay where Fine Coat had pulled him, stopping only when I saw some of the fabric buried under a trunk.

I rolled the trunk away, barely feeling its weight. Canvas-covered bolts lay beneath; one was partially open, revealing a glimpse of crimson in the debris. I threw it over my shoulder, ignoring Father's shout of protest. Two more bolts followed, along with several books and a wooden box of Father's supplies.

And then I found what I searched for—the pieces of it—under the last bolt.

Mama's music box lay shattered, its tin heart spilled out beside it. The thin bands of metal that had sung the simple notes were crimped and bent at odd angles.

"No . . ." I breathed out and in, out and in, my chest tight with the pain of it.

"Let me get the cloth, Saville!" The fury in Father's voice didn't scare me. He grabbed my shoulder, trying to pull me away from the wreckage.

I shook him off and tried to pick up the pieces of the music box, but my fingers trembled too much.

Father's grip on my shoulder tightened painfully. "Out of my way, girl!"

I wrenched free and stood so quickly it startled him. I was nearly as tall as he was, and he hated that I could look into his eyes. It was only Father and me for a moment, as the merchants surrounding us faded away.

My own anger rose up to meet his, not a bit softened by the small trickle of blood down his temple. When he tried to reach around me, I stepped to block him. He could forget his precious fabric just once.

"Let me past, Saville!"

"No." I shook my head, glad for the strength my anger gave me. "Not until I pick up Mama's music box."

I held his gaze for one more heartbeat. Then, before he could decide whether to slap me in front of the crowd, I knelt and gathered the pieces of Mama's last song. When I was finished, I stood a moment longer between Father and his fabric.

He hated even that delay.

Then I walked away from the wreck, the fragments of the music box cradled in my skirts. Father shouted orders about his fabric and the men around him sprang into action to salvage what they could.

I moved through them like a ghost, unnoticed by all but one.

Luca limped up, favoring his bad hip, and handed me a small burlap bag. He tended the caravan's fires and drove the wagon that carried the food. He'd tended to me, in his own way, the entire journey.

I transferred the pieces to the bag and tied it shut, trying not to think that I'd lost the music box and Mama's song. And I was going to lose Luca, too.

"I'm going to miss your stories," I said, rubbing my thumb over the burlap's roughness. It was the closest I could come to saying I'd miss him.

"It looked like that young merchant was telling you a fine story," said Luca.

I followed his gaze. The other caravan was already traveling on toward Reggen, taking with it Lynden and Fine Coat and the poor young man who'd whispered of monsters.

I sighed. It had been fun to laugh with Lynden.

"Don't make me tell you about the time the caravan was caught in an early snow and I spent two weeks peeling boards off the sides of wagons to cook and feed the men," warned Luca.

I turned to him, knowing he was gathering one last story for me.

He grinned. "They never knew the difference. Thought it was nothing more than tough travel bread."

"I don't believe it," I said. I could feel the sadness build at the base of my throat, grief for the music box and myself, and for never hearing another of Luca's stories. But I spoke as brightly as I could. "Even if your cooking *is* close to boards."

"The tale is true!" Luca whipped his woolen hat over his heart. "I swear it."

He told me the story as men collected the scattered cargo and loaded it onto other wagons. He was telling it still when the caravan moved forward once more. He even bribed a young merchant to drive the food wagon so he could walk with me.

"I'm tired of the wagon rattling my bones," he said with a wink.

Luca walked on with me, even when he'd finished the story. He didn't say anything else, and I couldn't. But I was glad to have him beside me, a Guardian of my own.

After a while, he prodded me. "Look, child."

We had crested the last low bluff before the Kriva River. A bridge as long as two fields arched across it to Reggen, which was tucked between the river and the cliffs that rose behind it. I understood why tales claimed giants had cut and laid the city's foundation stones. They were each broader than a man could reach with his arms spread wide, and they felt old, older than bones. Reggen's brick walls looked young by comparison, great-great-grandchildren of the foundation they were built upon.

And then there were the Guardians: two men, their bodies blurred by time, carved into the cliffs on either side of the walls, their feet near the Kriva, their shoulders rising above Reggen's walls.

"It's a sight, to be sure," said Luca. "Those two standing in the cliff."

"I like them," I said. "They remind me of kings."

"Or giants?" he teased.

I rolled my eyes. "Yes, giants. I've seen so many, you know."

"I think I saw one when I was younger," said Luca.

"You can't mean that!" I turned to him, as surprised as if he'd claimed to ride dragons.

He shrugged his crooked shoulders. "He was a great big man, that's all I know—half again as tall as most—with a forehead like a cliff and a nose like a bag of rocks. That's how I know those two aren't giants, like some claim. They're too pretty, too human. A giant would be more lumpy."

I laughed, glad for a chance to crawl out of the ugliness of the day. "Lumpy?"

"Lumpy. Do you think a giant would have fingers that could sew so well as your father?" Luca must have seen the anger in my eyes, for he plunged ahead. "Or a nose as straight and fine as that young merchant's you were talking with?"

Then I saw the clusters of bare trees along the Kriva's banks. They had sturdy enough trunks, but I'd never seen such branches: masses of slender limbs that hung like curtains or hair. Some nearly brushed the river. What would they look like in the spring, covered with leaves?

I pointed. "What kind of trees are those?" I thought I knew, but I needed to be sure.

Luca turned to see. "Willows. They're common enough. Love the water. Why do you ask?"

I shook my head.

But I couldn't look away.

Mama had named me after a place a traveler had spoken of. Saville was a tiny village, but the traveler had described it so well that Mama'd ached to see it. She'd named me after the village with the willows.

Now, at seventeen, I saw willows for the first time. For a few long breaths, they were all I could see.

Then I glanced over my shoulder. Father was arguing with the merchants about the cost of delivering us and our goods to an inn.

I scampered toward the bank, the bag gripped in my hand. A moment later, I slipped past the curtain of branches that bent close to the ground. I heard a few notes, I swear I did, as if the wind plucked the willow branches like harp strings.

Father would remember the music box soon, and he'd want it, and then we would fight because I'd never give it to him. Or he would look for it when I was away, and I'd return to discover the pieces were gone.

Better that they stay here. I looked around to mark the spot: three willows over from a tumble of boulders. Then I knelt at the base of the tree and began to scrape at the soil. Within a minute, I had a deep enough hole. I gently laid the bag in the ground and patted the soil over it, glad I'd found a home for Mama's song.

I looked at Reggen standing between its two great Guardians, then back at Father, already shouting with the merchants.
Even here, with no guild to crowd him, he had to fight. It would
be like Danavir all over again—the disputes with other tailors,
the arguments at night, sewing for him because no apprentice
dared risk his fury. I couldn't live like that again.

I wouldn't.

I wouldn't stay with Father for a moment longer than I had
to. I'd make a home for myself, somehow, even if I had to carve
it out of the cliffs.

Chapter 2

"Here it is," said Father.

We stood in a narrow street, looking at our new shop—a modest storefront with a green door and windows that faced the street. All of Reggen was made of stone, as though the city itself had sprung whole from the cliffs behind it. This shop, slumping between its neighbors, was no different, its building stones cracked from supporting its weight for so long.

I'd never missed the thatched roofs of Danavir more.

Father had brought his old shop sign all the way from Danavir. He plucked it from the hired wagon and hung it above a small, rust-colored door in the same building: *Tailor.*

Just *Tailor,* the way others would say *King.*

Then he unlocked the narrow door—*not* the green one—and tugged it open. All I saw was a flight of stairs more narrow than the door itself.

Sky above. He'd bought us a garret shop. We'd freeze in the winter and bake in the summer.

"What do you think, Saville?" He turned with a flourish, as if he'd opened the door to a castle.

I just stared, the early spring sunlight barely warming my back. I couldn't answer. Then I rushed past him and plunged up into the gloom. The stairs were steep and uneven, and I stumbled twice as I climbed.

When I reached the top, my breath puffed out before me. The garret was dark. One large window let in a pool of light that didn't dare spread beyond my place at the top of the stairs. There weren't rooms, just rope strung between hooks in the wall and a pillar to curtain off a sleeping area.

This was my new home. I'd have cried, but I was too angry for tears.

For the next hour, servants wrestled beds, cutting tables, and trunks up the stairs, while Father shouted instructions.

But it was Father's silence, after the servants left, that scared me. He stood in the middle of the dirty room, his hands pressed against his head.

"Father?"

He didn't respond.

"Did you hurt yourself yesterday when you—"

He jerked his head to look at me. "See to the fabric trunk, Saville!"

I didn't move.

"Now!" he barked.

I shoved the trunk against the far wall, scraping it across the floor's rough planks.

"Careful, Saville!"

"The fabric is *in* the trunk!" I shouted. "Pushing it across the floor won't hurt your precious cloth."

 19

Father took a step toward me. "I told you—!"

The words slurred in his mouth and he stumbled. Something was wrong—horribly wrong. A great length of fear unfurled inside me.

Father slapped his fingers over his mouth, as if he could force it to work. When he looked up at me, I saw fear in his eyes, too. He tried to speak as I helped him to his narrow bed. Halves of words tumbled out of a mouth he couldn't control.

"Father, I'm going for a physician, do you hear me? I'm going to get help."

My terror made the next hour seem like two lifetimes. It felt like months to find the physician, years to convince him to follow me.

I didn't think Father would be alive when I returned.

I dragged the doctor to Father's bed. "Do something!"

The doctor held a candle close to Father's face, pushing back his eyelids as if he could somehow look into his head, then moved the candle back and forth, ordering Father to watch it.

He couldn't.

I saw no sign of the man I'd known. Father just lay there. I didn't even know if he could see us.

"Apoplexy," murmured the doctor.

"What?" I asked.

The doctor waved his hand dismissively. "Apoplexy, the paralysis that comes when someone has been struck by God."

"Struck by God . . . ?"

"What else could the old doctors call it? It's an imbalance

of bodily humors. Bile builds up in the body, pressing against the brain. Finally, it causes great damage. A victim loses his speech, the ability to move, even."

I looked down at Father, his eyes wide and unblinking.

"But what do we *do*?" I asked.

He shrugged. "Some doctors drill into the head to relieve the pressure. Blood follows the bile, you see, and when the blood is allowed to drain away, the patient sometimes improves."

I nearly gagged. "Who would even try something so awful?"

"Katar has done great work with prisoners in Yullan, though fewer than half survived the procedure."

"Fewer than half survived having someone drill into their skulls? I wonder why."

For the first time, the doctor noticed that I was not pleased with him. His eyes narrowed as he looked around the room. "It's a good thing this happened to a tailor—"

"*The* tailor," I corrected, thinking of Father's sign.

"You'll need fabric, lots of it," the doctor said. "You'll have to diaper him like a child."

He seemed to take some satisfaction from my horror.

"You don't want this bed ruined, do you? Change him often, girl, or it will create sores."

"I'll take care of him," I said. The doctor wouldn't see me cringe again. "Then what?"

He glared at me, disappointed by my reaction. "He either dies, or he recovers."

"Recovers? How long will that take?"

Another shrug. "He may be able to speak again. He may be able to walk. Or he may just stay there, in the bed."

I looked down at Father. *Time to recover or to die . . .*

Later that night, I knelt beside Father, watching him. He hadn't moved in the hours since the doctor left. I'd never seen him so still in all my life.

Even then I couldn't feel sorry for him. I couldn't feel anything.

I rubbed my eyes with the heels of my hands, as if that would blot out Father lying as still as a corpse on his bed and this awful garret—the room I'd planned to escape.

There'd be no leaving now.

After a long while, I looked up and knotted my hands to stop the shaking. I felt tears but blinked them back. With a deep breath, I stood, barely certain that I could, and took stock of the room: trunks scattered, tables clustered in the middle of the room.

It was time to set up shop.

Chapter 3

A week after Father fell ill, I sat in front of the big window, our last few coins in the palm of my hand. Soon we would be out of money. Father lay in bed, rigid even in his sleep, his hands curled into claws. He'd clung to life with badgerlike tenacity, but he would not sew for a long time.

I dropped the coins into my lap and rubbed my eyes. I might be able to sell the fabric, but I doubted I could get a fair price for it. And how could Father sew once he recovered if he had no fabric left? In Danavir, I could have found work with a friend. If Father had secured even one commission here before his apoplexy, I could have finished it.

I pushed the coins in my lap around with a fingertip. Then I stopped, my finger on a small silver coin.

What if I secured a commission for the tailor of Reggen and then sewed it myself? I held the idea, felt the weight of it.

A girl couldn't gain a commission. She wouldn't be allowed to measure a man, let alone be trusted to sew for him. I scooped the coins up from my lap and poured them into Father's money purse. They made precious little clatter—there was more purse than coin.

I could dress as a boy, as Father's apprentice.

I sat perfectly still. I didn't even pull the drawstring of the purse closed.

I could sew, I knew, but to make myself into a young man? I was tall enough. My face wasn't very feminine—I could thank Father's jaw for that. I didn't have to be a knight. Just a tailor.

Ridiculous. I closed the purse and almost put it away. Almost.

I opened the purse again and shook the coins back into my hand. *Look at them. You have money for two weeks. You don't have the luxury to sit and hope something will happen.*

I closed my hand over the coins and walked to the cutting tables to examine Father's equipment: the shears, his box of pins and needles—long pins for thick fabrics, needles as fine as hair for sewing silks. I knew how to use each and every one.

I set the coins on the table. Then I opened Father's trunk and pulled back the canvas cover of the first bolt—a deep plum velvet. I made myself touch it, palm flat against the cloth.

So much would change if I dressed as Father's apprentice. I'd have to tell our landlord that Saville had gone to visit family elsewhere. And if Father never recovered, I'd be trapped.

But he would. He must. In the meantime, we had to eat.

I moved to the trunk in which Father kept his already-sewn garments. They weren't fine, but they were useful when a client needed something quickly. I picked up a shirt and held it in front of me. It would do. I spread it out on one of Father's empty tables, and studied it the way a knight would survey an opponent, my finger twirling in my hair. *My hair!*

I reached for the shears.

When Father woke the next morning, he saw his new apprentice. He didn't recognize me at first, his eyes wide in alarm.

"Father, it's me." I stepped toward him. "I'm going to find work for us—for me—until you can sew again."

He examined me like a suit he'd crafted, as if looking for stray threads or crooked seams. But I was prepared for his scrutiny.

I'd wrapped a length of muslin around my chest as tightly as I could. I'd cut my hair to shoulder length and tied it back at the nape of my neck. I kept one lock and hid it in the bottom of one of the trunks. Mama liked my hair. Foolish as it seemed, I couldn't bring myself to burn all of it. But of all the changes, it was the cravat that I hated the most. The length of silk tied around my neck felt like a hand squeezing my throat.

Father's eyes slid over my hair, the cravat, the shirt and breeches that hung on a boyish frame . . . and he nodded.

It wasn't love. It wasn't even kindness. But it was the closest he'd come to approval in years.

For the rest of that day, I wore the garments so I'd grow used to them. But the clothing was nothing compared to walking like a lad.

I couldn't do it. And I couldn't afford scrutiny the next day when I would go to the castle. The castle. I'd decided it would be easier to gain an audience with the king while he held court than to secure an appointment with a noble family.

But every time I moved like a girl, I imagined being discovered. I saw the suspicion on the king's face, heard him shout to the guards. . . .

I could barely keep the fear at bay.

I was practicing my walk that night when I noticed Father. He was beside himself with fury and flicked a finger with all the emphasis of waving his arm. He wanted me to try again.

I gritted my teeth. I hated obeying him, but I hated the thought of failure more.

So I walked the length of the room, then looked at Father. He blinked his eyes twice: *no*. The finger flicked. I walked again . . . and again.

Each time was better—my anger gradually pushed the fear aside. But it wasn't good enough for Father.

Finally, after an hour, he raised his eyebrows as if my performance would have to do.

Somehow, that was worse.

"I am all that stands between us and starvation!" I seethed. "Would it be so terrible to give me a *thimbleful* of encouragement?"

Father's gaze snapped to me, bright and burning, and he shook his head. *No*.

"Just you watch." I clenched my fists. "I'll gain a commission from the king himself. Your daughter can manage that much."

The words were more breath than bravery, but I needed to hear myself say them. I needed to think I could be as badger-like as Father.

Father would have none of it. ". . . entiss," he whispered, ". . . entiss."

"What?" I asked.

". . . entiss!" he hissed.

Apprentice.

I wasn't his daughter. I was his apprentice. For a moment, I couldn't move. Then I pulled in one breath. And another.

So be it.

"I think . . ." My throat was so pinched that my words cracked. "I think since I can't afford to make a mistake, I should call you Tailor. Always. It will be easier that way."

He blinked. *Yes.*

"Good night to you, then, Tailor."

I would never call him Father again.

Chapter 4

I left the shop the next morning with a satchel full of swatches and string for measuring the king. The king! Anything would be possible if I earned a commission from him. Father would see.

And if I failed? If I was discovered?

I tried not to think about it, but tasted fear like metal in my mouth as I walked uphill to the castle. The streets passed in a smear of stone doorways and windows—everything in this awful city was stone.

Finally, I stopped at the palace's gate, high above the rest of Reggen. The cliffs behind the castle filled my vision, broad as the sky. And the Guardians? They filled the cliffs on either side of the castle, their stone eyes looking out to the east and west as if watching for invaders.

They were the one bit of stone that I didn't mind. Looking up at them was like watching a storm gather itself and roll toward me. I'd never felt tinier, but I didn't mind so long as I could keep looking.

I pulled the satchel close and walked through the gate into the castle courtyard. It was a hive of activity, with rivers of people flowing to and from their work. I watched until it became familiar to me. Only nobles came and went through a door protected by two of the castle guard.

How could a tailor's apprentice reach the king?

Then a workman gave a package to a noble, who carried it through the guarded door.

That's what I should do.

But who would carry my gift? A lady might notice the girl beneath the apprentice's clothes. But the nobleman with the purple coat and lace cuffs? He'd only see the value of a good velvet.

I approached him and bowed. "Please, kind sir. Will you take a tribute to the king for me?"

He sniffed as if he'd smelled something rotten and walked away.

I scurried after him. "He'll reward you! It's a gift finer than anything he has seen."

The nobleman stopped. "Why don't you take the tribute yourself?"

Stupid, stupid! I'd been too eager. I drew myself up. "My master, the Tailor of Reggen, wishes that his noblest fabric be sewn for the king himself." I pulled a swatch of the indigo velvet from my bag. For the first time, I relished the way sunlight tangled itself in the fabric. "This will be invitation enough once the king sees it."

The noble looked closer, eyes narrowed. I had him. "Where did you get this?"

"It belongs to the Tailor. Please, take it to the king. He will be as impressed as you have been."

The man tore his gaze away from the velvet to scowl at me. "A bold claim, for one who can't yet manage a beard!"

I flushed but would not back down. "I don't need a beard to sew for the king"—I looked the nobleman up and down—"or to tell that your tailor worked *very* hard to hide your narrow shoulders. Next time you need a coat, you should come to my master."

I held my breath, worried I'd gone too far. Then the man burst into a high, braying laugh.

"Now I believe you! Why are all tailors so outspoken?" He held out his hand. "I'll take this to the king. Who sends it?"

I gave him the velvet. "The apprentice to the Tailor of Reggen. But if you want the king's good favor, tell him you discovered me yourself."

The nobleman laughed again. "Well thought, lad!" Then he disappeared beyond the gate.

An hour later, a page arrived to fetch me. He led me through wide, sunlit corridors to King Eldin's suite.

"Through this door," he said.

I gulped and nodded—and promptly collided with a dark-haired man. In the sea of foreign faces, his was familiar. I knew him. . . .

Fine Coat.

Sky above, it was Fine Coat.

I ducked my head. He might remember the girl who told

him not to talk so loud, who hated his stories of crushed houses and boiled bones.

"I beg your pardon, my lord! I wasn't watching. . . ." I didn't dare meet his eyes.

He shifted his weight once, twice. "Don't worry yourself."

And then he was gone, taking whatever courage I'd possessed with him. This wouldn't work. The king would see. He'd know. I couldn't—

"Your Majesty, I present the Tailor of Reggen!"

A hand flat against my back pushed me forward. I took two great, stumbling steps, and looked up into the eyes of Reggen's king.

Chapter 5

The king was furious. He sat behind an ornate desk at the far side his suite and glared at . . . an older man who stood beside me.

He swept me a disdainful glance, then turned to the king. "Now is not the time for new clothes, Your Majesty!"

Sky above, I'd walked into an argument. I looked around the king's quarters. The noblemen wore the carefully neutral expressions of those determined not to notice what happened right under their noses.

Then I saw that the king held the swatch.

Look down, I thought. *Look at the velvet.*

The king merely twisted the cloth in his hands. "Why am I expected to send soldiers because Verras found a man who jabbered about *monsters*?"

Monsters . . . for a moment, I was back on the road to Reggen. I could feel the young man's hand on my wrist as he lay in the wagon, whispering about monsters and the man he couldn't best. Surely, the king spoke of someone else. . . .

The old man's reply pulled me from memories. "He was the only witness to the attacks, King Eldin."

"Witness?" jeered one of the king's guards. "He was delirious! And now he's dead."

No. It couldn't be that poor man. I needed to think he'd found some refuge from the fear that haunted him.

And who would make such heartless jests? Or dare speak to a noble so? The guard wasn't much older than the king, but he was as insolent as an eldest son, sure of his father's inheritance. His grin widened when the king laughed.

"Your Majesty!" barked the old man.

The young king hunched his shoulders like a child unwilling to give up his toy. "This whole discussion of armies and monsters from the north is tiresome, Lord Cinnan! There's no need to send scouts." The king waved a hand. "Even if an army was approaching, they couldn't cross the River Kriva and breach our walls."

Finally, the king looked down at the velvet in his hands. He ran a finger over it, the color shifting beneath his touch. And then—at last—he looked up at me.

All thought of monsters and armies fled. The king held my future in his hands.

This is bread, a way to live, I told myself as I bowed low. *You can't afford to be afraid.*

I straightened from my bow, tall and proud, the way tailors stand. I knew the king would want a coat sewn from the indigo velvet.

King Eldin studied me. "You're a tailor? You don't look old enough."

I can make you look like a man. I wore the thought like a fine coat. "I am his apprentice, Your Majesty."

The king's mouth drooped into a pout. "Why doesn't he come himself?"

My future depended on the perfect reply. When my gaze dropped to the velvet, I knew what to say.

I stepped forward and lowered my voice as if sharing a secret. "Your Majesty, he sent the thing he valued most."

The king laughed. "You?"

"No." My confidence filled the room. I spoke the truth, after all. "He sent his fabric. It's like a child to him."

The answer disarmed the king, and I pressed my advantage. "The Tailor requests the honor of making a coat for you. Will you give him that great pleasure?"

Lord Cinnan glared at me. "He requires no payment for *so great* a service?" He turned to the king. "Your Majesty, there is no time for this! Yet another village, Alma, was razed. We have no idea who is behind these attacks, only that they are drawing closer to Reggen—"

If I had met the man in any other place, I would have liked him. He reminded me of Luca; he had the same sort of eyes. But I couldn't let him distract the king. If I left without a commission, I might never have another chance.

"The Tailor does not require payment *now*," I announced.

Lord Cinnan looked ready to send me away but I hurried on. "The Tailor asks that you allow him to create a coat for you, Your Majesty. He'll entrust you with the fabric he values most. You won't have to pay until you have worn the coat and found it worthy."

I stepped forward again without the king's permission, though I kept my head tipped deferentially to hide my face. "May I observe the fit of your coat, sire? I see that it pulls across the back. Does it make it difficult to move your arms?"

The king blinked in surprise. I grew bolder, stepped behind him, and placed a single finger between his shoulder blades. "Here, I think. It must not be very comfortable."

He half turned, and I yanked my finger away and bowed. "I apologize. I meant no disrespect."

"You're *good*," he said.

"That's why the Tailor sent me." I wanted to press for a fitting but resisted. Not yet. Speaking might break the spell.

Lord Cinnan was not so wise. "Your Majesty, please! Send a few men. Lord Verras is concerned. Perhaps if you read his reports—"

"He is wearisome!" snapped the king. "And his reports bore me. Read them yourself and tell me what you think tomorrow."

Lord Cinnan stood there, reproach in his eyes.

"Leave!" shouted the king.

Lord Cinnan did as commanded—with a look that made King Eldin flush.

A stifling silence filled the suite. Finally, the king motioned to the insolent guard. "I am finished with audiences today, Leymonn. Send them away."

 35

"A wise request, Your Majesty," he murmured.

"Only you understand the burden of the throne!" the king whispered.

Leymonn bowed, then called out, "His Majesty calls this audience to an end! He wishes to be left alone!"

The nobles streamed out. After a moment, the king, his guards, and I were alone in his suite.

"Good riddance to them all!" exclaimed King Eldin. He grinned as if he had won a battle against a great opponent. "Lord Cinnan is tiresome, and he gets angry when I am not as dull as he is."

I could see how soft the king's arms were. I had felt his doughy back. King Eldin couldn't win a battle against a blindfolded squire. Still, I answered as if he was a great ruler.

"I hope you will not find *this* tiresome, Your Majesty: I must measure you for the coat."

"Of course. I should very much like clothing that—" He paused, and I saw he was unwilling to admit that his figure needed assistance.

I swallowed my irritation. "Clothing that matches your royal dignity?"

"Yes! You understand me perfectly." He peered at me. "Are you sure you are capable? How old are you, apprentice?"

"I am—" I was seventeen, but I didn't look like a seventeen-year-old lad. "I am nearly sixteen, Your Majesty."

"I find that hard to believe."

That is the least difficult thing I need you to believe, I thought. Then I had a flash of memory. I tilted my head and ran my fingers over my jaw, the way Father used to when he had finished shaving.

"It isn't hard to believe, Your Majesty. My beard's coming in. It won't be long now."

The king laughed so long that I decided I truly disliked the man-child. I ducked my head as if embarrassed and, when he stopped laughing, mumbled, "You have to look close, that's all. You can see it then."

The king was still chuckling when I left an hour later.

Weary as I was, my heart wouldn't slow as I walked back to the shop. I was certain someone would discover that a girl had masqueraded as the Tailor's apprentice. The moment I entered the shop, I untied the cravat with trembling fingers, tugged it loose, and flung it onto one of the tables.

I pulled in a deep breath and walked over to the Tailor's bedside.

His eyes were the most alive part of him—and they burned with questions he could not voice.

"I did it," I told him, chin raised. "I gained an audience with the king. I left with his measurements and a commission."

The Tailor didn't even blink.

"One of the men from the caravan was there." I wanted the Tailor to know how dangerous the morning had been. "The one who pulled you from the wagon. He bumped right into me. And there were others arguing about armies. But I wouldn't let the king be distracted. I made him believe I could sew him a coat that would make him look like a king. And I can."

I felt a rush of guilt. What if there really were invading armies and I'd filled the king's head with promises of new clothing?

But the Tailor didn't care that Fine Coat might have recognized me or that the king had been preoccupied with talk of an approaching army. He stared at the trunk that held his fabric.

I shook my head. "It's the indigo that he wants, Tailor—a coat of the indigo velvet. But I need to make the form first. You—and the velvet—will have to wait."

Chapter 6

After the indigo coat came the black one with breeches that made the king look slim as a knight. Then he demanded something truly magnificent. So I crafted a regal coat of ruby brocade that would have looked clownish in the hands of an amateur.

The king's commissions kept me busy for over two months, two tedious, frightening months. I spent the time sewing, always sewing. Every visit to the castle, I risked meeting Fine Coat, risked being discovered. I was safe only in the garret, though the dark room never felt like a refuge.

The Tailor was still confined to his bed, barely able to speak. He spent his days watching me sew, and I watched the street beyond our window.

Sometimes, that patch of the outside world wasn't enough.

So one early summer day, as I set the collar of the king's new gray silk coat, I indulged in a daydream.

I imagined looking out the window and seeing not Fine Coat, but Lynden. *He walked down the street with his easy stride and open face. I was myself again, the Saville he met on*

the road. *He was delighted to see me, looping my arm through his and telling me of his travels and—*

It was a good daydream. Too good.

I focused on the king's coat, stabbing the needle through the silk, stitch after stitch. I wasn't the girl Lynden had known, the Saville who hoped to be free of the Tailor. I was Avi, who whistled because singing would give me away, whose fingers were calloused from sewing for a pudgy, spoiled king.

After a few seams, I looked out again to remind myself that Lynden wasn't there, that he never would be. Instead, I saw a boy huddled in a narrow strip of shadow. He was young, maybe eight, and looked lost and hungry. Very hungry. I stopped sewing, wondering if I should give him food.

Immediately, I heard the Tailor's voice, the one he possessed before his illness: *He's no business of yours.* I looked back at the Tailor, even though I knew he was sleeping.

It was the worst kind of haunting.

The Tailor hated softness. He'd hate the softness in me that pitied the boy. It was what he'd despised most in Mama. Sometimes I wondered if that was why he'd grown even more angry after she died: he hated the weakness of missing her.

The boy will be fine, I told myself. *He doesn't need my help.*

I wasn't like the Tailor: I wasn't worried about softness—I was worried about starving. But as I returned to stitching the collar, I felt that I'd cut something out of myself, something Mama would have treasured.

40

The next day, after the midmorning bells, the boy sat in the same bit of shade across the street. He didn't move for hours—until someone tossed a scrap at him. *Then* he scrambled after it but not quickly enough. A street cur, nearly as starved as the boy, scooped up the crust. The boy tussled with the dog, refusing to release it even when it swung around and bared its teeth. The dog attacked, and the boy scrambled away with a new hole in his tunic.

He'll be fine.

He fell back to sitting, pulled his knees close, and buried his face in his arms. I could see his shoulders shaking, even under his too-big tunic.

I hadn't heard Mama's voice since she died. I didn't hear her as I looked down at the boy, my heart beating so fast I could feel it in my fingertips. But I knew what she'd say. I knew it in a place deeper than the Tailor could ever reach.

I slapped the coat down on the table and took the stairs two at a time. Cart-churned dust clogged my throat as I ran across the street and stopped in front of the child.

He didn't look up, though he must have sensed me standing so close.

I said the only thing that came to mind: "Come with me."

He slanted a skeptical look up at me before burying his head in his arms again.

"I can help."

Nothing.

"I *said,* I can help."

He shook his head, which was still buried in his arms. We might go on like this all day. I took the boy by his right arm, lifted him to standing, and marched him toward the shop. He began to struggle then, but he was as frail as a nursling.

"Be still!" I told him. "I'm going to feed you."

He continued to struggle, and the part of me that wasn't worried about drawing attention to myself liked him the better for it. Up the stairs we went. We hadn't traveled more than a few steps before he went limp. I all but carried him up the last stairs, and he crumpled onto the floor when I released him.

"I'm not going to hurt you."

He shook his head.

"Stay there," I said, and disappeared behind the curtain that separated the private quarters from the shop. I took up a knife to cut a few slices of bread, then paused. He'd been so light.

I returned with the entire loaf.

"Here." I put it in his lap.

He stared at the bread for a moment, then looked up. "Is it poisoned?"

"*What?*"

He shrugged. "Folks put out poisoned food for the dogs."

I pointed to the street. "You didn't ask that when you were tussling for scraps."

"The man had just taken a bite."

"This is my own bread. It's not poisoned."

Still, he stared up at me.

I sighed, crouched down, and tore off a piece of the loaf. Then I popped it into my mouth. The boy watched me, eyes narrowed, until I swallowed. Then he pulled in a shuddering breath and devoured the bread—while tears streaked the dust on his cheeks. He was crying: crying and eating.

"There's no need for that!" I exclaimed, dumbfounded by the change.

I grimaced, hating that I sounded like the Tailor. But I didn't know how to comfort the boy. I didn't know how to play a man and be anything but distant and angry. The Tailor had taught me many things, but how a man could show kindness was not one of them.

"You'll never survive if others see you cry," I added, in a softer tone.

"I'm not crying." The boy gave a great, noisy sniff and swiped at his face with his sleeve. "Sir."

It was too ridiculous to argue, so I tried a different tack. "What's your name?"

"Will."

"Have you heard the old song about dragons, Will? When a dragon attacks a town?"

I whistled a few bars between my teeth.

Another swipe at his face. Another bite. A nod.

"The dragon is killed when it flies overhead. People below can see the soft spot, the one place scales don't cover. When

43

the archers find that . . . well, the battle's over." I shrugged. "Crying shows your soft spot. It lets others know where to attack."

"Anyone could see I was hungry. No surprise, that." His tears had stopped, but the catch in his voice remained. He looked around the garret, saw the fabrics and clothes scattered about.

"Is anyone looking out for you?" I asked.

He winced, and I wanted to kick myself for being so direct.

"No one." He looked down at the floor. "Mama's dead. I don't know about Papa."

I almost asked another question. Instead, I waited. Will took two more bites.

"Mama died . . ." He looked up at the ceiling and blinked a few times ". . . almost four weeks ago."

"My mother died nine years ago."

Will looked at me—quickly, intently—before picking at his bread. "Papa's a tinker. We lived in Esker, three weeks from here. Papa told Ma and me that we needed to travel to Reggen right away. He'd heard something was attacking villages." Will looked up at me with wide eyes. "Folks talked about monsters or a black army. Pa was going to travel to Kellan for one last job to pay for our stay here. That was six weeks ago, and he hasn't come back."

Will stared at the bread. "I heard something about Kellan. Someone said it had been destroyed."

I'd heard similar talk at the castle, more reports that

worried old Lord Cinnan. Something was drawing nearer to Reggen, attacking the villages scattered over the plains as it approached. There were no bodies left behind, only bones— human bones. Fine Coat had been right, after all.

I hated Reggen, but Will's father had been wise to send him here, protected by its massive walls and the Kriva, which bent around the ancient foundation. Perhaps I could help keep Will safe, too.

I hadn't carved a place for myself yet, but I could manage a corner for Will.

"Would you like to stay here until you find your father?" I asked.

Chapter 7

"**You want me** to stay with you?"

"I do." I didn't realize how much I wanted it until the the words were spoken. The past months with the Tailor had been like living in a cave, one I'd shut myself into. Mama would offer this boy a place. I'd pattern myself after her.

The Tailor's bed creaked and groaned.

Will froze. "What's that?"

"I need help." I took a deep breath and motioned to the curtain that partitioned off the Tailor's bed. "The Tailor is sick. It's hard for me to sew and take care of him."

Will made no effort to hide his suspicion. "You don't know me."

"I don't. But I'm willing to risk it."

He had no idea how true those words were.

He straightened his shoulders under the dirty tunic. "I might be dangerous."

All sixty pounds of him. But I didn't say that. I didn't even smile. "A man who works with shears and needles all day is dangerous, too. You're smart enough to know that."

Will's face brightened at the veiled threat, and he nodded

approval. Then he looked behind me at the table piled with fabric. His face crumbled. "I can't sew."

"You can fetch water and bread for the Tailor. I'll make sure you have food to eat and a place to sleep." I waved at the cutting table. "We could set up blankets for you under there."

"I have to go away every morning."

I raised my eyebrows. "You'll need to earn your keep."

Will flushed and looked down. "Pa said he'd meet us at the fountain near the gates at morning bells. I have to be there, or he won't know where to find me."

"You'll have to draw the water before then, understand?" I spoke as gently as I dared.

"I can do that." Will looked around the room once more, then grinned and tore off another huge chunk of bread. "You have a deal, Sir."

"My name is Avi," I told him.

"I like Sir," said Will, and held out his hand.

I shook it. "So do I."

The shaking from the Tailor's bed grew even louder. I glanced at Will. He shouldn't see what would happen next. I dug a coin out of my pocket.

"This will be your first test," I told him. "We need more bread. For some reason, it's disappeared."

Will grinned.

"Go and get two loaves and some milk from the farmer near the gate. He boils it first."

 47

I paused a moment before dropping the coin onto Will's grubby palm.

He looked up at me. "I'll be back, Sir. Don't worry."

As soon as Will had scampered down the stairs, I swept aside the curtain between the shop and the Tailor's bed. "His name is Will, and he's going to stay. He should have a home."

The Tailor's eyes widened, and his hand clenched into a weak fist. "No."

I clenched my own hands. "I'm not asking you, Tailor."

"No . . . no . . . no." He almost chanted it.

I sat beside him and leaned close. "I have given everything—everything!—to keep us alive. But I will not give this boy back to the street. I will not dishonor Mama by doing something so callous."

The Tailor flinched as if I'd struck him.

I pressed my advantage, felt the edge of cool fury in my voice. "Look at me, Tailor, and remember how much you need me. If you cannot be civil to this boy out of the goodness of your heart, you will do it out of consideration for your stomach. Do you understand me?"

A week later, Will walked up, a bit of hair in his hand—the hair I'd hidden in the trunk.

"You're a girl," he said in a canny, calm voice.

I hid my surprise as I rested my sewing in my lap. "You find some hair and decide I'm a girl?"

Will blinked to hear his argument put so plainly and looked down. Then he dashed forward, holding the hair up to mine.

"It matches," he announced. "You walk funny, sometimes. I noticed that first. And your voice goes high. You're a girl."

There was no point arguing with him. I'd have his loyalty in exchange for the truth.

"You're right." I picked up my sewing again. "Now throw away the cutting scraps."

"What?" I heard him step back. "Why?"

"Because I told you to."

"That's not what I meant!"

"Why am I a girl?" I said, hiding my smile. "It's the way I was made, I suppose."

He faced me, hands on his hips.

I took the hair from him. "How did you find this?"

"I like finding things." He jutted his chin. "I'm good at it, too. Most people hide secrets deep, like you did, so I look under things. And there's lots of room for 'under' in a trunk. If you really wanted to hide that hair, you should've left it on top."

I held the hair up in a sort of salute. "How does a tinker's son know so much about finding things?"

"Tinkers like to know how things are put together. People, too." He shrugged. "And there was something about you I couldn't figure out. Now"—Will screwed his face up into as fierce a gaze as he could muster—"why are you dressed like a boy?"

 49

"Ah. Now that's a better question." I twirled the length of my hair around a finger. "I'm the Tailor's daughter. We came here from Danavir just as winter was breaking."

"That's no reason to wear pants."

"Hush!" I scolded. "The Tailor was skilled, so skilled that he began sewing differently from Danavir's tailors' guild. The nobles liked it, but the guild did not."

Will rolled his eyes. "They fought over *clothes*?"

"The old way of sewing put as much brocade and velvet and lace as possible onto a coat—to show off the fabric. The Tailor liked to show off the man wearing the coat. He knew how to make a man's shoulders look broader, his hips trim." I shrugged, just like Will had. "He fought the guild and lost. That's why we came here. Reggen doesn't have guilds. But then the Tailor fell ill. So I became Avi."

"Just like that?" Will asked.

"I helped the Tailor in Danavir when his apprentices left. It wasn't hard to dress as his apprentice. We already had lads' clothing. I just needed to cut my hair."

"Wasn't your hair I wondered about. How do you hide—?"

"*That* is none of your affair. Enough to say it doesn't hurt that I know how to shape clothes." I leaned forward until I had Will's full attention. "What do you think will happen if some-one discovers I'm a girl?"

"Oh, you'd be in trouble! Men wouldn't like finding out a girl measured them. They'd hang you, sure. Folks don't like being fooled."

50

I didn't think they'd hang me. It would be a slow sort of death. It's hard to live if you can't work.

I leaned even closer. "And how would you eat if I couldn't sew?"

Will looked thoughtful. "I'd find a way."

I held his gaze.

"I won't tell, if that's what you're worried about," he said. "This is your soft spot, isn't it?"

It was only one of my soft spots. "If you tell . . . so help me . . ."

"I won't. I like finding things, but I like fooling people more."

Chapter 8

Rumors of an approaching army circled Reggen as summer began, like crows around a carcass. I heard stories in the streets as I walked to the palace to consult with the king. I heard whispers in the palace itself.

There were no witnesses. Not even the rangers, who extended King Eldin's rule into the lands beyond Reggen's walls, returned bearing news. The villagers who straggled into the city couldn't tell us what they were fleeing, for they hadn't seen anything. One old man sensed a darkness in the north. Someone's neighbor's cousin had seen monsters.

Will listened for news of Kellan and visited the fountain each morning, his face tight with worry every time he returned without finding his father.

I trusted Reggen's walls and tended to the Tailor, counting the days until his strength would return. Week after week, I told Will the Tailor would recover.

Week after week, I believed it.

Then, one morning, the sunlight streaming harsh and bright through our window, I watched the Tailor try to feed himself. I held the bowl of milk-soaked bread beneath his chin while he gripped a spoon in his fist and brought it, shaking, to his mouth.

The Tailor's hands had always been strong, his long fingers nimble. He'd been able to guide a needle through any sort of fabric with stitches so fine you could hardly see them. Now he could hardly move the spoon.

The Tailor would never hold a needle again—I knew it.

And I would never be free. I'd have to play his apprentice until he died. He'd dragged me to Reggen, and his illness had trapped me here, pinned to this garret room.

I'd been a fool to think I could get away.

I stood slowly, still holding the Tailor's breakfast, the milk dancing against the lip of the bowl.

I didn't turn when the door slammed, and Will thundered up the stairs.

I heard Will slide to a stop. "Sir?" he whispered.

I stared at the Tailor as the shaking spread through me.

"Sir?" said Will, louder this time.

I dropped the bowl and turned on my heel, dashing toward the stairs.

"Wait!" Will stepped in front of me. "Where are you going, Sir?"

I took him by the shoulders and shook him—shook him because I had to leave. If I talked, I'd fall to pieces and never be able to gather them up again. But I released Will just as quickly, horrified at what I'd done.

"Stay with the Tailor," I croaked.

I ran down the stairs and into the street. I'd go to the willows and sit in the shade where I'd buried Mama's music box. I'd pretend I could hear her voice and her songs.

I darted through the crowded streets, desperate to be outside Reggen's walls.

Yet I slid to a stop when I reached the gate. A single rider, dressed in black with a horse-skull helmet, galloped over the bridge. He held a staff decorated with bones, which made a hollow, clattering sound, like teeth chattering.

They aren't human bones, I thought. *They can't be.* But the skull on the top of the staff? That was human.

The black rider's horse reared as it approached the crowds, but he urged it forward. As he plunged into the midst of the people near the gate, the rider scattered pale leaves over the crowd. I looked down the road, anxious to see if other riders followed. No one.

He was only one rider, but I couldn't control the dread rising inside me.

I'd visit the willows another day. I needed to know what the rider had scattered.

As I pushed into the crowd, I saw that some people held pieces of parchment. Snatches of conversations boiled up around me.

"Who's this duke? Was he the one with the skull helmet?"

"Says he has a giant army."

"Who's foolish enough to admit he has a *small* army?"

"Princess Lissa would never have him—"

I plucked a sheet out of someone's hands and read, all thought of the willows gone.

The Duke of the Western Steeps,
Heir to the Ancient Emperor's Crown,
Holder of the Eternal Heart
greets the city of Reggen:

As Heir to the Ancient Emperor, I am the true king of your city, and I have come to claim it. I wish you no harm and would secure my throne through the most peaceable way possible: marriage. I will rule Reggen with Princess Lissa by my side.

If you deny my rightful place in your city, I will claim it through other means. I march before an army of giants, descendants of the giants that laid Reggen's foundation stones. At my command, they will be the army that dismantles your walls.

I will greet you as either your King or your Enemy in three days' time.

Choose wisely.

I reread the parchment, trying to make sense of it. I knew the Western Steeps—we'd skirted them on our long journey to Reggen. They were a stretch of desolate land far to the north, next to the Belmor Mountains: grim, gray peaks that rose straight out of the sea. Few explorers traveled their barren passes to reach the ocean . . . and the ancient emperor had ruled Reggen and the River Cities centuries ago.

But I'd never heard of the Eternal Heart in history or legend or song.

Who was this duke? And giants?

He couldn't be sane.

What had the young man in Fine Coat's wagon said? That there was a man who couldn't be stopped and there were monsters. This Duke of the Western Steeps, then, and his warriors—his *human* warriors.

I glanced up at Reggen's walls. I didn't care who this duke was. His army couldn't breach our walls. And how *dare* he even try? We had done nothing to him.

I realized in a rush that my hatred of Reggen had faded to a dull dislike. The city was mine, somehow, and the badgerlike stubbornness I'd inherited from the Tailor didn't appreciate anyone, not even a duke, claiming my city.

I stayed in the street till the sun slanted toward the west, hoping for more news of the duke. And then I remembered Will.

My heart dropped the moment I stepped into the garret and saw Will's face. He tried to run past me. I caught him, but he twisted away.

"Don't touch me, Sir! I'd have left already if it wasn't for the Tailor."

I held Will by the shoulders and knelt so I could look into his face.

"I'm sorry. I shouldn't have shaken you. I was—" *Half-crazy . . . and scared.* It didn't matter. Didn't the Tailor always have a reason for his outbursts? "I was wrong."

Will folded his arms. "You bet you were."

"I know."

The silence drew out. Finally, Will tipped his head toward the window. "What's happening? People have been crowding the streets."

It was his form of a truce. I sat cross-legged on the floor and studied him. How exactly was I supposed to tell a boy that Reggen might be attacked?

If the boy was Will, you just told him. I took a deep breath and waved the parchment. "A rider came into Reggen, scattering these. Can you read?"

"Not good."

I read the notice to him, then tossed it aside. "I don't think we need to worry. We'll be safe behind the walls. Even if there were a siege, the city has reservoirs that pull water from the river. But—you're not to play in the fields past the Kriva. Not till we know more."

"Does the duke really get to rule Reggen?"

"No. King Eldin is the rightful ruler, like his brother and father." I shrugged. "The duke can't be completely sane."

Will sat down, too. "What if he *is* coming with an army of giants?"

"There's no such thing as giants."

 57

"But there are stories about giants," he pressed. "That they laid the city's foundation . . . that they—"

"It doesn't mean the stories are true! I told you about the dragon but it doesn't mean one will ever fly over Reggen."

Will didn't seem to hear me. "I bet it was giants that attacked the villages. They're the monsters everyone talks about! What if they're the reason Pa hasn't come back?"

I put a hand on his knee. "People could mistake warriors for monsters, especially if they attacked at night. Giants don't exist."

Will shook his head. "You don't know that!"

For a moment, I almost believed him. Believed that monsters were traveling toward Reggen, that the Kriva wasn't deep enough and our walls weren't high enough to protect us.

Ridiculous. But I wouldn't argue with Will. He just needed to believe that his father hadn't been captured.

"Very well, then," I said. "Suppose giants do exist. Do you think they'd be able to sneak up on someone?"

Will stopped to consider. "No . . ."

"Your father, he sounds like a smart man. How would a giant sneak up on him? I'm sure there's another reason why he hasn't come yet." I nodded toward the door. "Why don't you run out and see if you can gather more news?"

Will looked relieved. There were few things worse than sitting still when the world was falling to pieces around you.

Even if it wasn't really falling to pieces.

Will was in fine spirits the next day when he returned from his midmorning trip to the fountain.

"The king thinks there are giants, too!" He flopped down on the floor and wrapped his arms around his knees, panting. "He does! He sent criers out, and they say that anyone who can defeat the giants gets to marry the princess. Marry her!"

"You can't be serious." I looked out the window. "*He* can't be serious."

How could Lord Cinnan let the king issue such a proclamation? It made the king look weak, desperate.

Will grinned. "You should ask him if he believes in giants when you bring him his coat."

"Don't be silly," I said. "This doesn't mean the king thinks the giant army is real. It means he's trying to keep the city calm."

"It's more interesting my way." Will popped up and looked over my shoulder. "That seam's crooked. You should use a double-back, whip-'em-hard stitch to fix it."

It was a game of ours: Will would find imaginary fault with my work and offer ridiculous advice. He'd outdone himself. I laughed until the tears rolled down my cheeks, laughed as if I wasn't trapped, as if I wasn't scared.

Will puffed out his chest, pleased. "I wonder why the king even keeps a tailor who sews so bad."

I swatted at him. "Do you want me to stitch your lips shut?"

He danced out of reach. "Bet even *that* seam would be crooked!"

"If my seams are crooked, it's because you distract me."

He put his hands on his hips. "You like it."

I rested the sewing in my lap, studying the boy. Will had just returned from the fountain, where there'd been no sign of his father. He slept in a nest of blankets under the cutting table and worried about giants. Yet he was grinning at me.

Poor little man, I thought, *if this seems good to him. What will I do when he leaves . . . ?*

"I do like it."

"I *knew* it!"

I pointed at some work on the cutting table. "Yesterday, I left you three vests to cut. Not one is ready for stitching."

"Can't cut them now. I'm going giant hunting. That's what I came back to tell you."

I looked at him—that long, slow look that announced he *would* do as I said.

He picked up the shears. "I'll go giant hunting after I cut the vests."

I bent over my work, absorbed with setting a sleeve, and listened to the whisper of the shears as Will cut the fabric. He often cut out the forms too quickly, leaving ragged edges and lopsided proportions. Yet he did a fine job that morning.

After a while, he asked, "Do you think I could catch a giant?"

"There are no giants, Will." I looked up from my sewing,

needle in midair. "Just how do you plan to hunt one?"

"With Tomas. And rope. He has the rope, so I had to let him come." Will put the shears down. "See? All finished."

He cantered toward the stairs.

"Make sure you're back by midafternoon bells!" I didn't fear giants, but I couldn't banish the image of the messenger. "And remember what I said: Don't go past the Kriva."

He yelped in protest, but I held up a hand. "I mean it! Set your giant traps close to the river."

"But there'll be people in the fields past the river! You won't let me go farther than a farmer?"

"No, I won't."

He glared at me.

"You're wasting time, Will lad."

One final glare and he was off. The shop seemed the darker for it.

Will didn't return by midafternoon bells. I passed the time by imagining the scolding I'd give him. The speech grew longer and louder when I went for bread and found that Will had eaten it all.

"I have to go out, Tailor," I announced. "Will hasn't left a crumb. He should return before I do." I snatched up a bit of new cheese to eat on the way and trotted down the stairs.

I was in the street when I heard the shouts.

"Giants!"

I shoved the cheese in my pocket and headed toward the gates.

"In the fields! Giants!"

"Close the gates!"

Will's friend Tomas darted past, wide-eyed with fear. Alone. He held a torn length of rope in his hand.

"Tomas!" I caught him by the shoulders. "Where is Will?"

He looked up at me. "He wouldn't let go of the rope, even when they got close."

Chapter 9

I pushed my way toward Reggen's gates—gates wide enough for four wagons. Would a giant be able to squeeze through?

If there were giants.

The huge doors were still open, but I heard the *clang, clang, clang* of a chain as the portcullis lowered. I shouldered through the crowd until I reached the wooden grate.

Out over the bridge, near the road that led through the farmland, stood two men.

They were men, just men. Dressed in foreign-looking clothes. It was the summer heat shivering up from the bridge, a trick of the eye, that made them look tall as trees.

Then one of the men brushed his shoulder, and the oak beside him whipped back and forth. I gasped. He wasn't standing far in front of the oak. He stood *beside* it—and was nearly its height.

Giants! They approached the bridge, moving like huge draft horses, slow and strong. But they didn't look ferocious for all their size. One even carried a rag doll.

And then I realized it was not a doll.

One giant held a boy by his foot while the second prodded

 63

him with an enormous finger. The child hung limp, his shirt falling over his face. I knew that shirt, even from this distance. I'd sewn it.

Will. The boy was Will.

I couldn't hear the crowd around me. I could hardly breathe. Another prod brought Will to his senses, and he began thrashing in the giant's grip. I squeezed the rails of the portcullis until splinters bit into my hands.

"No, Will," I whispered. "Be still. Be still!"

Will's struggle seemed to irritate the giant holding him. He shook Will the way a laundress would shake out a shirt.

Will screamed, an animal sound that cut through the shouts of the crowd. Then he went limp again, dangling from the giant's hand.

I screamed, too, as I fought my way through the masses. I had to reach the door beside the portcullis. Two guardsmen stood there, mouths agape. Watching, only watching!

I elbowed past them and ran across the bridge, my feet hardly touching the stones. The world narrowed to the giants before me and the roar of blood in my ears.

When I reached the other side, I skidded to a stop and scooped up some stones from the roadside. Then I charged the giants, hurling the rocks at them. One flew past the ear of the giant holding Will. He took no notice. The next was better aimed. It hit the creature on his nose.

He hardly flinched.

"Put! Him! Down!" I shouted, heaving a rock with each word. "Leave him alone!"

Both giants stopped—like wind-tossed trees suddenly turned to stone—and looked at me.

I stumbled back a step or two. Their faces looked human, except for their eyes. Their pupils were slits, like a cat's. I noticed—even then—that the one who prodded Will wore a well-sewn jerkin of gray leather. He looked like the younger of the two, with smooth cheeks and dark, curling hair. The other giant, the one who held Will, wore poorer clothing, with a pick strapped to his back. What would I do if he decided to use it? The pick was huge, stretching between his vast shoulders.

They were huge, as tall as six men. My head didn't even reach their knees.

I didn't care.

I glared up at them. They stared down at me. And Will hung limp from the giant's hand.

"Are warriors from your land so puny that they fight stripling children?" I shouted. They looked at each other.

I jabbed a finger at them. *"Put . . . him . . . DOWN!"* My voice was even louder than before.

"Oma would not like this," said the one who held Will. He had tawny hair and a trimmed beard. His melodic voice surprised me. I'd been expecting something nearer a grunt.

The young one narrowed his eyes, as if he didn't agree. But he didn't try to touch Will again.

Thank goodness for Oma, whoever he was.

"There is no glory in hurting a boy!" I shouted. "Now put him down!"

The young one put a hand on the bearded one's shoulder,

as if to hold him back, but the bearded one shook him off, and held Will out at arm's length. His grip on Will's foot began to relax. I could see his huge fingers release. . . .

"No!"

The giant looked at me.

"*Set* him down," I said. Would he really listen to me? "Don't drop him."

The bearded giant tucked his chin slightly, a close cousin to a nod. Then he crouched, forearm across his knee. It seemed to take an age to fold himself up. Finally, he set Will down so that his head touched the ground first, while his limbs flopped around him.

Then the giant straightened like a tower being built before me. He stepped away and watched as I ran toward Will.

"Talk not to the *lité*. Kill them before their voices can touch us," rumbled the young one. "The duke said—"

Lité? Was that what they called us?

"I'll not kill it," said the one with the beard and pick. "No matter what the duke said."

Their voices were low, like the last purr of thunder before it fades away entirely. I could feel the rumble of it in my chest.

I reached Will and dragged him back toward the bridge. He had to get to the city.

"I will look after the boy!" I called as I tugged at Will. "Then you may deal with me if you wish." I set Will down and waved a fist at them. "*If* you can!"

66

I couldn't believe myself—or that the giants had actually listened to me. I only knew that if I kept talking, they might keep listening and Will might be saved.

I knelt beside him. He was pale, his right foot bent at an awful angle. I looked toward Reggen's gates for help, but no one had followed me across the bridge. Not a soul.

"Will," I whispered. "Will!"

He didn't answer, so I lightly slapped his cheek. Nothing. The giants were beginning to shift their weight and mutter. I didn't have much time.

"Forgive me. . . ." Before I could think better of it, I prodded his crooked foot.

He woke with a shriek.

"Shhh!" I clamped a hand over his mouth, scared of provoking the giants. "Quiet, Will! As you value your life, be quiet."

His eyes were glassy with tears, but he nodded. I pulled my hand away.

"Listen to me," I whispered. "You must get back to the gates. I don't care if you think your foot will snap off. Go as quickly and as quietly as you can. Do you hear me?"

I looked back to Reggen's gates. Still, no one came for him. For us.

Cowards.

One last look at Will. One quick squeeze of his shoulder. "Go!"

I stood and walked back toward the giants. For the first

time since running across the bridge, I was afraid, the sort of fear that melted the marrow in my bones and made it hard to move.

I had to give Will time. My legs might be weak, but I could shout easily enough.

"Now!" I bellowed up at them. "Do what you will!"

The young one flinched, then lifted his foot in one sweeping arc. I dove away as the boot crashed down where I had been standing. The boot rose again and I threw myself to the side.

But the boot never fell.

"No!" The bearded one pulled the young giant back with a commotion like a small landslide. "Kill not!"

"The duke commanded—" The young one pushed the other giant away and he staggered back, the ground trembling beneath us. I'd never seen such strength, such force. I'd been a fool to think they moved slowly. The bearded one found his footing with a growl, and the two giants faced each other.

I pushed myself to standing and backed away, pulling in great, gulping breaths. *What was happening?*

"You will not kill! I will not let you." The bearded one shook his great head. "What would you tell Oma?"

After a moment, the young giant reluctantly lowered his hands. The earth trembled as both giants turned to me.

"What do you want, *lité*?" asked the bearded giant.

I wanted them to go away. No, I wanted them to never have come. I wanted to keep thinking giants were creatures from stories. But I needed to give Will time to escape. I couldn't fight the giants, and I wouldn't run. I glanced around me: fields, willows, river . . . stones.

Stones. The cheese in my pocket. That was it.

I cupped my hands around my mouth and shouted, "I challenge you to a game of strength! I dare you to break a rock with your hands!"

The one with the beard chuckled and reached behind him to touch the pick the way some men rub a luck charm. He must work with stone. Maybe he could—

"No!" I shouted, fists on my hips. "Breaking a rock is too easy. Our children do that before they're finished with their mothers' milk! I challenge you to squeeze water from it!"

Both giants walked to the river and snatched up boulders. Three paces there, three paces back . . . each stride must have been the length of two men. A moment later, the young giant's boulder exploded into dust and pebbles, and I threw my arms up to shield my face from the debris.

I rubbed the dust from my eyes, desperate to see again. The giants hadn't moved.

The bearded one shook his head and told the young one, "Too fast. You work too fast."

He held his boulder aloft, nearly above me, and I scampered back a few paces. Then he began to squeeze the stone, his eyes closed, his head tilted to the side as if listening. His knuckles grew white from strain.

The young giant stood near, dusty hands hanging loose at his sides. They were good hands: strong, with tapered

 69

fingers, the sort of hands that knew a trade. He might have been a tailor. I'd never expected to see a craftsman's hands on a giant.

Even so, I'd seen what those hands had done to Will. I could imagine what they would do to me. They were big enough to pick me up, fingers meeting around my waist—

I saw it pick you up, the young man in Fine Coat's wagon had said, *just like you were a doll. . . .*

No. I wouldn't let the fear seep into my bones again.

I looked up at the bearded giant's boulder. A small patch on the bottom of the rock had darkened. I thought it was a shadow. Then a single drop of water gathered. The young giant, also watching, didn't react. Perhaps he couldn't see. I glanced over my shoulder at the bridge.

Will was not even halfway across.

"There!" The young one's shout pulled me back. "He did it! I heard the water fall."

"Did you see it?" I asked.

"Ha!" he snorted, and it reminded me of a bellows. "How would we see something so small? But I heard it."

He heard it? Their hearing is that keen? He clapped his friend on the back. They both turned to me.

My mouth was dust dry, but I shouted anyway. "Only one drop? I could squeeze a handful of water if I wanted! But I am tired, so I'll choose a smaller rock. I'm ashamed to admit it, but I may only squeeze three drops today."

The bearded giant, still sweating from his exertion,

chuckled and shook his head. "It is a nervy little *lité,*" he said. "All spirit and sinew. It is good not to kill it."

The young giant's brows lowered. "The duke . . ."

I didn't give him time to finish.

"Now you'll see my strength!" I ran to the river. Once there, I quietly dropped the cheese from my pocket and toed it around in the dirt until it was covered. Then I picked up the fist-sized hunk and held it aloft. "This is the stone I have chosen!"

Both strode toward me like a slow-moving avalanche. I yelled and stumbled back, heart thudding against my ribs, arms raised against them, as if *that* could protect me.

Nothing happened. Instead, both giants dropped to one knee. They peered at me until their cat eyes were almost crossed, ready to see if I could squeeze water from a stone.

They were close enough to touch.

No, not touch. Though they bent close, their faces were still far above the ground. I'd have to stand on someone's shoulders just to reach the young one's chin. I'd never been so frightened, so awed. It was like having the sun and moon fall out of the sky and hang just above me. Their breath gusted against me, slow and steady.

The bearded one rested his left hand on the earth, palm down, to steady himself. His arm rose up like a tree, at least twice as wide as my body. I could see the muscle and sinew.

"*Lité?*" he asked, and his voice rumbled through my chest. "We await you."

I looked up into his face. His brown eyes looked half-focused, as if he were farsighted. The young one's blue eyes were also half-focused. *Could they even see me?*

"Its heart beats fast," said the young one. The bearded one nodded.

Sky above. They could hear my heart. I pressed my free hand against my chest. *Just keep talking. . . .*

"Watch!" I commanded, and held the cheese aloft.

Their heads moved closer, and I began to squeeze. The dust had absorbed all of the cheese's moisture. For a moment, I didn't think I could squeeze anything from it. But water gathered underneath it almost as soon as I tightened my hand. A drop fell to the dusty road.

The giants jerked their heads in surprise.

"You heard it, didn't you?" I shouted, wrapping the last of my courage around me. "Now listen for the other two. I am ashamed to take so long."

They eyed me warily until two more drops of water plunked into the dust. Then they jumped up, surprised. It was like a small earthquake, with hills rising into mountains and blocking out the sky.

I hardly flinched this time when the earth shook.

A glance behind me: Will was moving more slowly now. Still, no one came to help him, though I saw movement along the tops of the city walls.

I couldn't leave yet. What if the giants followed me back across the bridge?

All thought fled as the air shattered around us. I dropped to my knees, hands clapped over my ears. The giants shouted with a sound like thunder. When I looked up, leaves showered down over us. A few stunned birds fluttered to the ground.

A new crater pocked the road beyond us. A cannon! The city had fired a cannon at the giants while I stood there. *Cowards. Idiots!*

Another explosion as a second cannon went off. I hunched over, but the younger giant swept his arm through the air as if swatting at something. It wasn't until he opened his palm that I understood what I'd seen.

He'd caught the cannonball.

He straightened with a growl and lunged toward the bridge, ready to hurl the cannonball at Reggen's walls, but the bearded one held him back.

No! Will had to get home first.

I turned toward the city, waving my arms. "Stop! Stop!"

I thought I saw movement around other cannons, but I couldn't look for long. The giants were muttering again, and I swung to face them.

"Look!" I called to the young one. "One trial of strength proves nothing. Let us have one more."

I thought of the birds that had fallen from the tree, of the cannonball in his hand, and I knew what the trial should be.

"Let us see who can throw a stone the highest." I motioned at the cannonball. "If you are feeling weak, you may throw that."

He dropped it immediately.

The bearded giant laughed. Without a word, he swept up a boulder and heaved it at the afternoon sun. My eyes burned and filled with tears as I tried to follow its path.

The young giant muttered encouragement while we waited for the stone to fall. I felt it strike the earth while I wiped the sun tears from my eyes.

"Is that the best you can do?"

The giant huffed in surprise, then muttered, "It always shouts. . . ."

Of course. I must sound loud if they could hear my heart.

"Perhaps you should try a smaller stone," I told the young giant.

He shook his head and picked up a boulder as big as the one his friend had chosen. He'd tried to stomp me to oblivion moments before, but I felt a twinge of respect that my taunts hadn't swayed him.

He slowly drew back his arm. With a terrific grunt, he launched the boulder toward the sky. It took longer to fall to earth. As the giants pounded each other on the back, I looked for Will. Someone was finally carrying him toward the gates.

Now for myself. I needed enough time for Will to reach the gates. I ran to a small brown bird under the blasted tree, then paused. It wouldn't work. They'd see the wings.

They'd *hear* the wings.

I looked back at the wall, toward the cannons. I realized I didn't want the cannons to find the giants: the young one who

74

talked about the awful duke but didn't mind my taunts; the bearded one who saved my life. I didn't want them hurt. I just didn't want them here in Reggen.

Perhaps I could arrange it so they—and the army that followed them—wouldn't return.

"You may return to the duke after I make my throw," I said. "I will let you live since you spared the boy. But you will know, after I throw this stone, that we can match you strength for strength."

I saw frantic activity on the walls; soldiers swarmed around two cannons. I plucked up the bird and almost whispered an apology until I remembered the giants' hearing. The poor thing quivered in my hands and I stroked its head with my thumb. I willed it courage and safety—and most of all, flight.

I looked behind me and saw a soldier move to light a cannon.

"Now," I shouted, "listen and tell me if this stone *ever* falls back to earth!"

I tossed the bird into the air, far enough that it would fly when I threw it, but not hard enough to hurt it. I saw its wings spread, brown and gray against sun-bleached sky, as the cannon roar echoed around us.

The giants ducked away from the cannon noise but didn't run.

"I saw it," said the young one, pride in his voice. "It should fall soon."

But my bird rose higher and higher. After a minute, it still

 75

hadn't returned. The giants muttered to each other in their own language.

"It hasn't fallen, has it?" I shouted.

Another warning shot flew past. The giants grimaced at the cannon's roar.

"Go back to your duke," I shouted. "I'll tell my people to stop their fire."

The young one nodded. "You are a greater warrior than we expected."

I laughed, arms wrapped around my belly, as if I'd never heard a finer joke. I needed them to believe me. I needed them to never return. "*Warrior?* I am no warrior! Tell your duke I am a tailor. You will encounter men far fiercer than me if you attack this city."

Chapter 10

I watched the giants stride away down the road, trembling as the terror I'd ignored roared over me. I could taste the dust from the shattered boulders when I licked my lips.

But I wouldn't turn away from the retreating giants. They might return. And I feared I'd forget what I'd seen: giants too graceful to be monsters, with voices like thunder, legs like trees, and hands that could snap a boy's leg.

Will.

I ran unsteadily toward the gate. The day felt slow around me, as if the sunlight were honey thick and I could not push through it. The bridge over the Kriva had never seemed so long.

Now that the giants were gone, people poured out of the gates and onto the bridge. They rushed toward me, toward the lad who had faced the giants. The lad. I stumbled midstride, trying to make sure I ran like a man and not a frantic girl.

The wave of people engulfed me well before I reached the gates. Some of the crowd shook their fists and shouted threats at the horizon, where the giants had disappeared from sight. Others pounded me on the back or cheered.

"Brave lad!"

"You did just what I'd have done! Pity I didn't get here in time to help. . . ."

"They know what Reggen is made of now!"

Where had these people been when Will dragged his shattered foot across the bridge? And where was Will? I elbowed through the crowd, trying to find the end of it.

I couldn't.

The news must have spread quickly. The farther into the crowd I pressed, the more the story of my encounter with the giants changed. I had not traveled ten paces before I heard people clamoring about an actual fight, how a lad faced two giants with his bare hands. A minute later, I had killed seven with one blow.

A man grabbed my arm. "Well done, lad! That will show them—"

Several men tried to lift me to their shoulders. I thrashed until they released me, and then ran deeper into the crowd.

How could Will have moved so far past the gates? The fierce strength I'd felt when facing the giants drained from me. I wanted to cry. And that made me angry, a petty, waspish anger that wanted to sting every person who jostled me.

"Will!" I called, turning in a circle. "*Will!*"

The crowd quieted.

"Where is the boy?" I asked.

One man, a blacksmith still wearing his leather apron, heard me. "You're the champion?"

I almost told him I hadn't done anything, but there wasn't time to explain. I nodded. "Follow me," he said. Then he shouldered into the crowd, shouting, "Make way for the champion!"

I followed in the path he created. He pushed people aside, shouting, "Make way for the giant killer!"

That was too much. I touched his shoulder. "I didn't—"

He was too busy picking up a smallish man and moving him to notice. And then it didn't matter: I saw Will. Part of him, at least, lying by the fountain. He was mostly hidden by a young noble who stood, arms crossed, between Will and the crowd.

I darted toward Will, but the nobleman blocked my way.

"Let me pass—!" The demand died in my mouth.

Fine Coat. I ducked my head, unable to move, hardly able to think.

"Let him see the boy!" hollered the blacksmith. "He's the champion!"

His meaty hand clapped me on the shoulder, and I stumbled forward against Fine Coat. I righted myself, but I didn't look up.

"*He* is the champion?" I heard the disbelief in Fine Coat's voice and felt the tickle of fear between my shoulder blades. He must be looking at me. "Who are you, lad?"

Don't you dare wilt now, I told myself. *Will needs you.* The last time Fine Coat had truly seen my face, I was Saville, a girl bundled against the cold. He'd been preoccupied with boiled bones, crushed houses, and the young man in the wagon. He

 79

wouldn't guess the truth—unless I gave him reason.

So I raised my head and met his gaze as if I really had killed seven giants with one blow. "Who are *you*? And why won't you let me see the boy?"

Fine Coat scowled. "I'm the one who brought him here! And I need to know about the giants. How many were there? I saw two, and then—"

I didn't have time for his questions. Will hadn't moved once. I tried again to elbow past, but Fine Coat grabbed my arm.

I yanked myself free and glared at him. "I have to see Will! He's hurt."

Fine Coat planted himself in front of me. "And I need to know what's happened. There's not much time!"

I opened my mouth, about to tell him I didn't care. Then I saw the set of his jaw. He wouldn't let me pass until I answered his questions. I ground out an answer.

"There were two giants, and now they are gone. Not killed. Gone." It seemed important that he know the truth about my role as giant killer. "That's all."

Fine Coat narrowed his eyes, as if he suddenly recognized me. "Do I know—?"

I didn't give him a chance to finish the question. I pointed at Will. "He's hurt! If you have any honor, you'll let me help the boy."

For a moment, the nobleman stood there, studying my face.

I couldn't breathe around the fear, but I folded my arms and glared up at him.

One heartbeat. Two. Then he let me pass.

"It's the champion!" Someone lunged forward and tugged at my shirt, yanking me off balance. "Show us your arm, giant killer!"

I twisted to free myself, but Fine Coat was faster.

"Stand back! Give them room!"

I heard the ring of a sword being drawn, and I sensed the crowd pull back as Fine Coat moved to stand between us and the crowd.

"Will?" I knelt beside him.

His eyes opened. Focused on me. He swiped at the wetness on his cheeks, his face taut with pain. "It hurts, Sir."

I tried to keep the fear from my eyes. His right foot was twisted at a grotesque angle. Small tremors kept rattling his frame, and he was pale—too pale. I wanted to push his dust-filled hair back from his eyes, but didn't dare indulge in such a feminine gesture.

"I told you not to go giant hunting," I whispered.

"But you got me back and"—Will pointed to Fine Coat— "he carried me the last bit. I couldn't—"

I shook my head. "You are the bravest here, Will. Do you hear me? No one was as brave as you."

Oh, he was pale. Even his freckles looked faded.

"Did you kill them?" Will asked, though I could hardly hear his voice over the crowd. "They say you killed the giants."

I made a face, almost comforted that he was well enough to long for gore. "Don't be daft. The giants think I'm stronger than they are, thanks to cheese and a bird and the cannons."

He wasn't interested in such details. "Why didn't you kill them?"

"You *are* daft," I said. "Did they hurt your head as well?"

I put my hand on his forehead then—roughly, the way a man might. He was covered with cold sweat, and the dust that covered my hands left a rusty smudge on his face. I needed to get him out of the crowd.

I stood and yanked on Fine Coat's sleeve to get his attention. "He needs a doctor! He—"

A shout rose above the crowd. "Make way! Way for the guard on castle business! We seek the champion!"

Eight or ten of the castle guard inched toward us, escorting a thin-faced herald. The horses they rode liked the mob as little as I did, shying every now and then, their ears flat against their heads.

The guard in charge, a bulky man with small eyes, drew his sword and brandished it until the crowd parted. "We have a message for the champion! Make way for the guard and the king's herald!"

I'd just faced the giants. What could the court have to say about it?

Whatever it was would be more than a message. King Eldin would want to see me himself. I imagined being led to a bath, a page telling me I couldn't see the king looking so filthy. . . .

I couldn't go to the castle. Not as the champion. They'd find me out.

I tugged on Fine Coat's sleeve. "Please! I don't care about the castle. We must go. Can you take us home? I'll tell you everything that's happened, anything you want to know."

Fine Coat peered down at me, then at the guards. "What—?"

Stupid, stupid . . . I'd been too anxious.

I drew in a deep breath. "Please. I need to find a doctor for Will."

Too late. The small-eyed guard dismounted and stood before us, face flushed, sword held before him. He was not pleased to see Fine Coat.

Fine Coat was not pleased to see him, either. His jaw tensed and he folded his arms.

The guard wiped his shining forehead with his arm, and spat, just missing Fine Coat's boots. "Lord Verras."

So that was his name. He didn't flinch away, just nodded. "Pergam."

Pergam squinted up at Verras and spat again. The spittle landed on the boot this time. "Here you are in the middle of things again. It'll be my pleasure to tell Leymonn."

Lord Verras stood straighter. "I'll tell him myself. It *is* my job, after all."

Pergam peered at me and chuckled, a mean little sound for such a big man. "It's the small ones that are the fighters, every time." Then he turned to face the crowd and shouted, "Silence, you! Hear King Eldin's decree!"

 83

The herald spoke into the hush Pergam had created. "By decree of King Eldin, descendant of the Great Emperor, king of Reggen and all its territories . . ."

I turned to run, but stopped when I saw Will smiling up at me. I couldn't leave him. *There must be a way to carry him back home, to—*

Lord Verras tugged me back to face the herald. "Your name . . . ," he prompted.

I blinked up at him. What had I missed?

"They want to know your name . . . lad," said Verras.

I squared my shoulders and jutted my chin just a little. The herald looked at me expectantly.

"It's . . ." *Would Lord Verras notice the similarity between Avi and Saville?*

Pergam waved his sword. "Give us your name!"

"I'm a tailor!" It was no answer, but I didn't think Pergam or the herald would notice.

But I felt Lord Verras's attention, bright as the sun. He knew something wasn't right.

"Wait," he murmured, almost to himself.

Pergam and the herald didn't hear, or didn't care. The herald turned back to the crowd. "The valiant tailor is welcomed to the castle. He will be made a guest of honor there!"

"No!" Lord Verras stepped toward the little man, but Pergam shouldered into him. Verras was tall, but Pergam was broad—and all too happy to thwart Verras.

The announcement rolled on. "He will advise the king of

the weaknesses of the giant army. And . . . according to the king's proclamation, he will prepare for his wedding to the princess!"

What was King Eldin doing, giving the princess away to someone he'd never met? Had his fear of the duke and his army made him that stupid?

A cheer rose up from the crowd. *Idiots!*

"But I'm a—tailor!" I shouted.

The cheers rose louder.

"Oh, the sweet boy! He'll be a good husband to her, that one!"

"Not grasping like some of those knights."

Lord Verras looked as if he wanted to strike the herald. Instead, he plucked a wide-brimmed hat off the head of a field-worker and jammed the hat on my head, tugging the brim low over my brow. He wrapped his arm around my shoulder, as if congratulating me, and muscled me toward a horse.

I twisted away. "Will!"

Verras tugged me back toward the horse. "You need to leave. Now," he whispered. "And, for pity's sake, don't let anyone see your face."

I scowled up at him, but his expression stopped me flat. He knew. Somehow he knew.

"He's wearing my hat!" the field-worker shouted. "The giant killer's wearing *my* hat!"

The crowd around him pounded his back as if he had won a great prize. I looked back at Will. Two of the guards plucked

 85

him up as if he were a great pile of homespun. No one would carry a silk so carelessly.

Will shrieked.

I pulled away from Lord Verras, darting toward the men. "Careful of his foot!"

The guards thought I was a giant killer as well. One of them nervously half saluted me. I almost laughed, until I saw Will, his head lolling to one side. He'd passed out again.

And then Lord Verras was tugging me back, pushing me toward the horse. I looked over my shoulder. The guards were carrying Will's limp form toward another horse.

"Get . . . up!" Lord Verras commanded.

I didn't know how to mount a horse. I'd never ridden before. Verras bent down and put my left foot in the stirrup. "Up!"

He gave me a rough prod, and I lunged up onto the saddle. Lord Verras mounted another horse nearby and began pushing through the crowd.

"Follow me!" he shouted.

That was the last thing I wanted, but my horse was more compliant, carrying me forward whether I wanted it to or not. I looked behind me once more. One of the guards held Will before him on his steed.

"Verras!" Pergam's shout rang out over the crowd.

Lord Verras looked back but didn't stop. "I'm taking the champion to the king."

Chapter 11

Our horses broke into a canter when we reached the edge of the crowd. I clutched the saddle, convinced my horse was trying to pitch me off.

I almost wished it would. I'd fall, then disappear down a narrow street, and escape this horrible trip to the castle—and Lord Verras, who knew far too much.

I kicked my feet free from the stirrups and loosened my grip on the saddle. . . .

What would happen to Will if I ran?

I slipped my feet back into the stirrups. I couldn't leave him—but that didn't keep me from imagining what would happen if I were discovered.

We had almost reached the castle. The cliffs behind it loomed above us, with the Guardians carved into them, their faces turned toward any who approached the city. Time had blurred their outlines and chipped their faces, but their eyes, with the long, slashed pupils, remained untouched.

I'd looked into eyes like those as I'd shouted up at the giants. Whoever had carved the Guardians had *seen* giants. Perhaps giants had done the carving.

A cool shadow brushed my face as we rode under an iron

 87

gate. Castle guards clustered there. I thought they'd gather around us and demand to see the champion. Yet only one watched as we rode past, making no effort to hide his suspicion. "Verras! I should have known you'd miss the excitement! Where are Pergam and the champion?"

Lord Verras kept riding but called over his shoulder, "Pergam's close behind."

We entered a smaller courtyard where a man with close-cropped hair, armor, and a cape waited for us. Lord Verras circled his horse around to speak to him.

"I need twenty minutes."

"You have ten, if that."

Why did Lord Verras need time? I twisted in the saddle to better hear.

"King Eldin is impatient to meet the champion. He's to be brought to the throne room immediately." The man pointed at me on my horse, its tail flicking at the flies that billowed around us. "Is that—?"

"Yes," said Lord Verras. "*That* is the champion."

The guard gaped.

"Close the gate," commanded Verras. "It'll buy us a minute or two."

He urged his horse toward the far side of the courtyard, and, once again, my horse followed. *Impatient to meet the champion* rang like a bell inside my head. Soon King Eldin would discover that his champion was a girl, that there was no young man to claim the princess's hand. No one to tell the duke and his giants to leave.

I swallowed down my panic. I needed an ally.

Before us were two men dressed in gray, their clothing beaten by sun and rain until the fabric was the color of willow bark. Rangers—and friends of Lord Verras by the look of it. They watched us trot toward them, shifting their weight as if the cobblestones pained their feet.

Lord Verras dismounted quickly. "Two giants," he announced. He looked back at me and asked, "Which way did they go when they left?"

The encounter with the giants seemed years ago. I closed my eyes to better remember. "Down the north road through the smaller villages. The one that . . . travelers to Reggen take."

I'd almost told him it was the road we had taken.

"How tall were they?" asked the older ranger.

Verras shook his head. "I'm not sure. I'd say as tall as the oaks near the Kriva."

Lord Verras wasn't even looking at me. It was my last chance to escape—or find an ally. Perhaps I could slip away.

My legs shook as I slid off the far side of my horse, shielded from the rangers' view. A quick glance over my shoulder showed that the guard at the gate had disappeared. Maybe I could find the doorway he had used. *I could find . . . Lord Cinnan, the king's advisor. He'd never liked the Tailor's apprentice, but he was wise. He'd know what to do.*

"Shouldn't be hard to follow them." That was one of the rangers.

Lord Verras didn't answer immediately. I peered around my horse, wondering if he'd noticed I was gone. He was too occupied by his conversation with the rangers. "You don't have to go. I can't order you, and I doubt Lord Leymonn will require it."

Leymonn again. The rangers' faces hardened at his name. *Who was he?*

Finally, a ranger spoke. "But you think it would be good to follow the giants."

Verras nodded. "I do, Restan. Right now we have only the . . . champion's information." He stumbled over the word as he gestured to me. I quickly stepped into view and prayed I didn't look guilty. Lord Verras didn't seem to notice.

"We need to know how many giants there are," continued Verras, "and where they are. The king should know his enemy."

The older ranger—Restan—raised his eyebrows as if he doubted the king. Then he clapped Lord Verras on the shoulder. "Can't be left blind at a time like this. We'll bring news tomorrow night."

I saw Lord Verras's relief in the way his shoulders relaxed, in the breath he released. "Thank you."

The rangers bowed and left without another word. The young one looked back at me before he disappeared, his incredulity clear. I glowered at him, hoping I looked fierce enough that he'd reconsider his opinion of me.

Lord Verras turned. "We need to go."

I glanced over my shoulder, as if the strength of my wanting could make Lord Cinnan appear.

Lord Verras reached for my arm. "We need to go *now*."

I stepped back again. "But Will . . . They're not here yet."

"That's why we must leave. I need to talk with you alone."

Hoofbeats. *Pergam and Will must be close.*

I crossed my arms. "I don't want to talk to you."

Verras looked toward the gate and scowled. "I wasn't asking permission."

Once more, he wrapped his arm around my shoulder and marched me toward a doorway tucked between a kennel and stables. I could barely keep my feet under me.

"Let me go!" I tried to stop, scrabbling for a toehold. "What are you doing?"

"I'm trying to save the city."

I finally planted my feet and twisted away. His arm tightened, pinning me against him so that I couldn't move. I glared at him, expecting to meet his stony gaze.

"Please," he whispered.

I stopped, too surprised to struggle.

A second later, we were in the dark of a narrow corridor. I couldn't see after the day's brightness—only felt us turn left and then right and then right again. Lord Verras didn't slow, and he didn't release me, though his hold loosened as he threaded the damp and silent corridors. He must have decided I couldn't escape in the dark tangle of hallways.

That frightened me more than the giants. *I'm trapped,* I thought. *I'm trapped under the castle.* Finally, I saw light ahead. I looked for torches but couldn't find any. It wasn't until we stopped in a pale pool of light that I saw it shone from underneath a door. Lord Verras unlocked it and pushed it open.

"After you."

He couldn't be serious.

Then again, there might be something I could throw at him inside the room. I marched inside.

The room was cool and damp, despite a fire, and filled with dingy, mismatched furniture. Lord Verras locked the door behind us, and I rushed to a desk heaped with books. I snatched up a sturdy pewter candlestick and turned to face him.

He stood in the middle of the room, unperturbed.

I lifted the candlestick, just in case he hadn't noticed it. "Why did you bring me here?"

Lord Verras rolled his eyes. "I have a sword. If I wanted to hurt you, I would already have done so. A candlestick won't help you much."

I'd just faced two giants. I'd show him what a candlestick could do.

"Why did you bring me here?" I asked again.

Lord Verras simply eyed me from my boots to the top of my head. "Am I right? You're a girl?"

I'd expected him to attack, to accuse. His question shattered my confidence. I could feel the bravado stream out of me.

"*Are* you?" he pressed.

It would be silly to argue. He'd known since the fountain. I'd seen it in his face.

"Yes."

I half expected the fire to leap up or the ground to shake at my revelation. Instead, Lord Verras groaned and buried his face in his hands.

"How did you know?" I demanded.

He didn't answer.

"*Why?* Why would you—?" He paused, then continued in a calmer tone. "This is important: does anyone else know?"

I gripped the candlestick tighter. I doubted I'd leave the castle that day, but who would take care of the Tailor? I could see him in his bed, listening for Will and me to return. I closed my eyes against the image.

"It's a simple question," repeated Lord Verras. "Does anyone else know?"

"Two people," I said, pleased that my voice had not trembled.

"Who?"

I shook my head. "Not yet."

Irritation crossed his face, but he mastered it immediately. "You will stand before King Eldin soon—you cannot avoid it. I may be your only ally. And believe me, you will need one. This"—he waved a hand toward me—"makes him look very foolish."

"He does a fine job of that all by himself! Who declares a champion without even seeing him first? Is he that incapable of protecting Reggen?"

I knew the answer before the question was out of my mouth.

 93

"This is not a game." Lord Verras's even voice was more unnerving than a shout. "You have thrown yourself into the center of a possible war with this duke and his giant army. Whether you like it or not, King Eldin's proclamation set you up as the duke's adversary, and when you defeated the giants, you *became* the defender of Reggen."

I stared at him, openmouthed, but he didn't stop.

"If the city—if the *duke*—learns that the champion is a girl and that the princess will not be wed, they'll think there's no one to challenge the duke's claims. Reggen will tear itself apart, and this duke will think he goes unopposed." Lord Verras shook his head. "It would have been better if you'd never gone out."

"They had Will by the foot," I whispered. "They shook him like a doll!"

Lord Verras winced, but he wouldn't be distracted. "My duty now is to protect this city. I ask you again: who knows your secret? And *why* do I know you? I've seen you before, I'm sure of it."

I blinked, afraid, but the fear made it easier to fight back. "Why should I tell you? You practically ran from Pergam and now you're hiding here under the castle."

He flinched. Whoever he was, he must not have much authority.

I drew myself up. "I want to talk to Lord Cinnan."

Verras didn't answer. Perhaps he was too busy trying to figure out who I was: a girl he had seen who also knew the name of the king's advisor. Finally, he said, "Lord Cinnan is under house arrest."

I nearly dropped the candlestick. "Why?"

"The king found his counsel tiresome."

Tiresome. I'd heard the king use that word so many times. How would King Eldin react without a sensible advisor when he found out he'd been tricked by his own tailor and that there was no champion?

Lord Verras held my gaze. "I brought you here because I wanted to know the truth about you and the giants before you're taken to the king. Before you are peppered with questions until the truth comes out in front of every nobleman and soldier in attendance. There is no Lord Cinnan to speak . . ." He paused, choosing his words carefully. ". . . *wisdom* to the king. And we have minutes before I must bring you to the throne room. So tell me: who are you, and who else knows about you? I'll do my best to keep them safe."

I'd hung all hope of safety on Lord Cinnan. What was I supposed to do with this young noble?

"Who are *you*?" I sank down into a chair with patchwork upholstery, still gripping the candlestick. "You say you'll keep them safe, but can you?"

Anger tightened his voice, clipping the words. "I am Galen Verras, cousin to the king. I assisted Lord Cinnan."

I looked up in surprise.

"My job was—*is*—to gather information for the king and his advisor. I have cultivated friendships with many in the

 95

castle: lords, servants, guards, rangers. Now that Lord Cinnan is gone, I work under the new advisor, Lord Leymonn.

"He does not like me, and he does not listen to me. Still, I've used what little influence I have to learn what is happening with the duke and giants. Even if Eldin does not wish to know." He spoke the last words quietly, more to himself than to me.

Lord Verras pointed to the door. "I'll unlock it, and you can leave. Eventually, soldiers will discover you and take you to the king. But you'll have no protection. The two who share your secret will have no protection. And Reggen?" He shrugged. "Reggen will be defenseless. Is that what you would choose?"

Lord Verras studied me as if he could find the answer in my face—and he kept looking. A tickle of unease ran up my spine. It was the first time someone had seen *me*, and not the Tailor's apprentice, since Will discovered me weeks ago.

His gaze was nothing like Will's.

I forced myself to return Lord Verras's gaze with the same intensity. With all he asked of me, it was only fair. Dark, almost black hair. A nose with a small bump in the middle, maybe broken once. It kept him from looking too noble. He was determined—I saw that in the set of his jaw. But he was also worried, his gray eyes solemn, and I remembered how serious he'd been on that walk to Reggen. He'd guessed this threat was coming, and he hadn't been able to stop it—or even prepare.

"You faced two giants for that boy," said Verras. "I don't believe you'll walk away now."

He was absolutely right, and he knew it. Sky above, I disliked him! But I needed him, and if I had to choose between Lord Verras and Pergam . . .

I set the candlestick down on the table beside my chair.

"These two people who know about me. You must bring them into the castle and promise that they will be cared for."

Lord Verras closed his eyes a moment and sighed in relief. "I will. Though the castle may not be safe soon."

"It's the safest place in Reggen."

He nodded. "I give you my word. I'll keep them safe."

No mention of me. Couldn't he guarantee my safety? I thought of the king with his new advisor, this Leymonn, and suppressed a shiver. "Thank you."

Verras nodded again, but didn't answer. Then I realized: he was waiting for me to tell him. Just like that, I was supposed to reveal everything.

It was harder than running toward the giants.

I closed my eyes. I had chosen this, even if it felt like no choice at all. When I opened them, my voice was steady. "One is the boy who was hurt. Will."

Verras mouthed a silent *ah*.

"You'll make sure he's taken care of?" I pressed. "His foot . . ."

"Physicians should be seeing to him now. I'll make sure they are the court's best as soon as we leave this room. And the other?"

"Willem Gramton." *Why was it so hard to tell him?* I had to force myself to say each word. "You walked with him on the road to Reggen earlier this year. You pulled him away when the wagon wheel broke."

"The tailor, the one with the fabric . . ." He looked more closely at me then. "You're his daughter. The one who talked with Lynden about the Guardians." He smiled as if seeing something else. "That's all. . . ."

"What do you mean?" I asked.

"*That's all.* It's what you said when I asked you about the giants at the fountain. You said it when I asked you about the man on the road to Reggen—with the same glare. I *knew* I'd seen you before."

"You remember that from all those months ago?"

"That man had barely spoken a word, and then he started talking to some girl—!" Verras faltered when he saw my frown. "So . . . yes. I remember. Now tell me about your father. Where is he?"

Some girl. Lynden hadn't thought I was some girl. Why couldn't *he* have discovered me?

But I gave Verras directions to our shop. "The Tailor's sick. He can't move. He can't speak. He'll be scared. And angry. Very angry. You must promise that whoever brings him to the castle will bring the big trunk in his shop. It means . . ." My voice faltered. I looked down at my boots, trying to breathe around the pain in my chest. "It means everything to him."

"What happened?" he asked.

"He was struck ill soon after we came to Reggen. I dressed

as his apprentice to find work for us. We wouldn't have survived otherwise."

"You couldn't sew as a woman?"

I crossed my arms. "Noblemen don't appreciate having a
girl fit them. It isn't done—like advisors to the king hiding
under castles!"

He ignored the jibe. "And Will?"

"A boy shouldn't have to compete with dogs for food."

He nodded. I could almost see him stitching the story's
pieces together.

I heard it first: the sound of footsteps in the corridor.

"We need to leave," said Lord Verras.

"What do you mean?" I asked. "If we leave, we'll walk right
into them. And you said we were going to the king anyway!"

But Lord Verras was already sweeping aside a tapestry on
the far wall.

Chapter 12

"Follow me," he whispered. He stepped up onto a bench and squeezed into a recess behind it.

"You want me to hide behind a privy? Absolutely not."

Lord Verras looked down at me, his face like stone. "I'm done arguing with you, Miss Gramton. If you want to keep Will and your father safe, you'll come with me. *Now*."

I heard the jingle of keys. "Lord Verras! King Eldin commands that you and the champion join him in his suite!"

Verras had already disappeared. He'd just left, expecting that I would follow. I did hate the man.

I leapt onto the bench, turned myself sideways, and slipped into the narrow recess, pushing past a hanging of felt. I thought I'd bump into the walls of the chamber—or worse, Lord Verras.

But the recess was bigger than I'd thought. And dark. *Dark* didn't do it justice. Something fell on my shoulder, and I jumped. The pressure grew firmer and gave my shoulder a quick shake.

Lord Verras. His message was clear: *Be quiet.*

I yanked my shoulder away. I wasn't a girl who'd squeal in

the dark. Where were we? Was this a secret tunnel? I groped along the wall behind me with my left hand, but stilled when I heard the thud of a door being thrown open. Then voices. Though it did no good in the dark, I turned toward the opening, toward our hunters.

The edges of the felt glowed. The men must have swept aside the curtain to the privy.

"Did you really think he'd be in there?"

"He's an underhanded fellow. I wouldn't put it past him."

I looked back and saw Lord Verras in the pale gray light. He didn't move.

"Leymonn ought to get rid of him. Have you ever had Verras watch you? It's like you're being hunted—"

The voices faded and the light disappeared, but not before I saw Lord Verras's small smile.

His hand found my shoulder and then my forearm, closing completely around my wrist. He tugged me forward, and I followed like a child. I had to take small steps, feeling ahead by sliding my feet forward. Even then, I stumbled on the uneven floor. After a few turns, he released me, and I heard the sound of flint being struck. Those few sparks flared bright as the sun, bright enough to make me blink. Then Lord Verras held a lantern aloft.

We weren't in a tunnel. It was a cave.

It seemed open, but there were so many . . . pillars. I didn't know what else to call them. We stood in a forest of stone that looked like it had been poured from the ceiling. But it wasn't like standing in a forest. I'd never worried that trees would tumble down on me and bury me in the dark.

Lord Verras began talking, but I kept looking for the end of the cave. I didn't want him to see how scared I was.

"—built the palace against the cliff," he said. "That room was Lord Cinnan's. He knew about these caves and had the privy built in front of the entrance. He knew no one would want to look beyond it." I heard the satisfaction in his voice and saw he'd lost the tightness around his mouth.

He liked the cave. Liked it. He reached for my arm, ready to go farther in.

I pulled away. "We're going to walk through the caves?"

"It will be the only chance I have to talk to you before we reach King Eldin. Think of it as a shortcut. Stay close."

What a stupid thing to say.

"Do you really think I'd wander away from you?" I asked as I followed him. "That I'm silly enough to lose myself in this hole?"

He didn't bother to reply, just pressed farther into the darkness, his lantern making the shadows of the stone forest dance. "We'll reach Eldin soon. Tell me what happened."

I sighed, then settled back into the memory as I picked my way through the cave.

"The giants had Will," I said. "The older one was holding him upside down, by his foot. . . ." I hated the way my voice shook. You could hear everything in this cave. "So I ran out and told them to put him down."

102

"And they *did*?" he asked.

I shrugged, even though he couldn't see it. "I was yelling and throwing stones. I think it surprised them. The younger one tried to stomp me."

"They were tall enough to do that?" asked Lord Verras. "I couldn't tell."

That was what he focused on? Not that I'd almost died, but how tall the giants were?

I gritted my teeth and pushed on. "My head almost reached their knees. He had to bring his foot up high, but . . ." I saw the young giant's boot above, felt its shadow cross my face. My breath knotted in my chest, the memory so vivid I almost dove away.

Lord Verras's voice pulled me back. "When I reached the bridge, they were throwing boulders. Was that a ritual of theirs?"

"Nothing like that!" I laughed, and the sound chased away the image of the boot. "It was a game of strength. Will needed time to get back across the bridge."

I told Lord Verras about squeezing water from stone and throwing rocks so high they forgot to fall back to the earth.

"The giants believed you?" he asked.

"Yes."

"I've read everything I could about them—stories gathered from older times. All the tales describe them as witless brutes." His voice grew distant and I knew he was thinking. "Perhaps they became that way over time. The giants that laid

 103

our foundation stones—if it was giants—must have been intel-ligent."

"*These* giants weren't witless."

He looked over his shoulder as if he didn't quite believe me. "They thought you could squeeze water from a stone."

Enough. I'd help him, even follow him through caves. But I wouldn't be treated like a child.

"You're not thinking, Lord Verras! What did the giants wear?"

He turned to me, irritated. I didn't care.

"You remember what 'some girl' says months after she's said it," I taunted. "Surely you remember what two giants the size of trees were wearing?"

He flushed. I could see it even in the lantern light. "The bearded one wore a coat and breeches, with stockings and boots. The young one wore the same, except he had a jerkin—leather, I think." He folded his arms. "That was all I could see before I reached Will."

Sky above, he really did see everything. But seeing wasn't the same as noticing.

"Do you know how much work it takes to tan the leather for that jerkin? Or the skill it takes to sew a coat? You have to mea-sure, which means they have some grasp of numbers. And you need thread to sew and yarn for those stockings, which means a farmer grew and then harvested some sort of fiber or sheared sheep. And then someone—an idiot, I'm sure!—carded the fiber and spun it fine enough that *another* imbecile could sew or knit with it." I raised my chin. "They are *not* witless."

The Tailor would have struck me if I'd spoken to him so. King Eldin would have had me beheaded. But after his first surprised look, Lord Verras listened, his gaze fixed upon my face.

"You're absolutely right."

I stared at him.

"Miss Gramton," he said, rubbing the back of his neck. "I meant it when I said I'd do whatever I must to save Reggen—even if it means listening to 'some girl.'" He half smiled. "Shocking you is merely an added pleasure.

"Believe me"—he swung around to follow the trail again— "if I thought it would irritate you, I'd go so far as to thank you. . . . Now, what else did you notice about the giants? How did they move? Act? Did they have any weapons?"

It took a moment to gather my thoughts as I scrambled after him.

"One of them had a pick. The other had a knife, but I didn't see anything else."

"So they possess some sort of ironmongery . . . but they didn't carry the weapons a soldier would."

I tried to force the memories into an order that would make sense. "And they talked about the duke. I think he wanted them to kill any humans—they had a word for us that I can't remember—on sight, but the giant with the beard said that Oma wouldn't like it."

Lord Verras glanced back to me, a question in his eyes,

but I didn't give him a chance to speak it. "I have no idea who Oma is."

"A captain in the army, perhaps? Someone who might challenge the duke?"

"I don't know."

Lord Verras sighed. "Anything else?"

"The young one caught a cannonball right out of the air. And their hearing . . . they heard my heart beating."

"What?" He stopped so suddenly that I nearly walked into his back. Then he turned, holding the lantern so he could see my face. "What did you say?"

"The young one caught—"

"No! The other part."

I licked my lips. "They heard my heart beating. They'd knelt down to see me squeeze water from a rock—the cheese, I mean. The young one could hear my heart racing."

"How do you know?" His voice was rough with curiosity and something I couldn't place.

"Because they said they could hear it. And my heart *was* racing. And . . . I knew they could hear it. I was sure enough that I feared they'd hear the wings of the bird I threw. That's why I waited until the cannons fired."

Lord Verras stared at me, as though waiting for me to change my story. But I couldn't. I stared back while water dripped somewhere in the darkness. Then I saw the fear in his eyes.

"I sent Restan and Tannis after the giants," he whispered.

"If the giants hear as well as you say, they'll know the rangers are coming."

"Maybe the giants won't hurt them," I said. "Maybe Oma—"

"Boiled *bones*! You remember hearing that on the road, don't you? Bones that looked as though they'd been gnawed! An army led by a duke who can't be bested. Esker . . . Kellan . . . wiped off the plains!" He pulled in a steadying breath. "Where was this Oma then?"

I had no answer.

Lord Verras lowered the lantern. Without a word, he started back up the steepening path.

I followed, lost in my own wretchedness. All I'd wanted to do was save Will. . . .

Lord Verras didn't speak until the path leveled out. "We're almost there. Is there anything else I should know? Anyone in the court whom you've sewn for? Anyone who might recognize you before Eldin learns the truth?"

I stopped. He was going to hate me and I didn't blame him. Why hadn't I thought to tell him?

He turned to face me, eyes narrowed. "What is it?"

My mouth was dry. "I sewed for King Eldin. Those new coats of his . . ."

"And when were you planning to mention that?"

"I wasn't trying to keep it from you!" I hated that my voice rose like a scared child's. "There was so much to tell: Will, the giants—It's not good, is it?"

 107

Lord Verras shook his head and blew out a long breath. "It might make Eldin more understanding about how the entire city could be tricked, or . . ."

"Or?"

"He might—" Lord Verras couldn't bring himself to tell a comforting half-truth. "I expect he will be angry that he was deceived . . . and that you saw him in a state of undress."

"That's what will decide my fate?" I fumed. "I've kept the Tailor alive. I've saved Will from two giants. And my life depends on whether the king is embarrassed that I saw him in a 'state of undress'? He's a conceited child if he thinks I was ever tempted by seeing—"

I snapped my mouth shut. Lord Verras was my one ally— and cousin to the king.

"Are you finished?" His voice was cold.

"I am." I was frightened that I'd said something so foolish. But not sorry, not one bit.

"Is there anything *else*?"

"I told the giants I was a tailor—and that there were men stronger than me in Reggen." It had seemed such a bold move at the time. But I didn't see how it would help me when I met the king.

It didn't even help me with Lord Verras.

He nodded, then continued on. After a few paces, I saw a lantern tucked behind one of the stone pillars. Lord Verras must have one hidden near every entrance to the caves. How many were there in the castle?

He stopped by the pillar and snuffed out his lantern. The darkness pressed against me, the way the cave would if it collapsed. . . .

Lord Verras's hand found my wrist and he pulled me after him. Much as I hated to admit it, the contact comforted me. Straight ahead, a few steps, then right, then left, then a light so dim I thought it was a trick my eyes were playing on me.

A muffled swish of heavy fabric as Lord Verras swept a curtain aside. We stepped into a small room—a storage chamber of some sort—then picked our way from behind two sets of shelves. Verras stopped, his hand on the door that would take us back to the castle. He squared his shoulders, as if he was preparing for a fight.

"Now what?" I asked, even though I knew. My heart was already racing.

"We tell the king. Make sure your secret doesn't go any farther. I'll do everything I can to protect you."

I wanted to stay in the caves. I didn't even care if I didn't have a lantern. "What do I do?"

"Walk in like a lad. Don't let anyone guess the truth until we're alone with the king."

"And then?"

"Stay ali—" He bit off the word. "Stay safe."

I hugged my arms to myself. "It's that bad?"

"It might be." Lord Verras opened the door. "Let's go."

I stood rooted to the floor like one of the caves' stone pillars, poured into place when the world began. It wasn't my fault that the king had been so foolish, so weak. Why couldn't the tailor just disappear? Why did I—?

Lord Verras turned back. "Miss Gramton—" He stopped when he saw my face, and I braced myself for his rebuke. "Above all else . . . no matter how much you think about it, you should never . . . *never* . . . discuss whether you were tempted by seeing my cousin in his underclothes."

Had he gone mad?

Then I saw a spark of humor in his eyes, right there with all the worry about giants and advisors. It accomplished what no reprimand could have—I discovered that I could move again.

I almost smiled. "Not a word. I promise."

He nodded once. "Excellent."

Chapter 13

Lord Verras and I threaded a few more narrow turns before stepping into a fine, wide hallway that I recognized. Sunlight poured through the arched windows, and a rumble like the Kriva rose up from the courtyard.

A man jogged up to meet us, then fell in step beside Lord Verras, talking quietly. A moment later, he hurried away. Verras nodded after him. "He'll see to your father."

There was no time to answer. Pergam scowled and left the guards clustered around the doorway to the throne room.

"We looked for you everywhere! Even in Lord Cinnan's"—Pergam spoke the name as if it had a bad taste—"old chamber. Lord Leymonn was not pleased."

"I brought the champion through the back corridors," said Lord Verras. "I thought the king would wish to see him before every servant in the castle did."

Pergam grunted, then ducked inside the hall to alert the king. The remaining guards barely acknowledged Lord Verras, though they stared at me, eyes wide with disbelief.

I wanted to run. I wanted to cry. Instead, I straightened my shoulders and put my hands in my pockets, as if I were bored—as if I wasn't trying to hide how they shook. *Make them think you're a lad.* I stared back at the guards, hoping they'd believe they couldn't scare me after I challenged two giants.

Pergam returned and held the door open. "His Majesty will see you now."

Lord Verras whispered, "Stay here. Don't come until I call for you." Then he walked in and pulled the door closed behind him.

Pergam, however, stopped the door with his foot. Lord Verras would have no privacy. I could hear his footsteps even above the roar from the courtyard.

I looked out the window. People crowded below, shouting for the—

"Where is the champion of Reggen?" called King Eldin. "Where is he? I want to meet the man who can defend us so well. He *must* tell me how he killed all those giants."

The king was frightened—I could hear it—and he was about to discover he had good reason. I clenched my hands in my pockets.

"Your Majesty." Lord Verras's voice was even and calm. "I must speak with you first."

"And *that's* more important than meeting the champion and learning how he triumphed?" It was a different voice. Slow, almost drawling. Contemptuous. Leymonn, I guessed. "You're supposed to bring me information, Verras, but I thought you'd have better timing than this."

"It's about the champion," said Lord Verras.

"Then bring him to me!" King Eldin sounded childish, even when enraged.

"Your Majesty, he has news that only you should hear—"

"I *will* see him now!" After a brief murmur, he added, "Out! All of you, out! I'll meet the champion alone!"

Nobles streamed out the door, staring openly as they walked past me.

"Tailor," called Lord Verras, "come meet your king."

I looked back toward the courtyard, where people called for the champion, wishing none of this had happened. Why hadn't a real warrior challenged the giants? Someone who could actually help Reggen?

Someone besides me.

I drew in a deep breath. *Stay alive,* I told myself. *Stay alive.*

I had found enough courage to run toward two giants. I could find it again.

I did not flinch at the hollow boom of the door closing behind me.

I felt naked approaching the king without my satchel of notions and cloth samples. King Eldin sat on his throne, leaning forward like a child waiting for sweets. Beside him stood a young woman dressed in a gown of silk so fine that the slightest breeze could catch it. Princess Lissa. Her face was set as if she expected to meet an enemy. She grew rigid when she saw me.

Don't worry, I wanted to tell her. *You'll be free sooner than you think.*

 113

The man on the other side of the king must be the new advisor, Lord Leymonn. He had a soldier's build, strong and confident. I looked closer. He *was* a soldier—or he had been. Hadn't he helped the king clear the throne room when I gained my first commission? Lord Leymonn looked ready to laugh when he saw me. It gave me strength to walk to the center of the king's suite. It kept my shoulders square, my head up.

Leymonn seemed to have the same effect on Lord Verras. He stood as he had in the midst of the mob, feet wide, arms loose at his sides. Like he expected a fight.

I hoped he could handle himself.

"So this is the champion of Reggen, the one who will marry Lissa and challenge the duke!" announced the king. I saw the worried pucker between his eyes, heard the clang of fear in his voice. "You must"—he glanced at Leymonn, as if trying to remember what he should say—"receive our thanks. And"—sounding more like himself—"you must help us destroy these enemies! Surely the duke will be an easy opponent after killing his giants."

Then he recognized me and blurted, "Bless me! It's my own tailor's apprentice, Avi! The one who brought me this coat! Why does Galen call you Tailor?"

The princess, Leymonn, and the captain of the guard must have seen some hint of the truth in the way Lord Verras stood, in my strained expression.

King Eldin did not, and he could not stay quiet.

He nudged his sister with his elbow. "I'd hoped for a bigger fellow, but this has advantages, too! You won't mind if I ask your husband for a little help with my wardrobe once he's defeated the giants, will you?"

Anger flared in the princess's eyes, but she didn't answer.

Lord Verras stepped forward. "There's been a complication, Your Majesty."

"A complication?" asked the king. "Are there more giants? Will we be under attack?"

Lord Verras opened his mouth to answer—

But I stepped forward. It was my secret. I should have the telling of it. "I'm a girl, Your Majesty."

King Eldin looked around the throne room, as if searching for another tailor. "What do you mean?"

I pulled in a deep breath, hoping it would be easier to say the second time.

"Your Majesty." I curtsied deeply, and when I looked up, I saw the king's eyes widen. "*I am a girl.*"

It was like running toward the giants all over again, except there wasn't sunlight. There wasn't the sound of the Kriva. Only silence, and the dim glow filtering through draped windows and closed doors.

Lord Verras interrupted the silence. I prayed he had words enough to fill it.

"It wasn't an evil-minded deception. She dressed as a boy so that she could keep her father's business and care for him when he was struck ill. Her name is Saville. *She* confronted the giants today."

 115

Leymonn laughed. Princess Lissa looked at me with something close to pity. But King Eldin just stared. I could see him trying to rearrange the future now that a girl was the city's champion.

Lord Verras spoke slowly, deliberately. "She cannot marry Princess Lissa. And no one outside this room should know her true identity."

"But I already declared that the champion should marry Lissa," mumbled the king.

"I'm afraid that is impossible. But we can help you decide what to do now."

"Decide? Decide?!" King Eldin shouted, leaping to his feet. "Why should I have to decide? It would have worked so well—a champion and a husband for Lissa. The duke would have no place here. And she's undone it all! She should go to the dungeon for such treachery!"

I braced myself for the captain to drag me away, for the doors to burst open and soldiers to rush in. I wished I'd seen Will. I hoped Lord Verras would take care of the Tailor as he'd promised . . . and I waited for the worst to happen.

But it didn't.

King Eldin pointed at me, clutching the arm of the throne with his other hand as if he would fall back without the support. "She shall be beaten! Then dragged through the streets every day for a month! And if anyone *dares* to give her a sip of water during that time, he will join her punishment!"

I glanced at Lord Verras. He shook his head ever so slightly. *Be still.*

Finally, the king wore himself into silence and slumped back into the throne. I released the breath I'd been holding.

"What will we do?" whispered the king.

"I liked the idea of no food or water for a month," said Leymonn.

The king winced as if he knew he'd sounded foolish.

Verras stepped forward. "We must assume that the duke and the giants are still a threat to Reggen. I'll discover everything I can about them so that we'll be prepared."

"At least we know they can be killed," said the captain. "Reports said she killed six or seven, but I imagine there were fewer. News is always changed by the time it reaches the castle."

I shook my head, but Lord Verras answered first. "She didn't kill them."

King Eldin's head drooped forward.

"There were two giants. Scouts, I would guess," said Lord Verras. "Saville outwitted them and they returned to their camp."

"I heard there was a boy?" the captain asked me.

"There was," I answered, glad for a chance to explain myself. "I couldn't just leave him, and no one else tried to help—"

"Where is he?" asked the king.

"Pergam brought him to the castle. His foot was badly broken," answered Leymonn. "Did you know the boy?" he asked, turning to me.

Something in Leymonn's gaze frightened me. I didn't want him to know how much I loved that boy.

 117

"No," I said, after a moment.

Leymonn raised an eyebrow, and I wondered if he suspected a lie. "So, there was a boy. She saved him by tricking the giants. It must have been *very* hard." No one missed the sarcasm in his voice. "Giants were always described as such intelligent creatures in the old tales. What a champion for Reggen! She didn't kill them, but she did confuse them."

I winced at the word *champion,* and Leymonn smiled.

Lord Verras ignored him. "Saville has shown that the giants have a weakness. She outwitted them easily. They left believing that a tailor—not a soldier, but a *tailor*—beat them in a contest of strength. And they took that message back to the duke. We have room for hope."

For a moment, the king looked like a child in need of comfort. "What do we do now?"

"Don't tell the city," said Lord Leymonn. "They're happy to have a champion. Let them think the tailor will protect them. He should make an appearance. It will put the people at ease."

The king nodded and turned to me. His gaze startled me more than his earlier shouting. "Let it be done. Reggen will see its champion within the hour. You can greet them from the balcony. No one should guess your secret from there."

The king paused as though he wanted me to apologize or thank him for not killing me. If I'd been playing the Tailor's apprentice, I'd have flattered him into a better mood. But I was no longer his tailor. I would not thank him for his threats—

or apologize for saving Will. There had been enough lying already.

I bowed. "As you wish, Your Majesty."

King Eldin flushed. "And when she is finished, take her to the dungeon."

"Cousin," protested Lord Verras, "she hasn't committed a crime! And I need to question her further about the giants. She has incredible insight—my scouts couldn't have gathered better information."

The king's eyes flicked to Lord Verras, but they held no warmth. "You forget yourself, Galen Verras. I am the king of Reggen! She'll stay in the dungeon for all the trouble she's caused. There's nothing to prevent you from questioning her there." He half smiled at me. "The dungeon is equipped with instruments that would help her answer truthfully."

"Well done, Your Majesty!" said Leymonn. The king straightened on his throne. "Very kingly."

I turned to Lord Verras and saw in his eyes that I'd go to the dungeon for so foolishly provoking the king. I tried to stand taller, to look braver than I felt, but it was hard to stand at all.

"No one has asked what I wish," said Princess Lissa quietly.

She had a low voice, which seemed at odds with her delicate features. But then I'd never heard her speak before. I knew so little about her, beyond the fact that she was near my age.

And that she was burdened with a pretentious, evil-minded brat of a brother.

"Dear brother, you forget: I was deprived of a husband today. I will have to stand next to the tailor on the balcony and, perhaps again, if another appearance is needed. I don't want her stinking of dungeon."

Perhaps the princess deserved her brother, after all.

"Someone may discover her in the dungeon, so I suggest that we make Reggen's brave little tailor disappear entirely." My heart stopped. "Give me a new maid, one to attend me during the day and sleep near me at night. Let Reggen search for the tailor. They'll never think to look at a servant girl. Should someone ask the whereabouts of the tailor, we can say that he is getting to know the princess."

Or perhaps Princess Lissa was canny enough to save me from the dungeon. For a moment, I was back in the garret shop and Will was telling me that the best way to hide my hair was to put it at the top of the trunk, in plain sight. I blinked the memory away and looked to the king, who hesitated, scowling a little.

"Surely, my request is a small one," said the princess. "Not half an hour ago, you were happy to bind me to a husband who would be able to fit your coats."

I longed to point out that a woman could do much worse than marry a tailor. There was the poor soul who would marry her brother, for instance.

"Please, brother." She spoke, as if the words hurt her. "I beg you."

King Eldin clearly preferred begging. "Very well. You may

have her as a maid. I will instruct your guards on their duty should she cause you any trouble."

Then King Eldin, flanked by Leymonn and the captain, left for the balcony without even glancing in my direction. I stood before the empty throne, unsure of what to do. Lord Verras and the princess were already talking.

"Thank you, Lissa."

She glanced at me and lowered her voice. "Leymonn is horrible. I can feel him watching me. But Eldin doesn't notice. He never does. And now we must fight an army of giants!" She put a hand on his arm. "Is it bad, Galen? This duke and his army?"

"I believe so. I hope to know more tomorrow." He must mean the rangers he'd sent out.

She nodded. "I wish Tor were still alive."

Torren. King Eldin and Princess Lissa's older brother. The one who had reigned only two years before his death put Eldin on the throne. Lord Verras's mouth tightened. Perhaps he didn't miss Torren as much as she did.

I was still wondering what his expression meant when I realized the princess was watching me. I smiled and held her gaze, ready to answer any questions she might have.

She raised an eyebrow and turned back to Lord Verras as if I weren't there. "When will you need her tomorrow?"

"As soon as she can be spared."

The princess chuckled. "I have no use for her! She can't fix my hair or properly attend me, I'm certain." A pause. "I'll make her an errand girl, to fetch for me and my maids. It will give her an excuse to go to you whenever you have need of her."

A guard appeared. "The king requires the princess and the champion to attend him at the balcony."

The guard might have been addressing Princess Lissa, but he gaped at me. I glared, and he looked away. *There might be some value to being a champion after all.*

"We'll come immediately," said the princess. She leaned close to Lord Verras, but I heard her nonetheless. "I have given you a pawn in this game with Leymonn. Play her well."

Chapter 14

"**P**lay me well?" I echoed as soon as the princess had swept out of the room. "What does that mean?"

Lord Verras sighed. "It means she'll do anything she can to block Leymonn."

"I won't be anyone's pawn!"

"No. You'll provoke the king all by yourself. She *saved* you."

"She wouldn't even look at me!"

"She's more concerned with limiting Leymonn's influence over the king." Lord Verras turned to leave, motioning me to follow. "Leymonn was a castle guard just weeks ago. When King Eldin grew frustrated with Lord Cinnan, Leymonn convinced the king that he would be a better advisor. Lord Cinnan was placed under house arrest that evening. Lissa is wise to fear that kind of ambition."

We were almost to the balcony. "Leymonn scared me, the way he asked about Will."

"He meant to frighten you."

"You think he'd hurt Will?" I stopped. "What do I do?"

"Right now? Go and keep the people calm. We need time

 123

to figure out who the duke is and what his army is like."

The mob by the gates had been frightening enough, and it had been celebrating me. What would the people of Reggen do if they discovered they had been deceived? If they realized there was no champion to protect them from the duke and his army?

"I don't trust the king or Leymonn." I folded my arms. "Or the princess."

"I'm not asking you to trust them."

Play her well, the princess had told Lord Verras. Was this what she meant? That he should gain my trust and then use me?

"I'm not sure I trust you."

He looked at me the way he had in his room—as if he were taking my measure. "I've dragged you around the palace and threatened you so that you'd do as I ask. And I would do it all again. But I haven't lied to you."

He waited, quiet and still. I'd trust him—at least for the evening.

I rubbed my face and grimaced at the red dust that coated my palm. "I wish you had lied, just a little. Something like, 'I'm sure he'll want to give you a medal, Saville. Don't even think about the dungeon.'"

Lord Verras chuckled. So he *could* smile. "Keep them quiet for tonight. Give them hope. When you're finished, I'll take you to see Will."

I nodded.

Guards had already swung open the doors to the balcony. I could hear the crowd, even over the murmurs of the nobles who'd gathered. The roar reminded me of the Kriva around the pillars of the bridge: a restless, rushing sound.

And it grew only louder when I joined Princess Lissa on the balcony. The shouts were a battering ram pounding against me. I felt powerless. I looked down at my feet, as if my courage had spilled out and I could gather it up. All I saw were flowerpots in the corner of the balcony, deep blue flowerpots like the ones I'd hoped to put outside the Tailor's door so many months before.

It wasn't courage, but somehow it was enough.

I walked to the edge of the balcony and I rested my hands on the rail, arms straight, the way I'd seen men do.

People filled the courtyard and the road leading to the castle. Had the entire city emptied itself to gather here?

"Champion! Champion! Champion!"

I noticed the children first, little ones sitting on their parents' shoulders. One girl waved a chubby hand at me and grinned like it was a festival day. Her father wore a workman's smock and gazed up at me, worried and unsmiling. He needed to see the champion, needed to be sure there was someone to protect his daughter against the giants.

And all he had was me.

I looked over the crowd, the men and women and children, all shouting, all waving at me. I wanted to tell them to think—*think!*—Could a boy really defeat giants?

And yet I waved back at them. Waved as if I really were the champion.

It made me sick.

I couldn't let them think I could save them. It was wrong. But Leymonn moved into view, folded his arms, and nodded. His message was clear: *Do what you've been told.*

Then another word rose up, competing with *champion.* "Kiss! Kiss! Show us . . . kiss!"

I looked back, uncertain.

Lord Leymonn tapped the back of his hand.

Ah, I could do that.

The shouts billowed around us like storm winds as I turned to the princess. She must have seen Leymonn. She pursed her lips, steeling herself to the difficult task, and extended her hand.

It was so smooth, not a sign of work. I wondered what it would have been like if I had been born to a different father, if I didn't have callouses from pushing a needle through fabric I'd never wear.

Then I bowed with a flourish like the lords I'd seen in court and pressed a kiss to her hand.

But the crowd didn't stop.

"Kiss! Kiss!"

"—s kiss!"

I heard the rest of the chant. "Fate's kiss! Fate's kiss!"

Had they made a tale of us already? Had they decided that, somehow, kissing the princess would put the world right?

126

I rolled my eyes. The princess saw it, and a tiny smile curved her mouth.

"Fate's kiss!"

I'd have none of it.

I didn't need to look at Leymonn. I'd already decided what to do. I faced the crowd, legs apart, shoulders back, and I bowed as I had when I was the Tailor's apprentice: a quick bend at the waist. Then I took the princess's hand and led her off the balcony. Soldiers closed the doors behind us, muffling the roar of the crowd.

Princess Lissa immediately yanked her hand away from me. "Bring my new errand girl to my maids' quarters this evening," she commanded Lord Verras. She rubbed at the smear of red dust I'd left on her hand. "And be sure she's *bathed*."

I stared after her, jaw clenched. That dust had come from facing two giants.

Leymonn glanced at the princess, then back to me. "You're good, Champion. That should keep the city happy for a while, don't you think, Your Majesty?"

King Eldin didn't answer. He stared at me and, for a moment, I thought he looked jealous. Then he turned away abruptly. "Come with me, Leymonn."

The advisor flinched, anger flaring in his eyes before he smiled and followed the king.

And then it was just Lord Verras and me in the dim room. The clamor of the crowd leaked through the closed balcony doors. Had I looked at Will that day in the street the way Lord

Verras looked at me now—as if he needed to *do* something with me, but wasn't sure what?

My shoulders sagged. I couldn't play the champion any longer. "Well?" I asked. "What now?"

"Now," said Lord Verras, "I take you to Will."

Chapter 15

I followed Lord Verras through a blur of narrow hallways and staircases. I kept remembering the balcony, hearing the crowd, seeing the hopeful faces of the people below.

"That was horrible," I murmured.

"You did well," said Lord Verras.

I slanted a glance at him.

"They think there's a champion, a real champion! They think I can save them. And I can't!"

"No," he said, "you can't."

Did the man ever try to soften the truth?

"But you did well," he added.

"You said you wished I'd never run out to face the giants." I'd resented the comment a few hours ago, but after looking out at Reggen from the balcony, I understood.

"I don't know a soul who would blame me for saying that after all the trouble you caused. But—" Lord Verras sighed, and I saw how weary he was. "I won't be in any mood to repeat a compliment, so listen well, Miss Gramton: you showed more bravery than a soldier when you saved Will, and you noticed more than most scouts during your time with the giants. Then you stood before the king and returned alive, despite your foolishness. So. As I said, you did well."

I almost stopped, right in the middle of the corridor.

He cleared his throat, as though he was unused to giving such praise. "It just would be easier if you were a man. Much easier."

I smiled and gestured to my clothing. "If only you knew how many times I've thought that."

We reached Will's door before Lord Verras could answer. He rapped softly, then opened it. "The champion wishes to speak to the boy."

A physician stepped out of the room. I nodded at him, hoping I looked the part.

"How is he?" Bless Lord Verras for asking. I couldn't find my voice.

"His ankle—and his leg just above the ankle—were broken. We set it when he passed out, though there may be many small breaks that we could not tend to. He's been given a draught for the pain and is sleeping now."

"Will he walk again? It looked—" I couldn't finish.

The physician's gaze flicked away, then back to me. "I hope so, but I can make no promises."

The corridor swam and I blinked away tears.

"Thank you, Cannon," said Lord Verras.

Then he led me into Will's dim, windowless room. One wall was solid stone, as if it was part of the cliff the castle stood against. That comforted me. I liked the idea of Will being far from the throne room. I hadn't been in the castle long, but

I'd seen enough to feel that it wasn't safe. Not with someone like Leymonn advising the king. A fire lapped at the edge of a small hearth, throwing shadows against the bare wall and over Will's bed.

The bed linens covered him, but not his broken foot. Those smooth blankets startled me more than Will's pale face. He was more likely to get tangled in his blankets than lie so still beneath them.

I stopped in the center of the room, half expecting him to kick back the linens and leap from bed.

Lord Verras closed the door behind us and pulled a chair beside the bed. "For you," he whispered. Then he took the other chair and dragged it behind me to the far corner of the small room. "For me. This is all the privacy I can offer you."

I couldn't look away from the still form on the bed.

The chair creaked as he sat down. "He's brave. Strong. He was almost across the bridge before I reached him. I don't know how he did it."

Will pulled in a whiffling breath. How many times had I heard that from his nest under the Tailor's cutting table? I almost smiled, and found I could move again.

I twisted my chair so that I could sit as close to him as possible. He slept on, his freckles stark against his pale skin. Pain still pinched his face, but the trembling that had shaken his body when he lay near the fountain had stopped.

How I wanted to hold him close! Then I realized I didn't have to pretend here.

There was no one in the room left to fool.

 131

I reached out and rested my palm against Will's forehead. It was dry and warm, no fever. I pushed his unruly hair back from his forehead. His eyelids fluttered, but didn't open. I wouldn't try to wake him, not yet. I took one of his hands in mine, and softly combed his hair back with my other.

"Sir?" Will's whisper was so thin I barely heard it.

He looked at me with sleep-clouded eyes. "I thought you were Ma at first."

"She used to do this?" I asked, still sweeping his hair back. He nodded.

"How do you feel?" I asked.

A shrug.

"The doctors think you'll be just fine. You'll have to lie still a while, though, or your foot won't heal. Do you think you can manage that?"

His eyes opened wider. "How will I go to the fountain to look for Pa?"

I kept my voice firm. "You can't. Not for a while. If you try to walk before you're well, you might not be able to walk at all. You'll have to wait, do you hear me? You need to heal."

He nodded again. "Maybe I can wait a few days."

"Good." After a little while, he scowled at me and whispered, "Sir, you shouldn't do that. What if the doctor comes back and sees you?"

"Sees what?"

"You doing what Ma did with my hair. They'll know you're not a boy for sure."

Lord Verras's chair creaked as he shifted his weight. Will

heard it and jerked away from my hand, trying to see into the shadows behind me.

"They know now, Will. They already know."

He pushed himself up onto his elbows, worry pinching his forehead. "I didn't tell them, Sir. I swear I didn't!"

I pressed him back onto the pillows. "They just figured it out. It would have happened sometime."

He pushed himself back up, trying to see who else was in the room. The chair groaned again, and a moment later, Lord Verras stood beside me.

"Hello, Will."

Will's face grew serious, even though his head swayed a bit from the draught. "Are you going to hang Sir?"

Lord Verras blinked. "Who?"

"Sir." Will pointed at me. "That's what I call her. So . . . *are* you going to hang Sir?"

"No," said Verras. "We aren't."

The answer didn't satisfy Will. "Is Sir in trouble?"

Lord Verras answered immediately. "Not with me."

"But maybe with someone else?"

A pause. "Maybe."

The answer satisfied Will, who accepted it with a grim nod. I sensed Lord Verras weighing how much he should say. "We're going to hide her for a while. So the giants don't find out the champion's a girl. She's going to dress as a maid and stay in the castle. If you see her—"

"I'll act like I don't know her," Will finished.

"Good," said Lord Verras. "Very good. And I need you to

 133

tell me about the giants tomorrow. Everything that happened. Can you do that?"

Will's mouth thinned, and I caught my breath. *What was he remembering?* But he nodded immediately.

Lord Verras held out his hand to Will, who shook it solemnly. I looked at the nobleman. His face was set, as if he'd just made an agreement with another man. No silly smirk that adults sometimes wear to humor children.

"Till tomorrow." Lord Verras released Will's hand gently and returned to his chair.

Will flopped back in bed and scowled at the ceiling. "Here I am, stuck in a bed," he muttered. "Who'll help you?"

"I'll be fine," I told him, pushing away every thought of dungeons and spoiled kings. I didn't want Will to see even a shadow of fear on my face. "Truly. Don't worry about me."

But Will didn't believe me. He just looked up, dark circles under his eyes. He'd fought against the doctor's draught for too long.

"I'll listen," he said finally, "and then I'll tell you what I hear. Folks talk around children. They don't think we pay attention. But I already know the doctor doesn't think you could stop an army of giants."

"He's an intelligent man, then." I pulled the too-neat blanket up to Will's shoulders. Then I swept his hair back from his face, wishing he'd give in to his weariness. "Listening is a fine idea, so here's your first assignment: I'm going to sing you a song, and you're going to listen to every word. I couldn't sing before, but I will now. I have a fine voice, young man. You tell me if I don't."

Before he had time to argue, I began to sing the song I had whistled for him that first day we met. The song about the dragon and the brave bowman who killed it.

At first, I was too aware of Lord Verras behind us. But then I thought about how long it might be before I saw Will again. I thought about the giants outside the castle and the villains who walked inside it. I thought perhaps this room still wasn't a safe enough place for Will.

And I knew, certain as sunlight, that I'd shoot every dragon from the sky for him if I could.

I closed my eyes and sang about fear and fire, scales and wings and curved talons as the dragon attacked the village. I sang about the bowman who saw the destruction, who stood grim and still as he aimed the arrow. Who didn't flinch as the dragon dove toward him. I sang about the silence afterward, as smoke cleared and the sun rose. I sang every verse, and Will grew quiet.

"That's a good song," he whispered when I'd finished.

I smiled. "I told you."

The chair behind me creaked as Lord Verras stood. We'd run out of time.

"I have to go now," I said. "You won't try to walk before you're allowed?"

"Sure," said Will. "But you'll be back soon, won't you?"

"I don't know. It might be a few days." I tried to sound

more certain than I was, but Will must have seen my doubt. He opened his mouth to say something, but I spoke first. "Listen for what they say about me or the giants. You can tell me when I visit next."

"Whatever you say, Sir." Before I could stand, his wiry arms wrapped me in a fierce hug. "Don't let them hurt you."

I hugged him back, pressing my cheek against his forehead. "I won't."

The last thing I saw before Lord Verras closed the door was Will's pale face, like a moon in the dark room.

"Now what?" I asked Lord Verras.

"One more visit," he said. "Your father."

I rubbed my eyes with the heel of my hand. "The *Tailor*."

Lord Verras opened his mouth, then closed it. "I had my men bring the trunk as you asked."

I nodded and followed Lord Verras, too exhausted to notice the route we took. We finally stopped outside another door. The Tailor lay on the bed, awake. His eyes widened when he saw me. I walked to him, one halting step after another, until I stood at his side.

His mouth was white with fury, his eyes wide. He was angry. I didn't take his hand.

"I don't have much time, Tailor, but—" I didn't know what to say, and looked over my shoulder at Lord Verras. Why did I think he could help me find the right words? "Do you remember how Will and I talked about giants? Giants came to Reggen today. They had Will, and I made them release him. So

I have to stay at the castle. I don't know how long. But you'll be safe here."

I looked down at him.

"No . . . ," he said, venom in the rasping word. "No. No." His eyes rolled as they took in the room.

My throat tightened, as if I still wore a cravat. I looked around the room for the first time. A cot sat in the corner, for whoever would tend to him. And the chest with the Tailor's fabrics stood at the foot of the bed, where the Tailor could not see it.

"Why couldn't Leymonn know about *you*? Ask about you? Will should be hidden," I whispered to myself.

Then I walked to the chest and pushed it to the wall nearest the Tailor's bed. It was very heavy, but my fury made easy work of it.

"There," I said. "You can see it now. That's what you wanted, isn't it?"

He blinked once: *Yes*.

"Then—" I almost called him Father, but the word could not rise past the tightness in my throat. "I pray it comforts you, Tailor."

Chapter 16

Weariness pulled at me the moment I left the Tailor's room. My anger had given me strength to see him, but it spent itself as quickly as it had sprung up.

The corridor tilted and I leaned back against the wall while Lord Verras pulled the door closed behind us. I'd never fainted before and didn't plan to start.

"What do I do now?"

"Sleep."

The rest of the evening blurred together: bending over a basin, sponging the red dust away, lads' clothing scattered at my feet. The feel of a skirt catching and swirling around my ankles as I walked to my new maids' quarters. Lying in moonlight, my body too tired to move and my mind unable to rest.

And finally: dreams. Dreams of dust and heat and crowds. Of giants with voices like thunder. And dragons, so many dragons. Too many to shoot from the sky.

I woke to someone shaking my shoulder.

"Will?" I threw back the bedcovers, looking for the cutting table and his nest of blankets.

"Who's Will?" a girl asked, hands on her hips. She had pale skin, black curly hair, and a sweet expression.

I rubbed my eyes, not quite awake.

"You must have had quite a trip to Reggen yesterday." She shook her head sympathetically. "You need to dress quickly. The princess is asking for you."

Had something happened in the night? More giants? The duke?

Will.

I scrambled to my feet. "Is everything—is Princess Lissa well?"

I plucked my dress off its hook and tugged it over my head. I hardly remembered how to fasten a dress after wearing trousers and a shirt for so many months. The girl must have noticed my hesitation.

"Let me help you." She stood behind me, and I felt her fastening the back of the dress. "The princess is well. And we address her as *my lady*."

It was a short walk to Princess Lissa's suite. The guards flanking her door didn't even blink as Nespra, the princess's maid, led me in.

I looked around the room, worried that I'd see more guards there, eyes sober with a night's worth of bad news. But there was only the princess in a silk robe, sitting by the fireplace. She looked tired.

Nespra grabbed my arm and gently tugged me into a curtsy. I dipped down, wobbly and off balance, then quickly stood. I wanted to know about Will, about the giants. I stared at the princess, hoping for some hint.

Princess Lissa glanced at me, then reached for one of the pastries on a fine porcelain plate beside her. She knew that I wanted news. And she didn't seem to care.

"Nespra," said the princess. "I see you've brought Saville."

Nespra dipped her head. "I have. Is there anything you would have me get for her? She has only one gown."

Princess Lissa waved a hand dismissively. "I'll have Kara tend to that."

Kara, I decided, was the girl laying out a dress for the princess.

"In fact, Kara," said the princess, "we shall see to Saville right now. Please arrange her hair. She can sit at the bench beside the window."

I turned to the princess, astonished. A duke with an army of giants was camped somewhere near Reggen, and she wanted her servant to arrange my hair? The princess merely nodded at Kara, who led me to the bench and pointed for me to sit. A moment later, the ribbon was yanked from my head.

"Were you ill? Is that why it's been cut?" Kara asked. "I've never seen hair cropped so short before."

"Kara, I told you to arrange her hair, not comment on it," murmured the princess as she poured a steaming drink into a small cup. "Saville, I hear you entered the city just before the giants. Tell me about them."

I studied her. What did she want from me? "I hardly saw them."

"My lady . . . ," prompted Nespra with a smile.

"—my lady," I said.

Lissa looked at me, mouth set, eyes blazing. "Tell everything you noticed. I'm sure you know more than you think."

Was this a test? "They were nearly as tall as trees."

"Oh! The willows?" asked Nespra.

I shook my head, but Kara's small hand clamped down ovoer my hair, preventing any further movement. "The oaks. They were as tall as the oaks. The . . . tailor didn't reach their knees."

"The tailor . . . !" breathed Kara from behind me. "Tell us about the tailor!"

Princess Lissa pinned Kara with a glare. "I wish to know more about the *giants*, Saville."

"I heard their voices, just once," I said, "because I was right next to the gates. They sounded like humans, only lower. And they moved almost gracefully. They looked slow, but they aren't. One stride seemed to take several seconds, but then you realize they've just moved the length of many men."

"They had human voices and long strides. How *fascinating*," said the princess. "Surely, you can remember more important details."

What more did she want? A description of their faces? Anything else would betray me.

I shook my head. "I wasn't as near as the tailor, my lady. That's all I saw."

She half smiled, as if acknowledging a hit. "I wouldn't have Kara die of curiosity. You may tell her about the tailor now."

I was supposed to describe myself? I paused, trying to think of what everyone else had seen—what the princess had seen.

"He was dirty. He and the giants had been throwing . . . things." I didn't dare say more.

"Do go on," said the princess.

"But when he was closer to the gates, I could tell that he was . . . average." I tried to imagine how I must have looked to the crowd inside the gates. "Average height, brown hair. He seemed confused by the attention. But he had a good face, an honest one—" The words caught in my throat. How could I describe myself as honest after disguising myself for so long? Wasn't this a disguise, too?

The princess tapped a finger against her mouth. Finally, she said, "Average . . . honest . . . a good description, Saville. The champion is also brave, truly. I have seen enough to know that. Though I wonder if perhaps he is a bit naïve, too." She looked at me. "Time will tell."

"He is a lucky tailor, Princess, to marry so fine a lady as you!" Kara said.

The door swung open before the princess could answer. Lord Verras stood in the entryway, looking worried. "Lissa, I must speak to you alone."

Please don't let it be Will.

The princess's eyes widened, and she motioned to Nespra and Kara. "Leave us."

Nespra held her hand out to me. "Come, Saville."

Lord Verras shook his head, ever so slightly.

"Stay, Saville," said the princess. "I have an errand for you."

Once the maids had left, the princess asked, "What is it, Galen? What's wrong?"

"Is it Will?" I did not care that the princess glared at me for speaking out of turn.

"We may not have hidden Saville as well as I thought."

I looked at the door, half expecting soldiers to burst through it. Instead, Verras walked to me and touched me lightly behind my ear.

I twisted away. "What are you doing?"

"What is that?" He pointed at the place he had touched.

My hand rose to where his finger had been . . . on the birthmark behind my right ear, just below the hairline.

"It's a birthmark," I said. "Why are you—"

"It's Fate's Kiss," he said.

"*What?*"

"Fate's Kiss. It's what the crowd chanted last night. They didn't want you to *kiss* Lissa. They wanted to see Fate's Kiss."

"You can't be serious! They think it means something?"

He shrugged. "I sent a man out into the crowd last night to ask about it. Someone at the gates must have noticed the mark yesterday."

I sat down on the window seat. "There were so many people when I first reached Will's side. My hair was tied back

 143

and I didn't have a hat. Anyone could have seen it."

Lord Verras sighed. "By the time night fell, half of Reggen was convinced you'd been marked by fate to save the city."

I traced the spot with my fingers. It wasn't even the size of a small coin. "I hated it when I was little! Mama used to tell me that—"

He raised his eyebrows.

Mama used to tell me that I'd been such a precious baby that she'd kissed me all over when she first held me. And one of her kisses, one just behind my right ear, had stayed. So I shouldn't mind if other children made fun of it.

But I did mind, every jibe—until Mama died. After that, whenever I needed to remember how much she'd loved me, when the Tailor was especially bitter, I had only to touch the birthmark behind my ear.

Princess Lissa's sigh brought me back to the present.

"She made me not mind it so much," I stammered. "Besides, it's so small."

"It's a way to identify you," said Lord Verras. "Right now the champion is a thin lad about this high"—he held his hand up to his chin—"with brown or blond hair and a face that no one can remember, thanks to the hat I gave you. But they *do* remember the mark. They've named it! You have to take your hair—"

He didn't have to finish. I tugged the combs from my hair, undoing all of Kara's work. My hair fell to just above my shoulders, long enough to cover the mark. "I can't let anyone see it."

"No, you cannot." He looked at the princess. "And I can't risk anyone walking in and hearing me question Saville. I need to take her to my rooms."

I smiled. No more talking about the tailor while the world outside the palace spun toward war. And Lord Verras wouldn't expect me to curtsy.

"I'll help however I can," I said.

The princess eyed the combs that I'd dropped on the window seat. "I'd say you've helped quite enough already, Tailor."

Chapter 17

What a relief to escape! I would have faced giants again before telling him so, but I was glad to see Lord Verras. He might pepper me with questions, but he'd let me ask my own. I even enjoyed the bewildering path we took to his chambers beneath the castle.

Once inside the dark little room, he motioned me to a seat. Then he sat at his desk and found a pen among the debris. I thought of the tables in the Tailor's shop, with shears and chalk neatly arranged, and the box of notions with small compartments inside. The Tailor didn't have to look if he wanted an extra-fine needle or the long pins. They were always in the same place.

Was anything ever in the same place on Lord Verras's desk? It was covered with piles of papers and books. He opened a drawer and pulled out a new sheet of paper. Then he moved a small pile, retrieved the inkwell underneath, and opened it.

And he did it with complete self-possession. What had Lord Cinnan thought of the disorder? Perhaps he didn't care as long as Lord Verras could find what was required as quickly as he'd found the inkwell.

Lord Verras shifted in his chair to face me.

"I talked to Will this morning."

I leaned forward. "How is he? Did he seem better?"

"He was well enough to tell me—" he looked up at the ceiling—"he told me he was bored out of his head and asked for something to play with."

I smiled. "He's doing well, then. Give him something that's broken and a few tools to tinker with."

"I'll do that." Lord Verras handed me a dusty lump of cloth. "He suggested a project for you, too. His tunic."

I unfolded it and spread it out on my lap, running my finger over an ugly tear in the sleeve. I hadn't noticed any wound on Will's arm earlier, but I'd check next time I visited, just to be sure.

"I'll get you any supplies you need," said Lord Verras. "You might like sewing while you're here."

"I hate sewing."

"The king swears you're the best tailor he's ever had."

"I never said I wasn't good. Just that I hate it."

"But why?"

"Did you know that the only things that make the Tailor smile are his silks and velvets? I do not please him. He doesn't smile when he sees me. When he watches me sew, I can tell that he wishes he could hold a piece of velvet one last time."

Lord Verras's eyes widened.

I drew in a deep breath, hating the way it rattled. "All my life, the Tailor has loved his fabric more than me, more than

 147

my mother, I think—at least toward the end." My voice grew steadier. "That is why I hate sewing. How could I love my rival?"

I silently folded Will's tunic. This time yesterday, he'd been teasing me about crooked seams. Mending the tunic would be my way of holding him. But my throat was too thick to tell Lord Verras I'd do it.

Perhaps he knew anyway. His voice was kind when he broke the long silence. "Will told me about his father."

I nodded. "Will waits at the fountain by the gates every day at morning bells. He's waited three months for his father to return from Kellan."

Lord Verras's face was carefully blank.

"What do you know?" I asked.

"Kellan was attacked weeks ago, though we've only just learned of it. No one escaped to tell us."

I hugged Will's tunic to me. "I can't tell Will that. I won't."

"You shouldn't. His father may still be alive."

I took a steadying breath. "You think the duke's army attacked Kellan. And that it's marching toward Reggen."

"I do." Lord Verras pointed at a map hung on the wall. There were slashes in the plains between the Western Steeps and Reggen—*villages that had been razed?* I didn't know there had been so many. "That's why I need your help. Yesterday, you told me about the giants. Now I need to know about the duke. I need to know who's leading the army."

I stared at the table, trying to remember. "I don't know

much about him. I think he told the scouts to kill humans before they could hear us. The young one thought our voices could . . . do something. Hurt him? He would have crushed me, if not for Oma."

Lord Verras wrote down every word I said. His pen had a rhythm; the writing and dipping into the inkwell made a scraping sort of music. He wrote as if Reggen's safety hung on each detail. Every now and then he'd shush me to keep me from talking ahead of him, too engrossed in his task to realize his rudeness.

Finally, he glanced up at me. "Did they say whether the duke was a giant or not?"

"No . . . I don't know. They never said. I assumed he was human because Duke of the Western Steeps is a human title." I sighed and shook my head. "But maybe I heard wrong. I was so focused on keeping Will safe. Maybe the duke didn't want us killed. Or maybe Oma is a washwoman who tells them they shouldn't kill humans the same way we tell children not to pull the legs off ants."

"But what do you *think*? If you had to say right now?"

I thought back to when the giants first mentioned the duke, and felt the cold, creeping fear once more. "I think the duke wanted the giants to kill humans on sight without talking to us. I think he's human. And I wonder why the giants would listen to him. I could fool the scouts for a little while, but how could a man make an army of giants follow him across the plains?"

Lord Verras smiled, never looking up from his writing.

 149

"What?" I asked.

"Lord Cinnan used to say that to me after I told him everything I'd learned: *What do you think? Right now?* Sometimes what came out of my mouth surprised me. It *is* effective."

"Do you know what else I think?" I told him. "I think . . . I hope . . . the giants might not come back."

He frowned.

"You don't believe me."

"You don't believe yourself." He shrugged. "You hope the giants won't come back, but you think they will."

He was right, but I wouldn't admit it. "Why are you so sure, then?" I challenged. "And why do you keep asking about the duke?"

Lord Verras set his pen down, but didn't answer. He just looked at me, in that way of his that I was beginning to recognize, as if there were something in my face that he could measure or weigh.

"Because I told you everything I knew," I said. "Mostly, though, because you need someone to think with."

"What?"

"You know something about the duke. I'd wager velvet on it. And you were wondering if you should tell me." I sat back in my chair, making myself comfortable. "I was telling you why you should."

He smiled wryly. "You're proud of yourself, aren't you?"

I folded my arms. "What do you know?"

He scrubbed the ink that smudged his right forefinger.

"Four years ago, Tor came back from a counsel, where all the kings of the River Cities had met. He said that the Duke of the Western Steeps had demanded to join them. The duke claimed that all of the kings were descendants of the emperor and that he was also a descendant."

"But wasn't the original Duke of the Western Steeps a son of the emperor?" I asked.

Lord Verras shook his head, a gesture that said, *hush!* as clearly as if he'd spoken it aloud. "The original duke was illegitimate. That was why he was given such a wretched piece of land. No Duke of the Steeps has ever sat in the counsel—or demanded that honor—not in the two centuries since the emperor's death. It was a ridiculous request."

"What happened to the duke?"

Lord Verras stopped rubbing at the ink stain. "Tor said he was thrown out, that when the duke was finally dragged beyond the doors, he collapsed and wept like a child. Tor thought it was funny, but . . ." Lord Verras shrugged. "There were rumors the duke's people wouldn't have him afterward, that they pelted him with stones when he rode back to the Steeps. They turned him away from his own castle."

How horrible. It was foolish for the duke to make his claim in such an outrageous way, to just walk into a meeting and demand a place there. But to be thrown out and then rejected by his people . . .

"Then what happened?"

"No one knows. It wasn't as if the Steeps needed a ruler.

It's covered with small towns and villages that look after themselves. They don't want interference and they're too poor for bandits to bother with them. Lately, there have been rumors of a newer, stronger duke who claimed the castle. But he's made no move to communicate with Reggen or any of the other River Cities."

"A relative of the old duke?"

"No one knows. I was too busy with rumors of giants. . . . It was only when the rider appeared two days ago that the Duke of the Western Steeps was even connected to the approaching army."

"What do you think about this duke right now? Is he the same duke your cousin threw out?"

Lord Verras stared at his desk. I'd never seen a man work through a problem like him, as if his thoughts were so real he could hold them in his hand.

"I hope not. He'd have a score to settle. And he'd be crazy enough to use giants to do it."

"You *hope* not, but you think he is."

Lord Verras raised his eyebrows at my impertinence. Then he nodded slowly. "We'll know soon, one way or another." He picked up his pen. "Thank you for all you've told me. You may go back to Lissa now."

"Could I stay with the Tailor instead?"

"But you—" Lord Verras didn't finish the thought. Finally, he ventured, "This is about Lissa, isn't it?"

"She thinks I'm a pawn," I told him. "I won't be anyone's pawn . . . certainly not hers."

He put the pen back down. "How did it feel yesterday in the throne room to know that your life was in King Eldin's hands? That anything he declared would come to pass, and you were powerless to stop him?"

I didn't answer.

"Lissa has lived like that for years."

"He's only been king two years."

"It wasn't only Eldin. There's always a king."

I couldn't imagine being trapped like the princess while her brothers played with her life. But it didn't give her the right to do the same with others—with me.

And why did Verras defend her? I hated that he was so calm, so sure. Then . . . *Ah, that must be it.* Besides, I wanted to see if I could make him blush.

"You wanted to marry her, didn't you? That's why you know so much about her. And that's why she's so gentle with you."

He didn't blush, but his mouth dropped open and he squinted at me as if I'd spoken another language. He was flustered—truly flustered—and that was as good as a blush.

Maybe better.

"Me? No," Lord Verras stammered. "No! I am the third son in my family. My father was fortunate to even find a lady whose father would allow a betrothal." He sobered. "But even after the betrothal was signed, Lady Farriday's father wouldn't think of a marriage until I'd made a name for myself. So I was sent here to help my cousin and to work under the respected Lord Cinnan. Now that Lord Cinnan has been sent away, I wonder if Lady Farriday's father will still find me acceptable."

"What is she like?"

"The princess or Lady Farriday?"

I wasn't worried about impertinence. "Both."

He leaned back in his chair.

"I told you about my father, about why I dressed as an apprentice," I said. "Besides, the princess is not the only one whose life was decided for her."

He nodded and then, to my surprise, answered my question. "Lady Farriday is . . . I've seen her only once. She trains falcons, and I like that about her, that she works with such wild creatures. She's intelligent and"—he held a hand up to stop the question I'd begun to voice—"pretty enough. Prettier than a third son deserves."

Lord Verras sighed. "As for Lissa . . . she and I shared the misfortune of having older, *powerful* brothers used to getting their own way. It creates quite a bond. I've known Lissa since our nurses let us wander the gardens while our brothers tore around, beating each other senseless with wooden swords."

"I can't see King Eldin tearing around with a sword."

Lord Verras's mouth thinned, as if remembering something unpleasant. "No, not poor Eldin. Torren was the one with the sword."

Lord Verras glanced at me, turning away from whatever memory that had been resurrected. "But go. See the Tailor first. Get what you need for Will's tunic." Lord Verras unearthed a piece of paper and scribbled something on it. "Give this to the physicians overseeing your father."

I realized, all at once, how much I owed him. "Thank you."

He nodded and turned back to his writing.

He wasn't making this easy, but I wouldn't be a coward. "No. Thank you for . . ." *Fighting to keep me out of the dungeon yesterday; for not minding that I ask so many questions; for actually answering them.* " . . . everything."

Lord Verras peered up at me. He was flustered again, enough that I didn't know whether to laugh or take pity on him. Finally, he answered, "You're welcome. For everything."

All the way to the Tailor's room, I wondered: *what sort of nobleman is that unused to thanks?*

The Tailor was sleeping when I entered his room, and I sighed in relief. He'd hate what I was about to do. I tiptoed to the trunk and eased open the lid. A little thread would mend the tunic, but Will should have more . . . and for that, I'd need some of the Tailor's fabric.

Whoever had fetched the trunk from our shop had tucked the Tailor's notion box on top of the canvas-covered bolts. I used the Tailor's shears to quickly cut what I needed, listening all the while for a change in his breath, a rasping no.

Nothing.

I tucked the fabric into my satchel and closed the trunk, then walked to the Tailor's side. He lay perfectly still—

His eyes flew open.

I leapt back, hands gripping the satchel as if the Tailor really could wrench it and the fabric away from me.

He stared at me, his expression vacant.

 155

He didn't recognize me.

Of course. He'd seen me dressed as a boy for months now—ever since his illness. I smoothed my skirt over my hips and stepped closer.

"It's me, Tailor." *Tailor* still fit better on my tongue.

He started a little, and then his eyes narrowed.

"It's Saville."

He squinted up at me, but didn't move. *What was wrong?*

One of the doctors slipped into the room. "Tell Lord Verras that he had another episode last night."

I looked up at him. "What?"

The doctor shook his head, irritated. "It happened after Lord Verras and the champion visited. We're not sure how much Gramton can understand."

I shook my head. "No. He was—"

"His moments come and go," added the doctor. "We're caring for him as best we can."

I looked back at the Tailor. I'd wished he wouldn't notice me a thousand times since Mama had died. Why, then, did I feel so lost that he didn't know me now? It was like looking in a mirror and seeing no reflection.

I put a hand on his arm. "Tailor!"

He looked at me, eyes blurry with fatigue or illness.

Both hands on his shoulders now. I even shook him. "Tailor!"

He saw me then, his old self slipping back as if it were a coat his mind could wear for a moment. His gaze sharpened in recognition. I saw a flash of relief before the anger rolled over his face. He shook his head, left, right, left, right—slow, creaking movements.

"No . . . ," he whispered. His favorite word.

"Tailor," I said. "You're going to be fine. You just need to rest."

"No . . ."

Chapter 18

It didn't take long to mend the rip in Will's sleeve. It was the crest I created on the indigo velvet that took time. I'd never sewn anything like it.

Perhaps that was why I enjoyed it so much.

Will's crest was just like him. It had a tin trumpet for his tinker father, but if someone looked closely—and Will would—he would see that the squire held it to his ear, not his mouth. Perfect for someone who listened. And at the bottom of the crest? A trunk flanked by rampant lions. Will would notice that the top of the chest was partially opened. He'd know I remembered how he discovered my hair and his knack for finding things.

I used a basket-weave stitch to create texture for the lions' coats. Scraps of silk formed the body of the squire, and a satin stitch in the Tailor's precious silver thread gave the ear trumpet sheen.

I spent the entire morning in the princess's suite working on the project, then stitching it to Will's tunic. The princess seemed content to have Kara brush her hair hour after hour while Nespra read to her, but the quiet of the chamber wore at me. If I hadn't had Will's sewing, I would have gone mad.

I heard echoes of Leymonn asking about Will every time

I added a stitch. That memory was enough to make me keep my distance for Will's safety. But this tunic with its new crest would tell Will what I wanted him to know. He was brave. He was a knight.

He was the only reason I'd pick up a needle.

I'd finished sewing when we heard shouting from the streets below the castle. Nespra's voice faltered. Kara's brush stopped midway through the princess's hair.

The shouts grew more distinct. "Make way for the duke! Give way to the Duke of the Western Steeps!"

Nespra ran to the princess's side, but Lissa pushed her away.

"Go, Saville," she said, eyes bright and sharp with fear. "See who this duke is."

I folded Will's tunic and stuffed it into one of the ridiculously large pockets in my apron. Then I ran to a window in the corridor that looked out over the main courtyard.

The Duke of the Western Steeps was a man—only a man. And he entered the courtyard on . . . a wagon. A lone horseman accompanied him.

Why would the duke drive what looked like any farmer's wagon, heaped with canvas-draped cargo? Dogs streamed behind him, noses reaching toward the load. A few lingered in the road, snuffling in the dust, even licking it.

The duke leapt from the driver's box, ignoring the soldiers waiting to escort him to the hall. He waited for his rider to join him, then grasped an edge of the canvas and flicked it back before striding into the castle.

 159

After a few heartbeats, I understood what I saw in the bed of the wagon: the heads of two giants, swollen and distorted in the summer heat. The execution had been recent. Even from a distance, I could see that the wagon floor was slick with blood. The dogs had been licking up the drippings. I put a hand over my mouth, nearly sick with the horror of it.

Then I recognized the heads. Those heads had bent near mine. Those bird-pecked eyes had strained to see whether I could squeeze water from a stone.

I ran to Lissa, reaching her quarters just as two soldiers summoned her to join her brother in the throne room.

"What's happened?" she asked. "You're as white as your apron."

"He killed them," I said. "The duke killed the two giants I—" I almost said *outwitted*, almost gave myself away, right there in front of Nespra and the wide-eyed Kara. I swallowed. "The duke killed the two giants I saw the day I came to Reggen."

The princess shrugged. "Then there are two fewer giants for us to worry about."

I didn't reply. I couldn't. But I saw the two giants again, towering against the bright sun, heard their voices roll toward me and through me. They'd put Will down because I'd told them to. They hadn't killed me, even though the duke had commanded it.

And now they were dead.

Minutes later, I stood with Princess Lissa beside the throne, sunlight threading the edges of the closed windows. The door swung open, revealing a man silhouetted against the summer glare.

The doors closed with an echoing boom and the duke strode into the hall, holding a red-stained canvas bag with two melon-sized lumps in it. I thought of Lord Verras's gray-clad rangers. *Please, let me be wrong.*

A steward began to announce, "His Grace, the Duke—"

The duke interrupted him. "—of the Western Steeps, Heir to the Ancient Emperor's Crown, Holder of the Eternal Heart . . ." He swept the room with a baleful glance. ". . . and giant slayer."

He was tall and powerfully built, like a warhorse and his blue-black hair was tied back from his face. He was frighteningly handsome. Or just frightening.

King Eldin sat straighter in his seat. "You are welcome here."

Lord Verras's mouth tightened as if he could not bear to hear so monstrous a lie.

The duke laughed and began to walk the length of the hall to stand before the king. The soldiers gripped their weapons more tightly, the ministers' faces grew grim, and Lord Verras . . . Lord Verras just watched, taking in every detail. Was he trying to see if this was the duke who the dead King Torren had spoken of?

Though Lord Verras's eyes never strayed to the canvas bag in the duke's hand, I saw his clenched hands, the way he grew pale.

"I have come to claim what is mine, King Eldin," announced the duke. "The throne and your sister."

There was no ring of swords being drawn. No shouts of outrage. No challenge from the court—or the king.

King Eldin had no answer. I wished it were a grand silence, to show that the duke was beneath his notice, but everyone present knew that the king was too overwhelmed to speak. I heard the hiss of Lissa's sigh as she realized her brother would not protect her.

Lord Verras broke the silence. "You may be welcome in this room by King Eldin's grace, but we do not acknowledge any claim to the princess—or to the throne of Reggen."

The duke stared at Lord Verras. "I am *heir* to the ancient emperor."

Lord Verras planted his feet the way he had in the mob, the way he had when we revealed my secret to the king. "As is King Eldin. As was his brother. As was his father and his grandfather before him. They were *all* heirs of the emperor— and kings of Reggen."

The duke gripped the hilt of his sword. "We will continue this conversation later, you and I."

"You can't have anything!" King Eldin finally blurted out. "Lissa is already given to the . . . champion, as I promised. I will not go back on my word."

He could not have looked weaker if he tried, hiding behind the champion of Reggen.

The duke sneered. His voice filled the hall. "The champion? You cannot mean the little tailor who met my scouts! He was no hero. He merely tricked two who were easily confused. I, however, bring Princess Lissa two giants' heads as tribute." He bowed and I felt her stiffen beside me. "*I* am the champion."

He looked around the room, and his eyes flashed. Flashed like the eyes of heroes or villains in battle songs I'd heard as a child. I already hated the man, but it was hard to remember that with him standing so proud and certain, while King Eldin wilted on the throne.

His eyes flash, I reminded myself, *because the madness inside him makes him open his eyes too wide. He wouldn't look half so heroic if he had a weak chin.*

The duke spoke into the silence. "Did you know that the giants once held one king above all others? Halvor, their high king, could not be deceived. Tales say he could hear the truth in any creature's voice, even a human's. They revered him because throughout their long existence, giants have been defeated by trickery. They fear human cunning as wild creatures fear flames."

He stepped closer to the throne. "But I am not so easily tricked. When the scouts returned to camp with news of a tailor who squeezed water from stone, I was not amazed. And when I explained what had happened, my giant captains were not merciful."

The thought of giant captains seemed to rouse King Eldin. "How could *you* command giants? I don't believe it!" The tremor in his voice claimed otherwise.

The duke laughed. "Oh, you have done me a great service! Some of the giants had grown restless under my rule, but your . . . *champion* proved my worth. The scouts might be tricked by the tailor's words, but I was not. Your champion demonstrated to the giants that I, alone, protect them from the deceitful world of men."

That had been our only hope. Lord Verras had told the king that we could outwit the giants. It wouldn't matter how big they were if we could trick them. But my trickery had only sealed our fate.

No one in the hall moved, though perhaps that, itself, was a clue for the duke.

He smiled as if he knew his barb had found a home. "They cling to me even tighter now. They will do anything I say. And do you know what I say?"

He stepped closer to the throne, so close I was sure he could see King Eldin trembling. Two guards stepped in front of the duke to bar his way, but they gave me no comfort.

The duke appraised King Eldin as if the guards were not even there. "I say that they shall kill any human they see. It is the only way to protect them from a city filled with such cunning citizens. There will be no more contests of strength, no discussions—only swift death.

"I say that as ruler of the giants, and as the slayer of the giants who your tailor confused, I am due your throne and your sister's hand in marriage within five days' time, the fourteenth day of Temman. I will make camp outside your walls. On that night, you will come to my camp. You will sit with me at midnight and open the city's doors to me when the sun rises."

He stepped back and looked around the room. "If your champion wishes to prove his mettle, he may fight any giant he chooses. It may be easier that way, if your citizens watch him die. Then they will understand why your sister will not have him. But do not mistake me: whether you consent or not, I *will* have Reggen. I will either sit on this throne as husband to the princess Lissa, or I will build myself a throne out of the rubble and bones of a ravaged city. It *will* be mine."

Another bow to Lissa, another smile to King Eldin. "If your sister makes an extra effort to please me, I may even let you live."

He looked down at the bag in his hand, as if noticing it for the first time, and emptied it at the base of the throne. The heads of the two rangers landed with an awful, moist thud, leaving a rusty smear on the marble floor.

Lord Verras gripped the side of the throne as the duke's voice rolled on.

"I leave you a gift. You sent two riders near our camp. They believed they were at a safe distance, I'm sure, but as you can see . . ." The duke studied the heads the way I'd seen the Tailor look at a project he was particularly proud of. Then he shrugged and smiled up at the king. "I had to kill two of my scouts, King Eldin, because of your *champion*. It seems only fair you should lose two of yours. I brought you their heads—I leave you to imagine what my army did with their bodies."

Boiled bones . . . Lord Verras had said when he led me through the cave. *Bones that looked as though they'd been gnawed* . . .

Before anyone could answer, before the king could swallow, the duke turned and left.

Princess Lissa's face was white and drawn, as if she were already dead.

Oma, I thought. Who was the Oma the giants listened to? I had to know. The duke had left the hall, but I ran after him. I caught up to him as he stepped out into the courtyard.

"Your Grace!" I called.

He spun to face me. I was close enough to look in his eyes. They were bicolored—one blue, one green—and eerily empty. I felt that he was deciding whether he should kill me or not. I glanced away to the wagon behind him. We were so close I could smell the giants' blood, feel the fear claw at me once more.

But my fear made me angry, and my anger gave me courage.

"Why should I speak with you, girl?"

"I am lady-in-waiting to the princess."

He raised an eyebrow. "She lets you stray so far from her? I shall have to talk to her. She shouldn't let her treasures wander away. I never trust mine to great distances."

I swallowed back my revulsion.

"Please, Your Grace. My lady, the princess, wishes to know: who is Oma?"

The duke cocked his head. "*Oma?* Where would she have heard that word? Did her champion tell her that the giants whimpered it as he overpowered them?" The mockery in the duke's voice flashed like a knife.

"I never said he was a champion," I answered quickly, too quickly.

I thought the duke's laugh seemed like it would never end. "So you despise him as well! You show more good taste than the rabble that gathers around him."

I despised the champion more than he would ever know. It helped, though, that the duke wasn't aware of who stood before him. I almost smiled. Almost.

"I would think you would wish to please my lady, yet you still haven't given her an answer: who is Oma?"

He smiled. "Tell your lady that Oma was the last word on the young giant's lips. He was scared and fought. It took two of my captains to hold him for execution."

The duke chuckled to see me flinch.

I lifted my chin and asked him one last time: "Who is Oma?"

He made me wait. "It means *mother* in the old giant tongue. Didn't the princess's champion know that?"

Chapter 19

"Is there anything else your lady wishes to know?" asked the duke.

"No." I had to press my heels into the ground to keep from running.

The duke must have seen my struggle. He smiled.

Did he ever stop smiling?

I smiled back as if I weren't scared, as if I could stand there before him and the bloodied heads of the two giants all day. Finally, I curtsied and walked away. As soon as I was out of sight, I dashed back to the throne room, desperate to know what King Eldin planned to do.

The main doors were already closed. Just as well. I didn't want Leymonn to see me. He'd be far too happy to send the champion to fight one of the duke's giants.

I rounded a corner, moving toward the doors at the back of the throne room. A guard was already closing them, muffling the shouts coming from within.

"Wait!" I called.

The guard paused.

"I am maid to Princess Lissa! She would not wish to be left alone."

The guard looked over his shoulder, but I slipped inside before he could ask the princess.

The throne room was in chaos. Only Princess Lissa stood quietly behind the massive throne. Perhaps she was afraid she'd be sent away if anyone saw her. She waved me over, and I joined her, just as anxious to be out of sight.

"I won't retreat to my room and wait to be told of Eldin's decision," she whispered to me.

I had never agreed with her more.

"Who sent the rangers?" Leymonn's smooth voice cut through the clamor. I couldn't see him. He must still be standing at the king's side. The princess and I peered around, careful to keep out of sight.

Lord Verras stepped to the middle of the room and bowed, ignoring Leymonn. Verras's gaze rested on me a moment, and he shook his head. *Stay back.*

I nodded, and retreated farther into the shadows, pulling the princess with me.

"You sent them, Verras? On whose authority?"

The room fell silent.

"I assumed you would want news before you advised the king." Lord Verras clenched his jaw. "Was I wrong? Had you already decided what you would advise?"

The silence reminded me of an approaching storm, before the lightning has begun.

Leymonn's voice echoed from the corners of the high ceiling. "Your foolishness gave the duke opportunity! Look how he has frightened the court and the king!"

 169

Lord Verras shrugged out of his coat, never taking his eyes off Leymonn. At first, I thought he meant to fight the advisor. But Verras walked to the heads of the two rangers and dropped his coat over them, then looked at the king.

"Restan and Tannis were brave men. They wouldn't wish their deaths to dishearten . . . the city."

I wished I could see King Eldin's face, hoped that Lord Verras's words gave him courage.

"I should have you confined to your miserable rooms under the castle," said Leymonn. "You wouldn't be able to—"

"Stop it, stop it!" King Eldin's voice had a sharp, panicked note to it.

Lord Verras kept his gaze on his cousin. *Please,* I chanted to myself, *please let him find some way to strengthen the king.* Reggen deserved a king who would not run and hide.

The king's voice was steadier when he spoke again. "There's only a week. What can we do? Tell me."

One of the nobles, an older one with a medallion, glanced at Lord Verras, and nodded. Leymonn scowled at the deference given Verras, but did not speak. The man with the medallion stepped forward.

"The steward of the city," whispered the princess.

"Your Majesty, the Kriva runs through channels under the city. In case of siege, we would have enough water. I am more concerned about the walls themselves. I do not know if they could stand a direct assault from giants. Without more infor-mation"—another involuntary glance at Lord Verras—"we can't know for sure. But I believe the wall would be torn down before the city would run out of food or water."

The king did not answer. I wanted to walk out from behind the throne and shake him until he found some spark of courage inside himself. Lord Verras looked up at the throne, mouth set, as if he could will his cousin to answer.

Still nothing.

Another man stepped forward. He wore a leather breast-plate and had a close-cropped gray beard. He cleared his throat, looking toward the king, then beside him, to Leymonn.

"The minister of war," whispered Lissa.

Did Reggen even have an army? I knew only of the city guard and the castle guard. I would ask Lord Verras later.

"Your Majesty, we would need time to prepare for war with giants. We have five catapults—maybe eight if some can be repaired. They might hold the army off for a week, especially if the giants must cross the bridge to reach Reggen." He looked at Lord Verras. "Do we know whether they can cross the Kriva?"

Lord Verras shook his head. "Not for certain. If the sto-ries are true, they set Reggen's foundation stones. We should assume they can cross the river."

"Then our weapons might buy us a day or two. We'll need troops from our allies." The minister's gaze skimmed over the lumps beneath Lord Verras's coat on the floor. "I don't know if riders could reach the other River Cities quickly enough."

I thought I heard a low, shuddering breath from the king. The minister of war could barely hide his disgust. I didn't

 171

blame him. No captain would tolerate such cowardice in a soldier. "There is perhaps another way. . . ."

When the king didn't answer, Leymonn said, "Tell us."

"I hate employing such underhanded methods, but a small group of soldiers could attempt an assassination."

Another man spoke up. "And what happens to the giants, then? Do you think they'll just go away?"

"Do you have another idea?" the minister of war snapped. "Yes, the giants may go back . . ." He waved a hand toward the north. " . . . wherever! The duke has made a claim against Reggen, not the giants. They may not be intelligent enough to plan an attack on their own!"

They were. I knew they were. They might be easily fooled, but they were not stupid.

The ministers argued on, and still, the king did not speak.

Lord Verras waited until they grew silent. "You're assuming soldiers could even reach the duke." His voice faltered. "These rangers were some of the best. They could track their quarry quietly. If the giants found and caught them, your soldiers will not succeed."

Another shuddering breath from the throne. Was the king *crying*?

"There is another way. . . ." Leymonn's voice, low and sweet, as if he were coaxing a child from her hiding place. "Two, actually."

No one spoke. No one, I supposed, wanted to ask him to explain himself.

"What do you mean?" It was the king's voice, brittle as an old man's bones.

"We give the duke what he wants."

Everyone stared at Leymonn as if they didn't trust their ears. Then the room erupted.

"Give him Reggen? Give him the throne?"

"Let him marry the princess?"

"He means the champion! Just the tailor."

But Lord Verras spoke for them all. "You *cannot* be serious! You know the duke will not be satisfied until he marries the princess and sits on Reggen's throne."

"And kills the tailor," prompted Leymonn. "Don't forget that. But you misunderstand me."

"Tell us what you mean, Leymonn!" gasped the king.

"Escape. I've heard there are tunnels that lead out of Reggen. The king could escape."

"And you, too, I suppose?" asked a man I did not know.

"I'll remember you said that, Anders!" snapped Leymonn.

"What about Reggen?" Lord Verras asked. "The duke might raze the city."

"The king would return with an army to reclaim Reggen."

I didn't believe the king capable of leading an army. No one in the room did. But Leymonn might. What a masterful stroke that would be: escape the duke's wrath, then return with an army to drive him out of the city. If Leymonn won, Reggen would crown him king.

"The king cannot reclaim Reggen if it is demolished,"

argued Lord Verras. "We cannot leave the city defenseless."

Lord Verras did not take his eyes from the king. I'd never seen such hope, such pleading, such confidence. The blood-smeared floor, the king's frantic gasps echoing from the far walls, they all faded away. I wondered what would have happened if the Tailor had looked at me the way Lord Verras looked at his cousin . . . if I'd seen that trust just once in the Tailor's eyes.

"We'll discuss this later," said the king. "I must rest."

I released the breath I didn't even know I'd been holding.

"Your arm, Lord Leymonn," said the king. "I am weary."

"I am ever at your service." Leymonn helped King Eldin off the dais.

No man as young as the king should be so undone, so disheartened that he walked like an old man. He saw the princess and me as he passed, and motioned us toward him. I could see he was frightened beyond reason.

"You heard it all?" he asked his sister.

She nodded, lips thin with disapproval.

"Don't hate me," he whispered. "You can't hate me. Tor said this would happen, you know. That I'd bungle being a king if I ever got the chance. He said so, and he was always right. I know. You don't have to tell me. He's the one who should have been here. Not me."

Princess Lissa shook her head, as if nothing he said mattered. "I will not marry the duke, Eldin. I will not have giants dance at my wedding."

The king winced. "Take me to my rooms, Leymonn."

The princess watched as the king walked away, leaning on his advisor.

"Come, Saville," she said. "You may read to me. I am sure Nespra and Kara will be too worried to do it properly."

I curtsied, trying not to let my own fear show. I looked over my shoulder at the emptying throne room. Lord Verras stood alone, beside the covered heads of his two rangers. Why wasn't anyone helping him? They'd looked to him, the youngest one there, when King Eldin demanded answers from them.

"Now, Saville!" Princess Lissa was white around her lips, and who could blame her? We'd listened to her brother weep like a child. He would give her away to save himself.

But then, Leymonn had liked the idea of letting the duke *kill* me.

"My lady, I cannot go with you."

"What? Why?" She asked the questions with such force that I wondered if anyone had ever told her *no*. She was as spoiled as her brother in some ways. She didn't want giants to dance at her wedding, but she didn't seem to even think about Reggen or the souls that filled the city.

Another glance over my shoulder. Lord Verras knelt, tucking the edges of his coat underneath the bloody heads. He gathered them up, stood, and walked away, cradling the gruesome burden. Had he ever possessed an ally besides Lord Cinnan?

He needed one. Reggen needed him to have one.

"You are my maid, Saville!" Princess Lissa caught my arm, turning me back to her. "You will do as I say."

I tugged my arm from her grip.

"No, my lady. You said I was a pawn." I stepped away from her and was happy to see her flinch. "And from now on, I will play myself."

I left her standing there, mouth open, and ran to find Lord Verras.

 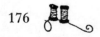

Chapter 20

After two wrong turns, I found him in the courtyard. There was none of the usual midafternoon bustle, only the retreating form of a ranger.

Lord Verras's hands were empty—and covered in the rangers' blood. He stared as if he didn't know what to do with them. As if he didn't know what to do with himself.

I stepped into the courtyard, blinking against the sunlight. Lord Verras didn't move, even when I stood beside him.

Finally, I put a hand on his arm.

He peered down at me, surprised. "Saville?"

Any other time, calling me by my given name would have been an intimacy. But he spoke so plainly, as if he needed something to hold to.

"You should go to your room, Lord Verras."

He nodded but didn't move.

I looped my arm through his, careful of his bloody hands. "Take me to your room. I don't remember how to get there."

He led me out of the courtyard so quickly I almost couldn't keep up with him. He sped down the dark corridor, turning left and right without hesitation. In no time we had arrived.

The coals in the fireplace threw little light. I went to his cluttered desk, found a candle, and lit it at the fireplace. I found another and lit that one, too. And another. It shouldn't be so dark.

By the time I lit the last candle, Lord Verras had settled into one of the chairs. I couldn't see his face, just his dark hair edged with candlelight. He kept staring at his hands, and he sat still, so very still. Something about him reminded me of Will that day in the street when the dog stole his food.

"They were good men," said Lord Verras without looking up, "good rangers."

"The best," I agreed. I had seen it in their faces.

I looked around the room and saw a small table covered in books. I quickly cleared the surface and set it in front of him. A basin and pitcher sat in the far corner. I filled the basin, and set it before him, too.

"You need to wash your hands now."

He nodded and moved to unbutton his cuffs and roll up his sleeves.

"Wait."

He didn't need more blood on his shirt. There had already been too much blood that day.

I reached for his hand and fumbled with the buttons. Once the cuff was loosened, I rolled it back over his forearm, aware of every time my fingers brushed his skin.

Then the other cuff. I could sense the rise and fall of his chest. I remembered how it had been when Mama died and it seemed like breathing was the only thing I could do, and sometimes even that had been too much.

"There." I gave the cuff a pat. When I glanced up, Lord Verras was watching me—looking at me like I was velvet.

I looked back, my fingers still on his cuff, and forgot to breathe.

Then he plunged his hands in the basin, the blood making dark clouds in the water. He worked quickly, no longer moving as if in a stupor. When he finished, he retrieved a towel. I used the opportunity to wash the blood off my hands.

"Why are you here, Saville?" His voice was emotionless.

I dried my hands, glad for the chance to think.

Then I set the towel down and told him the truth. "You helped me, so I helped you."

I picked up the basin, shouldered aside the curtain to the privy, and poured the water down the hole. "And . . . you need an ally."

He looked at me, incredulous, and laughed: a sharp, ugly sound. Then I saw his eyes and realized sometimes anger is the best armor. Sometimes, it's the only armor.

Lord Verras flopped down into the chair. "You are a fine girl, but you have a dismal grasp of castle politics. Go. Pick a better ally."

"That's my choice to make." *Fine girl, my foot.*

He shook his head.

I sat in the chair opposite him and made a show of settling in. "So. The duke has issued his ultimatum. What do we do now?"

He leaned forward. "*I* am going to make sure the duke doesn't set a foot inside the gates of Reggen again. And I'm going to start by figuring out who he really is."

"Good. Do you think he's the duke who King Torren told you about?"

Lord Verras didn't answer.

"I'm not going away, Lord Verras. I like this patchwork chair."

I braced myself for one of his measuring looks. But Lord Verras was surprised—surprised I'd come, surprised I'd stayed—and, maybe, for a heartbeat, glad.

Then he laughed, though it did not sound so sharp this time. "Have your way, then. Yes. I think he's the duke who Tor told me about."

"Why is—"

"Why is the fourteenth of Temman special to him? I don't know. Not yet."

I didn't mind that he interrupted me. I had news of my own. "I know what *Oma* means."

That got Lord Verras's attention. "How did you find out?"

"I asked the duke."

"You *what*?"

"I had to know, so I followed him and asked."

Lord Verras laughed again. "You asked, just like that?"

I didn't care about the asking. I cared about what I'd discovered. "*Oma* means *mother*. Those scouts didn't kill me because they worried what their mothers would think."

Fury erased any hint of admiration he'd shown. "It didn't keep the other giants from killing my men. Or your scouts. But then, maybe they had a different kind of mother."

"I don't know how to explain why the scouts were different, but it doesn't mean you can just ignore them. They weren't monsters!"

Maybe it was easy to be angry with him because I was already disappointed in myself. The scouts were dead because I'd tricked them. The rangers, too, because I hadn't remembered how well the giants could hear. I rubbed my forehead with the heel of my hand. No. That wasn't entirely true. The duke had a part in the deaths of all four. But it felt true, and that was almost as bad.

"What was the duke like when you talked to him?" asked Lord Verras.

I repeated the conversation, how he'd noticed my distaste for the word *champion,* how he'd gloated at the young giant's struggle before he died. "I wanted to run, standing that close to him. I felt like he'd pounce any moment and laugh while he killed me. His eyes didn't help, either."

"His eyes?"

"He opens them so wide. And they're different colors: one blue, one green. It adds to the effect, I think."

"That is . . . interesting."

"Why?"

"Think," he said. "Why would eye color matter to the 'Duke of the Western Steeps, Heir to the Ancient Emperor's

Crown, Holder of the Eternal Heart'?"

"I don't know anything about the Western Steeps or your emperor. Danavir was too far north, outside his rule. I only remember snatches of stories. Nothing *real*."

"The emperor had eyes of different colors," said Verras. "It was one of his most striking features."

"But even if the duke is a distant heir of the emperor, he has no right to Reggen."

"No," said Lord Verras. "No sane man would base a claim to Reggen's throne on something so small. That's not the point. When I first heard of the duke, I thought his titles were just arrogance. But what if he actually believes it? What if he intends to reclaim all the emperor's domain, starting with Reggen?"

"That's ludicrous!"

"I never said he was sane, just that he isn't playing a game. He believes the old empire is his inheritance, and he's come to claim it."

"All the cities and territories along the Kriva?" I asked. "Impossible."

"He has an army of giants."

The knock at Lord Verras's door made us freeze.

Before he opened the door, Lord Verras turned to me, and I saw that, somehow, he had accepted me as an ally. "The duke is copying the emperor. If we use that to our advantage, we may find a way out of this."

Chapter 21

Pergam stood at the door. He was just as ugly and unpleasant as he'd been by the fountain.

"Leymonn wants you, Verras," he said, then spat onto the carpet. "Fine thing for an assistant to the advisor to leave when a madman like the duke terrorizes the city."

"I was tending to the rangers." Lord Verras spoke carefully.

Pergam noticed me. "Wasn't all you were *attending* to, I'd say. If you're going to hide down here, find the champion for us."

Lord Verras's fingers tightened around the door handle. "Go."

"But—"

"*Go!*" Lord Verras slammed the door closed. "Leymonn has chosen a lieutenant worthy of him." He glanced at me. "Don't mind him."

"I don't." Pergam wasn't worth the spittle he'd left on the floor.

Lord Verras rolled his eyes. "I must go. Though I should have asked where Leymonn was before I sent Pergam away. . . ."

"And I should give Will his tunic." I pulled it from my apron pocket and showed it to Lord Verras.

He looked up from the crest and half smiled at me. "An ear trumpet and . . . a chest that's opening? The ear trumpet must be because he said he'd listen for you. But what does the chest between the lions represent?"

"You noticed?"

"My work is to watch, to make sure that King Eldin and the city are kept safe by seeing important things first. Yes, I noticed the chest."

I refolded the tunic and tucked it in my pocket. "Will found a lock of my hair in a trunk. That's how he discovered my secret."

Lord Verras laughed. It was the most heartening sound I'd heard all day.

I held it to me as I scurried down the halls to find Will. I'd felt safe in Lord Verras's room. But I'd witnessed too much blood and madness today to believe that Will was safe until I could see the truth for myself.

I was breathless by the time I stood outside his door. I tucked a strand of hair behind my ear and tried to hide the fear I felt. Then I knocked.

No one answered. After another knock, I opened the door.

Will wasn't there. Only the empty bed, its linens rumpled and thrown back. The bedside table was covered in the little toys and tools that Lord Verras had promised. But no Will.

Something was wrong.

I dashed down the corridor, straining for any sign of him. *Let him be safe.*

The passage changed as I moved out of the servants' halls, widening into a corridor with high ceilings and cut-stone walls. Golden evening sunlight filled the rooms I passed.

Will's laugh rang out, and I followed it.

The moment I crossed the threshold, two guards barred my way, their hands on their swords. I lowered my gaze and dropped into a curtsy, my heart throwing itself against my ribs.

"Miss Gramton!" called Leymonn. "We didn't expect the guards to fetch you from Lissa so soon."

Lissa? He dared call the princess *Lissa?* For a moment, I wanted to hide her as much as I longed to hide Will.

Will.

I rose from my curtsy, eyes taking in the room: an old nursery. Dolls, toys, wooden swords, play horses, and painted boats were all carefully arranged. There were even two wooden castles in the corner each armed with catapults.

Will sat in the center of the room, clutching a limp knight doll, his eyes wide as he looked up at me.

"Let her pass," said King Eldin from his seat in the corner.

"Thank you, Your Majesty," I whispered.

Will grinned at the young king and returned to his play. Only an idiot would think a boy of eight would smile so at an adult. Will was still acting the spy.

"We have been enjoying young Will's lively antics, Miss Gramton." Leymonn rested a heavy hand on the boy's head.

 185

Will scowled, but his eyes flicked toward me and he forced another grin.

"I haven't had the pleasure of meeting him," I managed, my voice brittle with fear.

Leymonn ruffled Will's hair so roughly that his head jerked side to side. "The king brought him a toy."

Will held up the rag doll knight and smiled widely. Too widely. He would have loved the castles, would have wanted to take apart the catapults just to see how they worked, but King Eldin had given him a silly doll.

And, all the while, Leymonn watched the boy like a hawk tracking its prey.

Time slowed around me. I tried to slow with it, to move so softly that the predator in the room would have no reason to attack.

"It's a fine knight." I knelt beside Will, glad the doll gave me an excuse to be near him. "May I hold it?"

"Here." For a heartbeat, I remembered Will with the giants, a rag doll in their hands. I blinked the image away, but before I could take Will's doll, Leymonn snatched it.

"Miss Gramton doesn't have time to play, I'm afraid. The king needs her."

I looked up at Leymonn and then the king, who perched uneasily in his chair near the castles. He waved a hand dismissively. "Tell her, Leymonn."

I stood slowly. I didn't look at Will, but I stayed beside him, hoping that would be enough to keep him safe.

"The city has grown restless after the duke's visit this afternoon."

Out of the corner of my eye, I saw Will turn away and begin to move the doll in some sort of pantomime. I knew he was listening.

I waited for Leymonn to continue. The silence was worse than his slick voice. Then I saw his smirk and realized that he wanted me to ask what was needed.

I'd rather wait all day.

Leymonn glanced at Will.

"The city is restless?" I prompted.

He smirked as if he'd won a game. "Yes, the city needs to see their champion."

"They don't have a champion! You know that."

Leymonn raised an eyebrow. "When I was a member of the castle guard, a man could be beaten for talking to his superior that way."

"Even if it was the truth?"

"Especially if it was the truth."

"I won't give them false hope." I looked at King Eldin, hoping he would say something. Do something. He turned away, staring at the wooden swords that hung on the wall.

Leymonn cleared his throat. "The king and I have already discussed this, Miss Gramton. He feels it is more a matter of giving the city time."

Time. So he could find a way to escape. I clenched my jaw against all I wanted to say.

"You owe your king whatever he asks of you." Leymonn wasn't smiling anymore.

I folded my arms.

He didn't look away from me. "Guard!" he commanded. "The boy is tired. Remove him."

One of the guards walked to the middle of the room and plucked Will up. Will yelped and dropped the knight doll.

"Careful with him!" I darted toward the guard, but Leymonn grabbed my arm and pulled me back. He smiled, baring his teeth. He'd found my soft spot, and we both knew it.

I'd never felt so powerless.

I looked at Will. He was breathing quickly, but his mouth was pressed tightly closed. He was determined not to show his fear, even with the guard's arms wrapped around him.

I turned back to Leymonn. "The city will have their champion," I whispered.

"What?" he asked. "I couldn't hear you."

"The city—"

"Don't worry about me!" interrupted Will. "My foot doesn't hurt so much now. The doctor put a special bandage on it." He reached over the guard's arm to knock on his foot. It sounded like he rapped against stone. "He says it's better than the starched rags they normally use. He says—"

"Quiet, boy!" bellowed Leymonn.

Silence filled the room, the quiet after a thunderclap. Will blinked, but didn't look anywhere near crying. I wanted to hug him.

And I wanted to belt Leymonn.

188

"What's happening here?" Lord Verras stood in the doorway, coatless, his sleeves still rolled up. He was furious, but he held the anger outside him, as if it was a wildcat on a leash.

I stood straighter just to see him.

"I was explaining to Miss Gramton what the king requires of her."

"I asked the king," said Lord Verras.

Leymonn's face turned red. "You serve *me*, the advisor to the king!"

"I serve the *king*." Lord Verras stepped into the room. "What is this, cousin?"

King Eldin flushed. "Who are you to ask what I am doing, Galen Verras? You remain in the castle only because someone must give Leymonn the information he needs."

Leymonn chuckled. "And yet I couldn't find you when I wanted to ask about this duke. I shouldn't have to send Pergam to fetch you."

Lord Verras's eyes flitted from the king to Leymonn, then to Will and me. He tilted his head. "I apologize. When I heard the boy cry out, I was alarmed. But, of course, you wouldn't hurt him."

"Never," said Leymonn. "Miss Gramton is already looking out for him. In fact, she was just leaving on an errand."

"I'll go out on the balcony again." I hoped Lord Verras understood every word I wasn't saying. "I wonder, though, if Will would be more comfortable if he was set down. The guard isn't gentle."

"I'll take him," said Lord Verras.

"No," Leymonn moved to block him. "You *won't*."

I folded my arms.

Leymonn understood my message. "Perhaps . . . you can escort the guard as he carries the boy to his new room, one closer to His Majesty's. King Eldin enjoyed this visit and would like to see him again, I'm sure."

Lord Verras looked at the king, who nodded. I wanted to wrench Will out of the guard's arms and hide him far away from giants and the castle politics that used him like a plaything. But I stood there, silent and limp as the knight doll that lay on the floor.

"I'm scared," whispered Will. Not once, in all the time I'd known him, had I ever heard him speak those words. He shot a look at Leymonn and added, "Of the giants."

King Eldin had been fiddling with his cuffs, but he sat straighter at the boy's comment. Lord Verras cupped Will's face in that way that men have, his palm close to Will's ear, his fingers curled behind the boy's neck. I wished I'd thought to hold Will so. I'd been so afraid to touch him, afraid it might betray my secret.

"There isn't a person here who isn't scared. It shows you have sense, that you can see what's coming. But if your heart is as strong as I think it is, you'll remember those who care about you. And you won't let the fear run you." For a moment, Lord Verras looked at his cousin, but the king would not meet his eye. Lord Verras sighed and looked back to Will. "Fear will try to chase you down—like hounds after their prey—until you are too tired to run anymore. You can't let that happen. When the time comes, you'll have strength to do what you must."

Will stared at Lord Verras, his brow pinched. "I don't know what I'm supposed to do."

"You'll know."

Will's shoulders relaxed. He gave the tiniest of nods.

Leymonn picked up the knight doll, and tossed it in the air. "You should go now before the boy gets tired."

"His name is Will," I snapped.

"Before *Will* gets tired. And you should do what the king asked of you, Miss Gramton." He smiled. "You should do it now."

I turned to leave, but looked at Will one last time. I was afraid to touch him, afraid to let Leymonn see how much I loved the boy. "You rest, do you hear me?"

He nodded.

I reached into my apron pocket and gave Lord Verras Will's tunic. "Thank you," I whispered.

He nodded, almost imperceptibly. "Of course."

As I left, I heard Will. "Thank you, Sir." My heart lurched to hear Will's name for me, and I blinked the haze from my eyes. "I had a good time here with you and the king and the knight you gave me."

 191

Chapter 22

Half an hour later, I was dressed in the clothes I'd never wanted to wear again. I tugged at my cravat and paced the room outside the balcony, rehearsing the lines Leymonn had given me. I ached to tell the people the truth: *There is no champion, there is no plan. The king is weak, and Leymonn? He will do nothing to save you.*

I stopped and looked around. The room was filled with Leymonn's cronies. They weren't the men who had guarded the king when I'd first visited the court, the quiet men who watched his every move. These new guards milled about, muttering among themselves.

And then Leymonn entered and the castle guard watched *him*. He approached the king and bowed.

"It's time," said Leymonn.

King Eldin walked out onto the balcony.

"People of Reggen!" Immediately the clamor in the courtyard quieted to an uneasy murmur. "An enemy . . . a great enemy has threatened our city. You have seen his riders. You have seen him."

I stood behind the king, hands clenched. His voice was so small. Reggen deserved better.

King Eldin straightened, like a puppet whose string had been yanked. "But you have also seen what one of your own can do against his giants! I give you . . ." Thunderous shouts and applause. King Eldin swept an arm toward me, finally finding his voice. ". . . our champion, the tailor of Reggen!"

I'd been given my father's name: Tailor. My stomach turned just to hear it.

In a heartbeat, Leymonn was at my side and mouthed one word: *Will*.

I walked out onto the balcony.

The crowd went silent. Every face was turned toward me. Then I imagined giants as tall as the city walls, moving through the crowd, great boots stomping these people. They shouldn't die just because the duke wanted the city and the king didn't know how to defend it.

The people wanted comfort. I closed my eyes and remembered what Lord Verras had just told Will.

"I know you are scared." I didn't shout. I didn't need to. My voice carried across the courtyard.

Leymonn coughed behind me. This wasn't what he'd given me to say. I didn't care. The people needed to hear it.

"I know you fear for your homes, your families, and your lives. Only a fool would say there's nothing to fear. But I ask you not to panic, for the duke will do everything he can to frighten you. Do not let your fear give him this city. Stand strong these next few days. I will do everything I can to help Reggen. The duke and his giants do not know what awaits them."

Neither do we, I thought.

I leaned out over the balcony and said it one more time: "Stand strong."

A roar rose up around me and the crowd began chanting, *"Stand strong! Stand strong!"*

I bowed once, the way I had when I'd first stood before the city, and then stepped back into the shade of the castle. The people needed courage, but the words I'd spoken tasted bitter as bile.

We had no defense against the duke and his army.

I did not return to Princess Lissa's suite until the next morning.

The moment she saw me, she dismissed Nespra and Kara. "Leave us. I wish to speak with Saville."

The girls scurried away, and I braced myself for the princess's displeasure.

"So you've decided to return," she said.

Did she have no idea what was going on? If I'd had a sword, I would have drawn it; I was that angry. Instead, I marched to her chair and . . . dropped into a curtsy. Perhaps she wouldn't kill me if I observed that one nicely.

"You needed someone to read to you. Lord Verras—the only man who defended you against the duke's claim—needed someone to help him attend to his dead rangers. He needed someone to help him wash their blood off his hands! Or would you have been willing to do that yourself, my lady?"

I saw anger flash in her eyes, but she wouldn't speak it, not even when we were alone. And then something else rushed over her face, taking the anger with it.

"They never ask me," she murmured.

"What?"

She lifted her chin, a regal expression that tucked anger and wistfulness and fear far away. "My brothers never expected me to do anything more than stand beside the throne. They would never ask me to help Galen wash the blood from his hands. I supposed I stopped thinking I could."

She looked down at her lap. "But it's no surprise that Galen was alone. Ever since Lord Cinnan was sent away, it's been unwise for other noblemen to associate with him. I think Galen's grown used to it."

It was the closest she would come to telling me she was glad I'd gone with him.

Princess Lissa shrugged. "After you helped Galen, what did my brother and Leymonn ask of you?"

All my earlier disgust at playing the tailor rolled over me. "They wanted the champion to speak to the people."

She raised an eyebrow. "And what did the *champion* of Reggen say?"

"He lied. The people think he can save them."

"He said that?"

I shook my head. "I let them believe that."

Her faced softened just a little. "I was right. You *are* naïve."

She leaned forward in her chair. "Do you know what my mother told me before she died, Saville?"

I held my breath, afraid that if I spoke too quickly, the moment might shatter. "No, my lady."

"She told me to take care that I didn't love my husband—it would give him too much power over me. She said I should be merely *fond* of him."

She paused, and I wondered if she ever tried to remember her mother's voice.

"You are more than fond of that little boy you saved, Saville. And for some strange reason, you are more than fond of this city. It gives people too much power over you."

She was right. Sky above, she was right.

"No one person can save a city," pressed the princess. "You shouldn't expect that of yourself. You shouldn't even *hope* for it. It will break you."

I sat down on a stool beside her chair and wrapped my arms around my knees. There was truth to what she'd said—and ugliness, too, though it took some time to see it.

"Hope . . ." I sighed. "My mother *hoped* the Tailor would be kind to her."

"Was he?" asked the princess.

"No. Never." I gathered up every memory I had of Mama, every scrap of every song she'd sung to me. "But she loved me—and she hoped good things for me. That's why I couldn't leave Will on the street. I had to want good things for him, too. I think it saved me."

Princess Lissa shook her head. "Who saved you? Your mother or Will?"

"Both . . . I think it was both." I looked down at my knees, then back to her. "I *do* want to save Reggen. You couldn't cut that hope out of me. Your mother's advice isn't easy. I'm not even sure it's wise."

Lissa sat back in her chair and smiled bleakly. "It has been easier to remain indifferent than I thought. My brother gave me to a tailor who is not a man." She looked out her window, the pale morning light washing over her face. "And if *that* scheme fails, I will be taken by a madman."

"Not taken, my lady," I said. "Don't assume that."

She raised an eyebrow. "Don't assume I would give myself so easily. But maybe *I* am too fond of Reggen. Perhaps I, too, would do something foolish to save it."

Before I could answer, the wailing began. It came from a thousand throats and rolled up the streets until it lapped against the castle walls. The princess and I saw our own fear in each other's faces. Slowly we stood and looked out her window, out across the city, across the Kriva, to the plain beyond.

It was covered with tents the size of houses.

"The giants have come at last," whispered the princess.

 197

Chapter 23

We were still looking out at the giant camp when Lord Verras entered the room.

Princess Lissa whirled away from the window. "Galen! Tell me everything."

"They arrived overnight. That's all we know. I'm going to see the camp for myself. There's a mob at the gates already, so I'll go to the wall on this side of the city and walk the ramparts. It will give me a chance to look from all directions."

The princess nodded. "Did Leymonn send you?"

"Leymonn has been more preoccupied with finding a way out of Reggen than the army that surrounds it. I sent a servant to tell him I was going and would return with a report."

"I wish he *would* leave," said the princess. "The giants are welcome to him."

Lord Verras glanced at me. "Will you come with me, Saville? Will it be difficult for you?"

I looked at the princess. *They never ask me. . . .*

"No, I'm not afraid," I said, and I wasn't. "I'll go."

Lord Verras nodded. "Find a scarf to cover . . ." He put his hand to his neck.

To cover Fate's Kiss.

"Here." Princess Lissa flung open a wardrobe. She pulled out a scarf and handed it to me. "You're fortunate, you know, to just walk out. I envy you." She stepped back and smiled. "I envy you both. It isn't easy to sit here and wait."

"Lissa . . . ," began Lord Verras.

She laughed, a lovely sound, even though I saw the fear in her eyes. "Go find a way to defeat this duke and his giants. I refuse to feel sorry for myself. And if you show me a crumb's worth of pity, Galen Verras, I'll chase you down the halls with a poker like I did when I was seven."

Lord Verras chuckled.

"Go! And bring me news when you return." She shooed us out the door.

When Lord Verras and I reached the ramparts below the eastern Guardian, I couldn't even look toward the camp. I needed a few moments to stitch myself together so that nothing I heard or saw could shake me.

I pulled in a steadying breath and turned to the cliffs, staring up at the Guardian's face. I'd never been so close to the great figure. It reminded me of standing before the scouts—feeling small as an ant, but somehow not minding because what you looked at was so grand.

"I wonder what the giants think when they look at the Guardians . . . ," I whispered.

"Hmmm?" Lord Verras looked downriver, where the Kriva flowed away from us, strong and smooth.

"It was nothing. Do you see something down there?"

"Nothing important. I swam there as a child, that's all."

"Did you?" I tried to imagine him near Will's age, laughing and splashing in the Kriva, but couldn't picture Lord Verras ever being so carefree. "Near the island?"

He squinted at the small island over a league away. "Rarely that far."

His eyes lingered on the river as if he was looking for something he'd lost. Or, perhaps, he'd never had in the first place. The princess had said he was used to being alone. Had he felt that way even as a child? I imagined a young boy with the same serious gaze, brushing wet hair out of his eyes. He had freckles. For some reason, I imagined young Lord Verras with freckles.

He pointed to a tumble of boulders on the far bank, between the city and the island.

"We'd go out to the rocks there, Torren, Eldin, and I. Then we'd swim beyond them. Tor and I would see who could dive deep enough to pull up a fistful of gravel from the river bottom. . . . What are you *looking* at?"

He'd caught me studying him.

I felt reckless standing so high above the city, so near the Guardian. "I'm wondering what you looked like as a boy—whether you had freckles or not."

He smiled, and I was glad I'd risked the question. His smiles—the real ones—had a comfort about them.

"Shorter." He chuckled. "I was shorter."

His smile faded as he looked toward the plains. "Are you ready?"

"Yes." And somehow, I was.

Every step took us closer to the camp and to the mobs below that shouted and wailed. The noise grew louder as we neared the gates: fear given voice until I could feel it in my body and blood.

Lord Verras and I stopped above Reggen's gates, looking out over the bridge across the Kriva. I rested my hands on the wall, not wanting to believe what I saw. The giant camp began near the horizon and ended on the banks of the Kriva, a tide pressing up against the river. Against us.

The fields and crops, the road to Reggen—all of it—were buried under tents. The land swarmed with giants. And at the center of it all stood a magnificent crimson tent: the duke's.

"Sky above," breathed Lord Verras.

Giants hauled provisions. Most carried tools, but some bore massive weapons: battle-axes or swords as long as several men. Those giants had something around their necks. I leaned over the wall to better look, though I knew it wouldn't help.

"What do you see?" asked Lord Verras.

"Some of the giants—captains, maybe?—are dressed differently."

He pulled a tube from his pocket and expanded it. "It's a spyglass. Look through this end."

 201

It took a moment to focus, but when I could see clearly, my stomach rolled. The captains wore collars of bones.

"Take it." I shoved the spyglass at Lord Verras. I didn't want to see any more.

His jaw clenched. "Bones."

"It doesn't mean they're human bones. . . ."

"Don't!" he bit out. "You *know* they are."

I did.

"They're really going to attack Reggen, aren't they?"

Lord Verras turned to me, incredulous.

"Don't look at me as if I'm stupid, Lord Verras. I'm the one who spoke to the scouts! I can't believe they'd just—" I shook my head. "We don't even know why the giants are here. What could they possibly gain if the duke takes Reggen? Why are they helping him?"

"I don't know," he shot back, "but it doesn't mean that they won't attack. Sky above, Saville! The duke said his captains executed your precious scouts. *Those* giants beheaded them! And you think, somehow, that they won't try to pull these walls into the Kriva?"

I had no answer—nothing I could wrap words around, at least. Death and violence clung to the bone-wearing giants. I could feel it across the Kriva. And the giants without the bone collars didn't seem to hate the captains. Perhaps I had met the only two giants with a spark of kindness in them. And yet . . .

"It's important that the scouts were kind, that they worried about *Oma,*" I said finally. "Please believe me."

For a long while, all I heard were the roar of the wind and clamor of the mob.

"I do, Saville. Can't you see how much I've—?" Lord Verras stopped and looked at me in that way of his, as if he were trying to see to the center of me. "I'm not saying they're monsters, but they've willingly followed the duke hundreds of leagues. He'll lead them over these walls, and they *will* kill us if we don't stop them. Help me stop them. Please."

Please. It was the second time Lord Verras had asked something of me as if I was an equal. It wasn't just that he used the word. He meant it. Leymonn might say *please* until burlap grew soft as silk, but I would never believe him.

I'd never trust him the way I trusted Lord Verras.

"What do you want me to do?" I asked.

He waved an arm toward the camp. "I'm going to make a map to study when I get back to the castle. But I need to watch the camp, too. Tell me what you see, just like you did with the bone collars."

"I'll do it."

"Thank you." He pulled a small book from his coat and an artist's pencil.

Trust Lord Verras to find a way to write without dragging the inkwell with him.

"Let's see," he murmured. "The camp is divided into squares. . . ." His mouth moved as if counting off the dimensions of the field. "Each square must have at least ten tents.

 203

Let's say two giants per tent . . . that would be twenty per square. There are—"

There were more squares than I could easily count. Lord Verras began scribbling a rough map in his notebook. I looked off to the left, upriver along the Kriva. A group of giants felled trees with one or two ax strokes. Other heaped them into great piles for campfires, I supposed. And still others . . .

"Lord Verras," I said. "Upriver."

Other giants waded far into the Kriva—the river that was supposed to protect us from invaders. They were plucking up boulders and dragging them ashore.

"How deep is the Kriva there?" I asked.

"It's fairly shallow. The center must be two or three times as deep. But, even so . . . I don't think it's enough. I always thought the river would protect us. That invaders would be forced to cross the bridge to reach the city." He turned to me, eyes wide. "This army could cross the Kriva. They could attack our walls from any direction."

"Can we stop them?"

"We might hold them off for a short while with fire or burning oil." He looked out over the plain, and I could almost see him watching a battle play out, wondering what would happen if the oil was positioned right at the gates or along the wall where the Kriva was the narrowest.

"One of the giants caught a cannonball," I reminded him.

He raised his brows as if to say, *You didn't think they'd attack.* "It would still make crossing the Kriva more difficult."

"You don't believe a word of that," I said.

"I don't believe it would work forever—a week at most. But I think it would give us time. I hope it will."

"Time for what?"

"For help to arrive from the other River Cities. Yullan is less than a week's ride."

"And how would any rider sneak past the giants?"

"I don't know," he said. "Yet."

We walked farther along the ramparts to better see the giants collecting rocks upriver. The warm wind roared up around us, buffeting my ears, tugging my hair from the scarf and beating it around my face. I welcomed it. After the clamor of the mob near the gates, the wind seemed a gentle companion.

After a while, though, I heard something else.

I put a hand on Lord Verras's arm. "Do you hear that?"

He rested his pencil in the crease of his notebook. "What?"

"Listen."

His expression changed the moment he heard it, too. "Singing."

We listened for the scraps of song that the wind tossed up to us. The melody was wild and strange, the notes strong and solid and as if other songs would break to pieces against them like ships on hidden rocks. None of the words sounded familiar, but the meaning was. I closed my eyes and saw hearth fires from a distance—a long distance.

Homesickness, if ever I heard it.

I glanced at Lord Verras.

"Longing?" he suggested.

"That's what I hear."

The song was soon replaced by one that was more warlike. I would have sworn I heard marching in it—and destruction. The first song had comforted me—surely creatures that missed home so much couldn't attack us. But perhaps Reggen had to be overthrown before they could return home.

Perhaps they didn't expect to return home at all.

I shivered and was glad for the distraction when Lord Verras pointed to an open area near the duke's crimson tent. "For military exercises, I expect. He's good. The entire city will be able to see what his giants can do. We'll be lucky if the people aren't ready to surrender after two days."

He raised the spyglass to take a closer look. I scanned the back edge of the camp and saw something that looked like pens. Had the giants driven cattle with the army for food?

I pointed them out to Lord Verras. "The far corner, near the horizon. What do you see?"

He focused the spyglass on the pens. "I see some of your captains—"

He stopped. "Men . . . women . . . babes, even. They don't seem to have much shelter. They—" He lowered the spyglass.

I wanted to protest that the giants couldn't be using humans for food, but I knew it was a lie. How had I been so simple? So stupid? This army would attack Reggen, and we had no defenses.

Without a word, Lord Verras collapsed his spyglass and

put it away. He tucked the notebook into his coat as he turned, striding back toward the castle.

I jogged to catch up. "Where are you going?"

"There's no point holding them off if no help comes. We can't send riders out across the bridge, but maybe someone can reach the cliffs behind the city. It would put the Kriva and Reggen between them and the giants."

"How? They're too steep to climb. And the giants would see."

"The caves," he said. "We need to search the caves."

Chapter 24

I knew the way to Lord Verras's room almost as well as he did. He reached for his keys, but the door swung open a handbreadth when he touched it.

He put a finger to his lips. When I nodded, he pushed the door open and I followed him inside.

Leymonn sat in the chair closest to the fire, his boots propped up on a low table. Lord Verras slammed the door closed behind us, letting its crash announce our entrance.

Leymonn jumped, then nonchalantly adjusted his boots on the table. "Ah! I've been waiting for you. What did you see, Lord Verras?"

"I'm surprised you asked. I thought you were more interested in a way *out* of Reggen."

"And I thought my question was clear enough: tell me about the giant camp."

"What do you really want?" asked Verras.

Leymonn tilted his head. "I want to make sure the king survives."

And his advisor, too, I thought.

"Your concern for Reggen is touching."

"I will not ask again," said Leymonn. "What did you see? What are we facing?"

I turned to leave, but Lord Verras caught my arm. "Stay, Saville."

Any other time, I would have been offended by the command, but I sensed it was more for Leymonn's benefit than my own.

Leymonn smirked. "I didn't expect you'd be so taken with the champion, but I don't mind as long as she doesn't distract you. Don't worry, Verras. I won't tell Lady Farriday when she comes to Reggen."

Lord Verras did not reply for one breath, then two. Finally, he answered, "I am not distracted, and if we survive these next few weeks, I'll tell Lady Farriday about Saville myself. The truth is that I see better when I'm with her."

Leymonn's eyes narrowed. If they had been swordsmen, I'd have awarded the match to Lord Verras . . . Lord Verras, who was never lavish with his praise, but still praised me. Who argued with me, but listened when I argued back. Who didn't smile—truly smile—half as much as I wished he would.

I thought of him telling his falcon bride about how we'd worked so closely. I knew he'd tell her everything, and I knew there would be nothing that could shame us.

But more than anything, I knew how much I'd miss Lord Verras when he no longer needed my help stopping an army of giants.

"Well, then," said Leymonn. "What did you *both* see?"

Lord Verras told him about the camp, the giants wading into the Kriva, and finally, the pens.

Leymonn schooled his expression, but not before I saw his fear. "We need a way out of Reggen."

"It's possible we could send a messenger to Yullan. Have him take a small dinghy out into the Kriva. We'd send him at night and he wouldn't use the oars, at least until the boat's past the camp—the giants might hear them."

"The Kriva's sound might help mask the noise," added Leymonn. "But don't choose a messenger you like, Verras. You might have *his* head delivered to you next."

A hit for Leymonn. Lord Verras's hands curled into fists, but he kept his voice even. "I know why the fourteenth is special to the duke. It's the date the emperor took Reggen. I found it in the archives last night. The emperor fought armies on the plains for weeks. Finally, the rulers of the city went to him at midnight. By morning, they'd negotiated a truce. The emperor entered Reggen that day, the fourteenth. We were the first of the River Cities conquered."

"You're sure?" demanded Leymonn.

"I am. Reggen wouldn't celebrate a defeat after the emperor died. When the calendar changed, the date became even more obscure."

"It fits," said Leymonn. "The duke wanted the king to join him at midnight. . . . You'll report what else you learn?"

"I need help." Lord Verras hesitated, as though the words pained him. "Lord Cinnan has read almost every document and book in the archives."

"No. Lord Cinnan will stay under house arrest and be happy that he is alive. I see no need to allow that man back into the castle. Am I clear?"

Lord Verras refused to answer.

Leymonn chuckled as he opened the door to leave. "I thought as much. I'll expect news from you soon."

Lord Verras locked the door the moment Leymonn left. Then he marched over to the desk. "Lord Cinnan had a map of the caves with other paths in and out of the city."

He riffled through papers and books, then peered at me. "You're wondering why I kept such a valuable map out on the desk."

I shook my head. "I'm wondering how you could possibly find it. I could hide a small giant on that desk."

He smiled and returned to digging. When he located the map, he spread it out before us—more a caress than an attempt to make it lie flat. I'd never seen anything like it—a series of caterpillars lying outside the straight edges of the castle rooms.

"Lord Cinnan had this made ages ago, though I think it was a retracing of an earlier map. Here is the entrance from this room." Lord Verras pointed to a spot, and then his finger traced a series of tunnels. "And this is the path we took to visit the king your first day here."

He stabbed a section just beyond those lines. "There used to be a tunnel that led to the cliffs, though it collapsed years ago. A similar path would be a safer way out of Reggen than a boat down the Kriva. We just need to find it."

"Without telling Leymonn? Without any other help?"

 211

"I don't want Leymonn to know about a route to the cliffs. He's too intent on escape."

I thought of all the people Lord Verras must know in the castle. "I'm sure you can find a few people to search the caves."

"I know of one."

I heard the answer in his voice. When I looked up, I saw it confirmed in his face.

"No. No! I hate the caves. It's like being buried one stone at a time."

"We have days, Saville."

I crossed my arms. "We *need* to visit the princess. You told her you'd come . . ." I sighed. " . . . and you can tell her that her errand girl will be busy."

Chapter 25

That afternoon, Lord Verras showed me how to systematically explore the tunnels. We would tie a rope to a rock formation near the entrance and unwind its length as we followed a path.

It was my idea to cut strips of linen and use them to mark the route instead.

Lord Verras liked the idea, though he warned me to secure the fabric. "Don't just leave it where it could slip." When I rolled my eyes, he'd smiled and added, "It's a fine idea, though. Trust a tailor to think of using fabric."

I was so surprised by the praise that I didn't even mind being called a tailor.

I hated the caves at first. I'd eyed the stone and wondered how it would feel to be buried beneath it. Yet the longer I explored, the more I enjoyed traveling among the stone pillars. It wasn't safe, but it . . . it reminded me of when the giant scouts had knelt before me. It was storms and mountains and seas; fear and joy twisted so tightly together I couldn't tell them apart.

The next day, while Lord Verras was occupied with the king, I explored the caves alone, searching for a tunnel that would lead to the cliffs.

And I found it.

I was so excited I could hardly tie the linen strip around the formation at the beginning of the new tunnel. Grinning, I threw the satchel of strips over my shoulder, collected my lantern and map, and picked my way back to Lord Verras's room.

The cave was covered with older markings, white blazes of paint that shone out in the light from the lantern. One day, when I had more time, I'd come back and explore the rest of the marked paths. But first, I had to tell Lord Verras. . . .

He was waiting for me when I squeezed back into his room.

"What took you so long? I was about to come after you."

"I found it."

"A tunnel?" He didn't smile as I'd expected. *Why was he so distracted?*

"*The* tunnel. I could see daylight at the end of it!" I shrugged out of the coat he'd made me wear. "It goes up to the top of the cliffs, though someone will have to clear away a small mountain of rubble first."

"Saville, you need to—"

"I could only reach my hand out of it, but I can't tell you how good the sun felt on my fingertips! I used a triple knot in the linen to mark where the tunnel branches off. You know what that looks like, don't you?"

"Saville!" He slapped the table to get my attention. "It's the Tailor. You need to go see him."

The walls of Lord Verras's room retreated till they seemed leagues away. And there still wasn't enough room to breathe.

"Now?" I whispered.

He nodded.

I turned back to the map. "There," I said, pointing to the passage. My voice sounded foreign to me. "That's it. I marked it with—"

"—a triple knot. I know. Just go, Saville. You need to go."

I ran to the Tailor's room, hardly aware of the corridors I threaded. When I reached the door, a doctor stood outside, face impassive.

"Where is Lord Verras?" he asked.

"He sent me," I gasped.

The doctor's forehead wrinkled. "Why you?"

I reached around him. "That is my business."

I stepped inside and closed the door behind me, leaning back against it. The sound of my breath slapped against the walls, loud as words. It wasn't until I saw the Tailor so still on the bed that I realized how restless he'd been even after the apoplexy. He was dead. He'd never lie so still otherwise.

I slid down the door and sat crouched on the floor, knees against my chest. I couldn't get a deep enough breath.

"No," I whispered against my clenched hands. "No. You can't leave me like this."

 215

I slammed my fists on the ground, glad for the sting and scrape of the stone floor, and pushed myself to standing. The room tipped around me as I walked to the bed.

Someone had pulled the blankets up to the Tailor's chest and folded his hands.

I looked down at his face, looking for . . . What was it I hoped to see? Some hint that he was sorry for dragging me to Reggen, so far from Mama's grave and my friends? A clue that he wished I, instead of the trunk of his precious fabric, had been by his bed these last days?

For the first time in my life, I stood in the room with the Tailor and wasn't battered by his anger, his disapproval. It was an empty, echoing sort of peace, like the quiet after shouting. I pulled the Tailor's trunk beside his bed and sat on it, peering down at him.

"Do you know how little I wanted from you?" I asked, my voice strong and steady, as though I could reach beyond death and make him hear me. "I wanted you to love me as much as your silks. I wanted to sit beside you and not fear what you'd do or say!"

All the words I had longed to speak to him. A life's worth. And they didn't change the silence, didn't make me feel lighter for speaking them. I laughed, more a ragged sigh than anything.

For the last time, I put a hand over the Tailor's. He was already cooling, his skin dry and rough. "Oh, Papa . . . ," I whispered. "It's too late for wanting, isn't it? It was too late years ago."

And then I was humming the giants' melody I'd heard out on the walls, the one that made me think of hearth fires and home. Except I sang of a father I'd never known and a home I'd never return to. The melody became a sort of tears. I keened the song until the strange syllables I remembered were as real as stone, more present than sorrow.

A long while later, I heard a knock, and Lord Verras slipped inside, closing the door behind him. "Saville, I'm so sorry."

The tears that wouldn't come earlier caught in my throat. How comforting it would be to have Lord Verras pull me close and—

I shook my head. "Please. Don't be nice. I'll—" *Break.*

He grimaced, then seemed to understand and perhaps even feel relieved.

"Why are you here?" I prompted.

"Leymonn has demanded that you come to the balcony and address the people. They're terrified. The duke has been putting on a show. The giants have been engaging in trials of strength since sunrise."

He raised his eyebrows: *should he go on?*

I nodded.

"I tried to tell Leymonn"—Lord Verras's gaze dropped to the Tailor—"but he wouldn't hear of it. You need to be on the balcony in an hour's time. After that, I promise you can go wherever you wish."

"What will happen to the Tailor?"

He sighed. "Most people are buried out beyond the Kriva, but now . . . we'll have to burn him, Saville. You'll have the ashes."

"When?"

Lord Verras swallowed. "Now."

Releasing the Tailor's hand was harder than I would have thought. I settled it back on his chest, then followed Lord Verras out of the room.

I did not look back.

Chapter 26

The shouts of the people beat against me as I stood on the balcony, their fear real as the summer heat. Yet neither their fear nor the heat could touch me.

I kept feeling the Tailor's cold hand beneath mine.

Finally, I roused myself and shouted something about courage and hope, and about how I would help them. I thought of the time I'd spent in the caves. That, at least, was not a lie. I hummed some of the giants' song as I left the balcony.

Lord Verras was waiting. "What song is that?"

"The first one we heard on the walls." I rubbed my forehead as if that might clear my muddled thoughts. "I like it."

"Like it?" he echoed. "Have you forgotten what we saw in the camp?"

I shook my head. "It was lovely and . . ." *It was all I had to hold on to.*

"I—I shouldn't have mentioned it." He stepped close, eyes worried. "Saville, go rest. You can stay in my room. I'll give you all the privacy you need. Just . . ." He shook his head. ". . . look to yourself."

I must take care of myself. No Mama to hold me close. No

friend in the castle to let me sit beside her and cry. I looked at the man before me, dark head bent, eyes that witnessed how deeply I grieved, even if I didn't want them to.

I'd see so little of him once the giants were gone. There'd be no reason to talk in his rooms or walk out with him on the ramparts.

There was no Lord Verras for me, not really.

He disappeared behind a blur of tears. I turned on my heel before he could see them and ran. He called after me, but I didn't stop.

And he didn't follow.

I went to his room anyway. I closed the door, locked it, and sat slowly in a chair—Lord Verras's chair, the one that smelled like ink. The grief was like a toothache: gnawing, twisting pain. I couldn't stay still, I—

Where had Lord Verras put the map? I wouldn't desert Will, but I could leave Reggen for a little, couldn't I?

I darted to Lord Verras's desk, wondering how he could find anything in those piles. Yet he'd notice if they'd been pawed through. He noticed every detail.

I didn't care.

I rummaged through the papers until I found the map and spread it before me, humming the giants' tune. I wouldn't take the tunnel to the cliffs. Or the one to the East Guardian's head. I finally found one that led to the river. I could swim out of the city entirely.

To the giants' camp.

I'd visit the giants. Hadn't I been wanting to all along?

I traced the path with my finger. It was one of the older tunnels, but it led to the banks of the Kriva right below where the walls met the cliffs.

Leymonn said the river might mask the sound of a boat. Why couldn't it conceal me? I'd swim toward the boulders on the opposite shore, where Lord Verras swam as a child. The roar of the water would be even louder there.

There was more to this war with the giants than the duke's claims to the throne, more than Lord Verras believed. And if I went on the adventure so I wouldn't have to sit and cry myself pale and tired, well, that was my choice.

I looked down at my clothing. The champion's pants were too fine for an evening in the Kriva. I went to one of the cupboards in the corner. Just as I'd suspected, Lord Verras had tucked some clothing away—he had everything here. I flipped through the pile until I found a pair of homespun pants, wrinkling my nose when I pulled them out. Where had he worn them last? The stables?

I glanced over my shoulder at the locked door, then quickly changed into the reeking pants, cinching them around my waist with a belt. One last look around the room before I left . . .

Will.

I went back to Lord Verras's desk and found a sheet of paper and ink. I *would* return safely, but Will deserved something, just in case.

Will,

I hope I'm able to come back and burn this note. But if you are reading this, I've failed, and I'm sorry. When you see your father again, be sure to tell him how brave you've been. He will be as proud of you as I am.

With all my

I paused, pen hovering above the paper. Hadn't I learned that words left unspoken wounded as much as those that were?

heart, and with all my love,
Saville

Chapter 27

I reached the beginning of the tunnel to the Kriva in no time. Holding the lantern aloft, I squinted down at the map in my hand. I wanted to race down the tunnel, but there could be no hurrying. I needed to mark my path with linen strips so I could retrace my steps when I returned. I reached for my satchel.

Nothing. I'd left it in Lord Verras's room. I looked behind me, shadows flowing like water as the lantern moved. All I wanted to do was leave the castle and listen to the Kriva, let it drown the grief inside me.

And then there were the giants.

"I'm not going back for it," I muttered.

I set the lantern down and pulled out the tails of my shirt. It was good linen and hard to rip. Perhaps Lord Verras's pants . . .

The worn homespun tore much more easily. I sat down and worked at the pants legs until I had a fistful of strips. Finally, I stood and followed the map through the tunnel, dropping a strip every few steps.

The path to the Kriva had not been lost, though I did have to squeeze sideways through two rockfalls. I had three strips of homespun remaining when I neared the tunnel's end.

I heard the song of the river first, the hushed roar of water. A few more steps, and I saw the slice of silver-blue moonlight. I snuffed out the lantern and tucked the map beside it.

Then I walked out onto the banks of the Kriva, picking my way through branches tangled with fishing twine, which shone like spider silk in the moonlight. Reggen's walls rose up on my left. I looked across the river. The far bank was dotted with giant campfires. Campfires I didn't have to visit.

I pulled in a deep breath, closed my eyes, and let the river sing to me while frogs chanted a chorus.

Then I opened my eyes and stepped into the Kriva.

I waded into the deep water as quickly as I could—I wouldn't splash as much there. Then, blessing the summers Mama had let me play in the millpond near Danavir, I let the current catch me and bear me downriver to the boulders Lord Verras had shown me. Water foamed around them, and I aimed for the bank just above them.

The current tugged at me as I drew near the boulders, and I let it carry me partway around them, their sharp edges jabbing my arms and shoulders. The moment I saw a handhold, I pulled myself up out of the water, hoping the river masked the sound of my flopping up onto that slab.

I rested there a moment, my cheek pressed against the stone. It was still warm from the sun and was strangely comforting, even as I listened for shouts that the giants had discovered me.

Finally, I pushed myself up. I couldn't see much—only

smears of movement against the campfires. The giants looked even bigger as the fire threw long, lurching shadows across the ground. Once, I thought I heard singing, but I wasn't sure. The Kriva kept the giants from hearing me, but it also muffled their conversations. Even so, I heard giants talking in the same low rolling tones as the scouts had, their voices like storms singing.

A long shadow fell over me.

I froze. *It's just the fire that throws the shadow so far.*

My heart would have nothing of it. My pulse roared as loud as the river—

Fingers thick as human legs wrapped around me, pinning my arms to my sides. The campfires tilted as I was yanked high into the air, too surprised to scream. . . . A great splash of water as the giant waded into the Kriva. I spluttered in the spray, trying to breathe.

It was going to drown me.

I fought, kicking and twisting. I even tried to bite one of the fingers, but the skin was thick as hide. The hand around me tightened, and my vision danced.

Finally, I felt ground beneath my toes, and the hand released me. I fell to my hands and knees, pulling in great gulps of air. When I raised my head, I saw him, a giant standing over me. I tried to scurry back on all fours, but collided with rock.

"Sit," commanded the giant in a voice like thunder. I could hear the flash of anger in it.

Why was he angry? My eyes never left his face as I reached a trembling hand behind me, feeling for a place to perch. I'd dive away if he so much as twitched, even though I was still within easy reach of those long arms.

I risked one look around me. We were on the island in the middle of the river, Lord Verras's island. A stand of trees shielded us from the giants' camp.

The giant folded himself to sitting, his feet almost close enough to touch me. Too close. In the moonlight, I could see he was clean-shaven, with a long straight nose and thick hair. A pick was strapped to his back. He didn't speak a word, but there was no hiding his fury. His breath rolled out in gusts, his hands were clenched. He looked at me as though I were a blight he longed to stamp out.

And he could if he wanted to. Finally, he leaned forward, elbows resting on his knees, and stared at me with a ferocity I'd never seen in the scouts' eyes.

"You will not hurt them," he rumbled. "I will not let you."

Panic turned my skin to gooseflesh. This giant *would* protect them, whoever they were. He'd do whatever he needed to keep them safe. I wanted to explain that I wasn't trying to hurt anyone, but I didn't think he'd believe me.

Then I thought of Lord Verras and how he often grew quiet when someone was angry with him. There was power in that silence. So I nodded to the giant but did not speak.

"You will not hurt my friends," the giant repeated. "The ones near the river."

I held up my hands to show I meant to harm.

"Will you not speak?" he demanded. "We are told your voices bring death, but I do not fear you or anything you might say."

"You have no reason to fear me," I whispered.

He flinched at my voice but immediately recovered.

"You carried me here," I said softly. "You could have drowned me or crushed me. How could I hurt *you*?"

Some of the fire left the giant's eyes. He folded his arms. "How, indeed?" he murmured.

He leaned closer until his face filled my vision. I could not look away. I didn't want to.

A flash in the corner of my eye. Something slammed into my ribs, and I flew backward off the boulder. I scrabbled in the shrubs, desperate to right myself, and leapt to my feet. What—?

His fingertip. He'd prodded me.

"What are you *doing*?" I shouted, too scared to mimic Lord Verras's wise silence. "That *hurt*!"

The giant reared back, surprised and . . . ashamed, perhaps? "Peace, *lité*. I meant no harm. Our scouts swore Reggen's tailor possessed great strength. And the duke . . . I thought all *liten* were stronger." He tilted his head as if he could hear something in the night air. "Please, I wish to speak to you."

I sat again. Slowly.

Lité. The scouts had used that word for me. I swallowed. "But the duke said—we've heard—you're to kill us on sight."

"I have no love for the duke." The giant made a low sound

 227

in his throat, too refined for a growl. "And I wish to hear a human voice."

And then I remembered the pens. It seemed a betrayal to meet this giant, to sense I could trust him, and yet know that this army kept humans! I grew too furious to be afraid. "You've had a thousand chances to hear human voices. You keep people in pens!"

The giant jerked back as though I'd slapped him. "You are angry?"

"Of course I'm angry! You keep humans like cattle! If you want to know what we sound like, listen to what they say before you eat them!" My stomach turned just to say it. "I've seen the bones your captains wear. And you want to protect your friends from *me*?"

He drew in a great breath and nodded to himself. I couldn't tell if he was pleased to learn I was angry or if he appreciated the explanation. "I have not seen these pens. They are guarded by the Deathless and I cannot approach them. We are told the voices of all *liten* deceive."

Deathless. Was that what they called the captains who wore the bone collars?

"Who are you, *lité*?"

Again, my heart raced. He'd mentioned Reggen's tailor. I didn't dare speak of sewing.

"My name is Saville. I am"—what was I?—"my father and my mother's only daughter."

"A she, then? I thought so." He bent forward so that his

head was near his knees, close enough that I felt his breath rush against me. He squinted, eyes trying to take in every detail. "But you are not dressed like a she, I think."

"It is difficult to wade in a dress."

"Yes. It must be. The water is big to you." He nodded. "You are the size of our infants, though you would look odd to them."

The giant chuckled silently, hands gripping his knees. Just as I gave myself permission to smile, he stopped and grew serious. "Now. Why are you here? It was not to speak with me, I think."

"I wanted to see what the giants were like."

"Giants? That is what you call us?"

"Yes."

He leaned back, his face retreating into shadow again. "Why else?"

Did he think I was spying?

No. I couldn't sense any of his earlier anger. For whatever reason, he didn't believe that I would—or could—hurt his friends. Then I realized that I did not mind telling this giant the truth. "My father died today. I didn't want to sit alone and cry. I needed to . . . go away. I wanted to see what the giants were really like. I have heard rumors of what your army has done, but . . ."

The giant sat still, head cocked, considering my words. Finally, he said, "*Uten.* We are *uten.*"

I smiled. "To see what the *uten* were like."

 229

"Good." He nodded his approval, then sat still again. "I hear . . . sadness. May your father's spirit find rest."

I found myself hoping the Tailor *would* find rest. More than that, I almost believed it was possible. I looked up at the giant. "You say you hear sadness and anger. What do I sound like?"

"That is the first good question you have asked," he said.

I pressed my hand against the boulder, felt his voice rumble through it. His voice was the most real thing about him.

"You sound like a bird from home, the little ones that nest in the mountain crags. Yours is such a small voice. But I hear more. What is it that you have not told me?"

I saw his pick lined with moonlight and thought of the scout who had worn one. What if this giant knew him? What would he think if he knew my lies had tricked the scouts and caused their deaths? He'd kill me, and I wouldn't blame him. Finally, I said, "I don't want to tell you."

He scowled. "What?" He wasn't angry. Yet.

Surprised, I thought. I repeated myself slowly. "I don't want to tell you."

"You refuse to tell me something?" He sounded tentative.

"I do," I said.

He grunted. "I could make you tell me."

I sat straighter. "No. You could kill me. But you couldn't make me tell you."

I watched him warily. His great head tilted as if he was listening for something.

230

"Do not worry, little one. Now I know everything I need to know. I hear your heart, and I did not think I would."

I put a hand to my chest. "You hear it beating, then."

He nodded. "Yes . . . but that is not what I meant. I hear . . . more. What you feel. And that surprises me."

"Why?" I asked.

"Your voice is so small. I thought I would hear only . . . the words." He shook his head. "If a bird—if a bug—spoke to you, *lita,* how would you know if it were happy? Or if it meant you harm?"

"But I couldn't hurt you, even if I did mean you harm," I said.

"You could if I trusted you."

His words were like a blow, driving the breath from me. I wanted to hide my face in my hands.

"But I do not believe you wish to harm me." He spoke slowly, as though he was discovering the truth for himself. "Go back to your city."

"You'll let me go?"

He shrugged. "What would you tell your rulers? That you spoke with a . . . what is your word? *Giant.* That the giant let you live? It would not change much."

"It might."

"I do not think so." He stood and I saw him silhouetted against Reggen's walls. "If you can return to your city, you deserve to live. I will go back to my camp."

I didn't want him to leave. Not yet.

"Wait. Please. I have two questions for you."

He cocked his head. "Yes?"

"What is your name?"

He smiled. "Volar, son of Kelnas. I cut the mountain halls for my people."

"I greet you, Volar, son of Kelnas," I said, and curtsied.

Another smile. He bowed from the waist like a tree bending in the wind. "Your other question, Hillock?"

"Hillock?" I asked. "Why do you call me that?"

His chuckle rumbled through the stone beneath me. "It is what we call our children. There are mountains and hills and then hillocks, smallest and softest of all. *You* are a hillock, little one."

A hillock. The name made me smile.

"Your question?" he prompted.

"What do you hear in your duke's voice?"

His smile disappeared. Standing there, he looked like one of the Guardians—a great, grim being carved in stone.

"Good-bye, Hillock," he said, and strode out into the Kriva. "I wish you a safe return to your city."

"What if I want to talk to you again?" I called.

He looked back at me, over his shoulder. "Come to this island."

"How will you know I'm here?"

"I will hear."

Chapter 28

A nd then Volar was wading back toward his camp.

I blew out a deep breath, trembling with relief and surprise and the sense that I'd stumbled across something as magnificent as a sunrise. I had to tell Lord Verras.

I waded into the Kriva, shivering as the water soaked my damp clothes. I slowly swam toward the cliffs, the current tugging at my shirt, carrying me downriver, farther from Reggen. I finally pulled myself up onto the rocky bank and crouched among the pebbles until my breathing grew even.

It would be a long walk back to the caves. But as I picked my way toward the city, snatches of my time with the giant flashed through my mind: Volar lined in moonlight, his laughter through the rock, the name he'd given me—*Hillock*.

A few hours before dawn, I quietly slipped back into Lord Verras's empty room, shivering. The fire had died to only a few embers. I stirred it and placed a narrow log on top.

Then I opened Lord Verras's wardrobe, looking for dry clothes. I could wear my old pants, but I needed a shirt. A quick search revealed an old, shapeless coat. I peeled off the homespun pants, grimacing when I held them up for inspection. They now barely reached below my knees. I grew a little warmer when I stepped into my old pants. Off came my damp shirt, and I looked down at the binding I'd wrapped around my chest. It sagged treacherously. I glanced at the door before unwrapping it.

I need to bind it differently next time I go into the Kriva. I draped the length of muslin over the back of the chair and pulled on the coat. It was rough, and like the pants, reeked of a stable. *Next time, I'll make sure I have clothing to change into.*

Next time. I was already planning to return to the island.

I plucked up my old belt, fastened it around the coat, then settled near the fire. Tomorrow night, I'd learn more about the giant army and why it followed the duke. I'd talk to this giant who heard the sadness in my voice, who called me Hillock, and wished that the Tailor would find peace. . . .

Peace.

I put my head in my hands and wept—great, wrenching sobs that started in my belly and bent my entire body around them. I couldn't stop and was too weak to try. I cried while the fire cracked and danced, wiping my eyes and nose with the sleeve of the shabby coat. When the grief finally released me, I curled up in the chair and fell asleep watching the fire.

"Saville . . . Saville . . ."

I woke up with a wild surge of hope that it was the Tailor, but could hardly open my eyes. *Why were they swollen?*

"Saville!" Lord Verras stood before me, holding his pants with the shredded cuffs in one hand and my letter to Will in the other. "What happened here? I thought you were going to rest!"

He took in the wrecked room: clothes scattered on the floor, yards of my binding draped over the chair, and me: hair loose around my face, wearing the champion's pants and his own smelly old coat.

I rubbed my eyes, trying to massage away the puffiness.

"Saville?"

I was still half-asleep, and I longed to sleep more. I'd had such nice dreams. . . .

He pulled up the other chair and sat in front of me. "What happened?"

"I left Reggen. I went out to spy on the giants."

He shot up. "You what?"

"I found your map. . . ."

"*Found* it?"

I dropped my hands into my lap and looked up at him. "I looked for it, and after shuffling through that wretched mess on your desk—"

"It's not wretched. . . ."

"I used the map to find a passage out of Reggen that leads to the Kriva. Then I swam to the giants' camp."

Lord Verras dropped back into the chair. "Are you out of your *mind*?" Then, as if he couldn't help himself, he asked, "What did you see?"

 235

"Not much. I tried spying on the giants from the Kriva, where they wouldn't hear me. Then Volar found me. He picked me up and—"

Lord Verras leapt up again. "They discovered you?"

"Stop jumping up and down like that. It's distracting."

"I'll jump up if I please!" he shouted. "Sky above, he could have killed you!"

"I had to leave," I whispered. "Just for a little while. And he . . . he was kind."

There's no time to be soft, I told myself. *It wasn't just because Volar was kind.*

I looked up at Lord Verras, determined. "He didn't believe the duke's warning that all *liten*—that's us—could kill them. He wanted to talk to me. I think he felt it was important that he could tell . . ." I shook my head. "No, *hear,* what I felt. I suppose you can't be tricked so easily if you know what someone is feeling. But they can't hear human emotion, so they can be tricked. Except . . . Volar *could* hear it, so maybe all the giants can and just don't know it. How would they, with the duke telling them to stomp us?"

I could tell Lord Verras was trying to make sense of all I was saying. "He just let you go?"

"He did. But that's not the important part. I asked him about the duke. Asked him what he heard in his voice."

"And?"

"I could tell he knew something wasn't right."

Lord Verras sat back in his chair, eyes on the far wall as he considered what I'd just told him. Then he said, "All this from one conversation?"

"Yes. It was . . . like recognizing someone you haven't seen since you were a child." I saw Lord Verras's skeptical look and hurried on. "I was scared at first. He was angry—told me not to hurt his friends. But he didn't hurt *me*. And he could have. And he talked about home and how I sounded like a bird and . . . you'd understand if you met him. I wish you had."

Lord Verras nodded as if he did understand.

"Are you strong enough to walk outside with me?" he asked. "The king wants to watch the giants and the duke from the wall today. He requested that we accompany him."

"He wanted *us*?"

"He requested that I come, and I said I'd bring you." Lord Verras must have seen the question in my eyes. "I told him I see better with you."

I wanted to thank him for seeing me that way, for meaning it, but he was pointing to a bundle perched on the desk. "I brought your dress. I'll step outside while you change. Then you can tell me more about this giant—"

"Volar," I said, reaching for my errand-girl clothes. "His name is Volar."

Chapter 29

An hour later, we were on the ramparts. I had hoped to hear more of the giants' songs as we stood high above the city. I had wanted to feel the wind rush around me.

There was no wind to break the heat. The sun bore down on us, sparking off bits of quartz in the walls.

But there was a song as we neared the gates. A terrible one.

The duke sat on a great throne outside his crimson tent. Giants had gathered in the clearing, hundreds of them. They sang a song that sounded like death, stamping to keep time. I could feel the ground shake, even though the Kriva flowed between us.

I turned to Lord Verras, eyes wide. He seemed so confident, so sure I could face this.

I swallowed the fear down until it was only a stone in my stomach and watched the giants.

The ones closest to the duke's tent—less than a hundred, I guessed—wore bone collars. "Volar called them the Deathless. They guard the pens."

Lord Verras nodded, eyes hard. "The Deathless. Those who wear death."

We could hear the crowd below. As Lord Verras and I neared King Eldin, I could see a ring of castle guard surrounding him, the princess, Leymonn, and . . . Will. He stood between the king and Leymonn.

No, he was *pinned* between them. I could see Leymonn's hand heavy on his shoulder, Will wincing at the grip.

I glanced at Lord Verras and saw my own fury reflected in his eyes. His anger was a still and quiet thing—something he kept outside him so he could do what was needed. I looked back at Leymonn, his fingers curled into Will's shoulder, and prayed I'd be there when Lord Verras let his anger loose.

The king didn't—or couldn't—look away from the giants. And Will?

Will looked over his shoulder at me and smiled. He patted his chest and nodded, his hand over the crest I'd sewn for him.

I pushed the thunder of the giants' song away and swallowed my fear once more, burying it so deep even Will wouldn't be able to see it. Then I smiled and tugged my ear: *Keep listening.*

He grinned at me, and I didn't mind the giants as much.

Until I heard a roar.

The duke motioned two of the Deathless into the ring. They faced each other, and with a bellow, grappled like animals.

The street below was packed with people of Reggen watching through the portcullis. Fear coated them like dust. I heard a few sobs as the giants continued to wrestle.

When I looked back to the encampment, the duke was giving another order. He pointed toward Reggen, and another Deathless charged down the road toward the bridge.

I kept waiting for the duke to call the giant back. He'd promised us till the fourteenth. I leaned over the edge of the wall, hands gripping the stones, not caring how much it hurt.

At the last moment, the giant turned away from the bridge and ran to the willows that edged the Kriva. He took a handful of the curtainlike branches and ripped them aside. Then he wrapped both hands around the trunk and heaved against it, his great back straining.

I heard the shriek of wood giving way. Then he lifted the willow up with one hand and turned to show his prize. The duke gave a signal. The giant turned back toward the city, willow still raised.

"He's going to throw it," I said.

"No," said Lord Verras. "It couldn't possibly reach the gates."

I knew better. I'd seen the scouts throw boulders.

Before I could reply, the giant hurled the tree.

The crowd cried out and the king whimpered as the tree arced into the sky toward us. Leymonn released Will, and dropped to his knees, head covered, to protect himself. The king would have done the same, but Lord Verras gripped his arm and held him upright. The willow was already dropping toward the ground—it wouldn't strike the wall.

But it struck the gates like a monstrous fist. The ramparts

240

shuddered and I nearly fell. Wails rose up from the people below.

"Is it breached?" shouted the city steward. "Go below to see if the gates are breached!"

Soldiers ran to the stairways. I couldn't see the gates, only the chaos of the crowd below. The people nearest the gate had tried to run, but those behind them would not make way.

"They're going to kill each other!" I shouted. "We have to do something!"

The giant who had thrown the willow stood facing us, laughing. He must be able to hear the shouts let loose behind the gate.

The mob grew louder.

I moved to Lord Verras's side. "What about the people below?"

He didn't respond. He remained beside the king, his arm around his cousin's shoulders. King Eldin was pale, his mouth working as though trying to say something, but failing to find the words.

Lord Verras looked over his shoulder. "There's nothing we can do. If we send more guards down, they'll be crushed."

"People of Reggen!" It was the duke. He'd left his throne and had walked to the tree-throwing giant's side. "People of Reggen!" he repeated.

I never thought I'd be grateful for the duke, but the crowd seemed to quiet. His voice had a similar effect on King Eldin, who pulled away from Lord Verras and stood taller. Leymonn

 241

recovered and rose, his hand back on Will's shoulder.

The duke spread his arms wide. Though he barely reached the giant's knee, he seemed to fill the space around him. In that moment, I understood how he could lead an army of giants.

"You see the strength of my army, Reggen! Why do you refuse to open your gates to me? If you take me as your king, there will be no violence, no pain."

And then, from the crowd, someone shouted, "The tailor will save us!"

It was more horrifying than seeing the willow flying toward us.

The soldiers kept scanning the ramparts, as if they believed the champion would suddenly appear. People took up the chant. "Tailor! Tailor!"

It drowned out the duke.

I put my hands on the wall and concentrated on the warm stone, its roughness against my palms—anything to distract me from the chanting. The king still stood, but he was trembling like a tree in a gale.

The duke motioned to the giant beside him, who nodded and walked back to the willows. Not again. What would the people do if another tree struck the gate and the tailor did not come to save them?

The king stumbled over to one of the guards and said something. The soldier seemed to hesitate, but the king insisted, so he raised his crossbow and aimed at the duke.

No. There was no telling how the giant army might react if

the duke was killed, but there'd be no stopping it.

I pointed, unable to be heard over the crowd. Lord Verras lunged toward the soldier. Leymonn blocked his way. Verras shoved him aside, but not before the soldier loosed the bolt.

It flew faster than sight, striking the duke with such force that he was thrown back.

A great cheer rose up from the crowd below, shaking the ramparts beneath us. King Eldin looked down at the duke lying on the ground, a blaze of pride in his eyes.

Lord Verras pulled his spyglass from his coat.

"Is he dead?" I asked.

Verras shook his head, as if irritated by such a silly question. "The bolt's in his heart. There's blood everywhere. . . ."

I'd thought the giants would go into a frenzy—shout a battle cry, rush the walls. Instead, the Deathless encircled the duke. They didn't touch him. They didn't even look at the city. They just stood, staring at his body. It was more frightening than an attack.

Lord Verras lowered the spyglass. "I don't know what they're going to do."

The captain of the castle guard nodded and motioned to his men. "We leave now."

The guards had just begun to flank the king and princess when a strangled cry rose up from the street. I looked back across the river and wanted to yell myself.

The duke was pulling the bolt from his chest. He still lay on his back, but in another moment, he pulled the bolt free.

 243

"No." Lord Verras raised his spyglass for a better look. "No, that isn't possible!"

The duke stood, still holding the crossbow bolt, and strode toward the city. He didn't falter, not once.

And the giants didn't seem surprised. This is what they'd been expecting. This had happened before.

Duke of the Western Steeps, Heir to the Ancient Emperor's Crown, Holder of the Eternal Heart . . .

Eternal Heart.

"Is this how you negotiate, King Eldin?" The duke's voice was as strong as it had ever been. "I expected better from you."

The king whimpered.

"Don't let him fall!" Lord Verras commanded the guards. Two rushed forward to support the king.

"You have no answer!" called the duke. "You will be able to hear mine, then." He spoke unintelligible words to one of the Deathless, who saluted, then chose a companion. Together, they walked back into the camp. Toward the pens.

The giants plucked out two humans and strode back to the shore, holding their captives so their arms were trapped against their sides. As the giants drew nearer, I saw that one carried a man who fought, kicking in the air. The other carried a woman. For a moment, I thought I heard her pleading with her captor.

I looked at Lord Verras. "Can't we do anything? Shoot the giants?"

He shook his head slowly. "They'd only get more."

"King Eldin, look what you have done! Your *champion* has not shown himself. You have foolishly fired upon me, a man who only desires peace. Such aggression, however, cannot go unanswered. Come now! Say you will give the rule of this city to a better man! Give it to me."

The king hung between the two guards, gasping. He could not speak. And I couldn't look away from the duke's prisoners.

There was no champion to save them—and there should have been.

The duke threw the crossbow bolt into the Kriva and raised his bloody right hand.

When he tightened it into a fist, the giants wrung the necks of their prisoners.

Even from the wall, I could see the sudden stillness in their limbs, the moment the thrashing stopped. The giants dropped the bodies and they seemed to fall forever. They were—they had been—people.

They fell like discarded rag dolls.

The world exploded with shouts and wails. King Eldin and Princess Lissa were hurried away. Leymonn jogged behind them, keeping the guards between himself and the ramparts.

Lord Verras scooped up Will, who had been deserted, and followed.

I stood at the wall a moment longer, looking out over the giant camp, hearing the screams of the mob. Hundreds of giants stood below me but I strained to find just one.

Chapter 30

I'd already changed into lads' clothes when Lord Verras came to his room that evening.

"I'm going out again," I said. "You can't stop me."

"Of course I could stop you. I could have guards hold you in a chair for the entire night."

I crossed my arms. "I'd never forgive you."

"I don't care if you'd forgive me. I'm far more concerned that you don't *die*."

"Volar doesn't trust the duke. He could tell if I was lying."

"You lied?"

"I didn't tell him everything when he asked who I was. But he still knew."

"I don't care."

"You say you want to know things, important things that will save Reggen, but you won't let me help! We have to know about the duke, now more than ever. I need to talk to Volar."

I expected Lord Verras to argue, but he just stared, weighing what I said, as though looking for something. Finally, he rubbed the back of his neck. "You think *I'm* the idiot. Fine. Go, talk to this giant."

He took off his coat, draping it over the back of his chair.

"But I'm going with you . . . Don't," he said as I opened my mouth to protest. He half smiled. "You can't stop me."

I glared. "Don't look so smug."

Shadows danced and flitted around us as Lord Verras followed me down the passage. We'd just squeezed past the first of the rockfalls when he spoke:

"You didn't tie them," he said.

"What?" I asked.

"The fabric strips."

It was a miracle he hadn't mentioned it before. "I all but ran from the castle last night. You're lucky I even marked the path."

Lord Verras just kept staring at the strips of fabric. After a few moments, I realized he wasn't going to scold me.

"So this is what happened to my pants . . . ," he murmured.

"I can't say how sorry I am." I nudged a strip of the dingy homespun aside with the toe of my boot. "I've never seen finer fabric."

He stared at me, one eyebrow raised, until I couldn't hold back my smile.

"I accept your apology," he said finally.

My mouth dropped open. *If he thought I really was apologizing* . . .

He smiled slowly, eyes crinkling at the corners, looking far too pleased with himself.

There we were, worming our way through a dark forest of

stone to visit Volar and save the city. I carried the Tailor's death like a boulder on my back, and Lord Verras? He knew he was Reggen's best hope, and that must have felt like a mountain.

But, oh, it was lovely to tease him about homespun pants. To have him smile down at me as if he'd never told so fine a joke—as filling as a feast. It was strength to keep going, even after all that had happened.

I almost rose up on tiptoe and kissed him, just for smiling like that.

Before I could bat the thought away, it had grown like an oak inside me, roots into rock, branches into the clouds. I imagined Lord Verras's arms around me and knew his heartbeat would be slow and steady when I rested my head against his chest.

I was so tired of being strong by myself.

Sky above, how stupid! He's a nobleman—and betrothed.

I turned on my heel so quickly that I stumbled and took a sliding step to catch myself. But my foot landed on another homespun strip and I slid a few paces, finally crashing against a stone pillar. My lantern skittered away and snuffed out.

"Saville!" A moment later, Lord Verras stood over me, lantern raised high. "Are you hurt?"

He held out his hand to help me but I ignored it. "I slipped, that's all."

Slipped was too small a word for it.

"You're sure?" he pressed. "You looked as if you saw something."

For a moment, I thought he knew. He saw so much.

"It was nothing," I said at last. "Where's my lantern?"

"There." He scooped it up, plucking off a strip of home-spun. "I'm not sure how much oil is left, though. Best save it for the trip back."

"Thank you. I won't be so clumsy again."

I turned and followed the trail of strips as quickly as my sore leg would allow. I didn't give Lord Verras a chance to speak until we stepped out on the Kriva's bank.

"We walk about half a league, Lord Verras. And then we swim."

He gazed across the river, before turning to me. "I think you should call me Galen. It doesn't seem right to go around Lording someone you have to swim with."

He wasn't making this easy. But I forced myself to hold his gaze. I even raised an eyebrow. "Lording?"

"It's an official term, I'm sure." He smiled. "Ready?"

"Yes, Lord Ver—"

His face fell a little.

"Galen," I corrected myself. "Let's go."

He nodded and followed me. It took us nearly half an hour to pick our way along the bank, moving as quietly as possible. The rocks lining the riverbed were slick, and the rushing water, even in the shallows, made it difficult to find our footing.

When we were close to the island, we waded in deeper. I swam once the water reached my chest, pulling myself along as quickly as I could. More than once, I struck my foot or leg

 249

against the boulders beneath the surface. Judging from the occasional whispered curse, I knew I wouldn't be the only one with bruises. Not long after, I pulled myself onto the bank, trying to catch my breath. Lord Verras joined me a moment later.

"I haven't been in the Kriva for years." He bent and massaged his shin. "Back then I remembered where the boulders were."

I saw how his shirt clung to him and realized that Lord Verras would never need a tailor's assistance to make his shoulders look broad. I rolled my eyes at my own foolishness and then realized my own shirt was no less sodden. I picked at it, tugging it away from me, not that it made a great deal of difference. My binding prevented any real immodesty.

He straightened. "Now what?"

"We sit and we wait."

"He'll just come? What about the other giants?"

"He said he'd hear me. I think he's the only one who hears so well." At least, I hoped he was.

It didn't take long to find the boulders at the island's center. Galen had hardly settled beside me when we heard a rhythmic splashing at the far side of the Kriva.

He turned to me, eyes wide. I nodded.

And then Volar stood before us.

Chapter 31

"Good evening to you, Volar," I said, my voice shaking just a little. "It's Saville. I've brought a friend."

Volar sat across from us. "Why does your friend not speak?"

"I am Lord Galen Verras. Saville wished me to meet you."

"And who are you, Galen Verras?"

He grew still beside me, thinking. Finally, he said, "I am cousin to the king. I provide his advisors with information to make the right decisions."

I grabbed Galen's arm. What was he doing?

Volar tilted his head, listening. "Tell me more, Galen, cousin to the king."

Galen's voice was calm, but his forearm tensed beneath my hand. "Saville thinks you know when we speak the truth." He paused. "I do not know you, but I believe her. I've told you the truth. Now you tell me: was I wise?"

Volar was silent. I was silent. Even the Kriva seemed to still while Galen looked up into the giant's face.

Volar released a gusty sigh. "You were wise."

And then I could hear the Kriva murmuring against its banks and the rattle of the wind in the leaves.

The giant looked up at the sky. "The stars are the only things here that remind me of home. Where I live, where we come from, we hear truth in stone. I am a mountain-breaker like my father before me. I have tunneled into mountains since I was as tiny as you, Hillock." I squeezed Galen's arm when I saw the question in his eyes. "When you have lived in and under stone, you learn its voice. You know whether it will crumble if you dig farther. You know if the rock is strong enough to support a great hall. You know it—you hear it—every time a hammer or pick rings against the stone." Volar shook his head. "Stone does not lie if you listen to it. Our people know this."

He tilted his head toward the Kriva. "Neither does water, though we are used to the sea and not this little trickle you call a river. Water can be as hard as stone, and those who go out in ships say that it speaks truth, as well."

"You have ships?" asked Galen.

Volar laughed and, once again, I felt it in the stones beneath us. "There is little food to be hunted or farmed in the Belmor Mountains. Our ships go out into the sea to hunt the great whales. Smaller vessels travel to shallow waters to harvest kelp. We would not survive without our ships."

"Then why are you here?" asked Galen.

"Here," said Volar, more to himself. "We are here because of the duke. Here where the stone is buried under soft dirt, where the water is so small its voice is a whisper. We are here because of the duke." Volar stared between his feet. "I will tell you the truth, cousin to the king, because you have told me the truth. We are here because some grew greedy. We ignored what the stone told us because we wanted greater halls. We dug so deep that the mountains themselves crashed down upon us.

"Two years ago, the duke marched to the foothills of the Belmor. He walked our valleys and told us he could restore our land to us—the cities of the plain our forefathers had built. All he needed was an army, and all we needed was a human leader who could discern human lies and protect us from man's cunning."

"Didn't it ever occur to you that *he* was lying?" I blurted out.

"Peace, Hillock," murmured Volar. "The duke vowed that he wore truth as a shield. It protected him from harm. He challenged the mightiest warrior to combat. I was not there to see it, for I was deep in the mountains. But I heard the stories. . . ."

I saw the duke pulling the bolt from his chest. I remembered how the blood flowed freely, but his face never grew pale and his step never weakened.

"Your warrior could not kill him," said Galen.

Volar shook his head. "The duke stayed the winter with us and then led our armies to the plains. Who would not believe such a sign? Our old stories tell how the high king's descendant will possess the strength of stone. The duke . . ." He shrugged.

"But what about your king?" pressed Galen. "Why wouldn't he be the high king's descendant?"

Volar's sigh was low, rolling thunder. "We had a king, though he did not possess Halvor's gift. None have in my time, or in remembering. *Uten* kings do not sit on a throne while the rest labor. Our king was a smith who worked iron in the heart of the mountain. He heard truth there, where few of us could venture. A month after the duke entered our valley, our king was found dead, his own sword through his heart."

"Who killed him?" I asked.

"Some *uten* believed it was his son, Ynnix, hungry for his father's throne. But it could not be proved. After the king's death, most believed that Halvor's gift rested with the duke. Perhaps the *uten* had grown so corrupt that none deserved to bear it."

Volar sighed again. "I tell you this so you understand why the *uten* would follow a *lité*. We needed a ruler to lead us from the undoing that was our king's death. But now I do not know. If this was stone, I would not cut farther into it. Perhaps I will go home to the mountains and the sea."

"You can't just leave," I said. "You can't let the army attack an innocent city!"

"Innocent?" rumbled Volar. "Two of our scouts were killed because of your city. Two good *uten* dead because of the lies of your champion. One was my sister-son."

Sky above, I'd killed Volar's nephew. That was why he'd been so determined to protect his friends. I didn't realize I was gripping Galen's arm so tightly until his hand settled over mine.

Volar's voice dropped as he retreated into the past. "I am told he swore he believed the . . . *champion* and not the duke.

And then he died. It is an awful thing to doubt the duke's word, it is . . ." He waved his hand. " . . . an act against the king."

"Treason?" suggested Galen.

"Yes. The duke hears truth. To doubt him is to doubt the high king's spirit." Volar shrugged, his shoulders rising and falling like a mountain shifting.

"But two *liten* were killed today," I whispered.

"The army will not listen to me, even if I had words to speak. I am only a mountain-breaker. The Deathless are the duke's captains."

"*Are* they deathless?" asked Galen.

"No." Volar shook his head. "But they must prove their loyalty. I am told they visit the pens to . . ."

He did not have to finish the sentence.

"But surely there are other *uten* like you! *Uten* who don't want this war!"

"*Uten* who will challenge the duke and his Deathless, Hillock? So far from the Belmor? The other *uten* cannot hear anything but words when *liten* speak. I have asked them this. So they will hold to the duke, who bears Halvor's spirit. They will trust him."

"Even if he tells them to slaughter the people of Reggen? You didn't kill me, Volar. And the scouts! They didn't kill the boy they caught. They let him go back to the city."

Galen squeezed my hand so tightly I almost cried out. I turned and saw the fear in his eyes.

Sky above, I'd mentioned the scouts.

He tried to fill my horrified silence. "What a man does on his own is different from what he will do when he is part of an army, Saville."

"What do you know of the scouts, Hillock? Of my sister-son?"

I wanted to run. I wanted to cry. I wanted to give Volar those last precious memories of his nephew—how he'd been a worthy adversary. How he didn't kill me because of Oma. Volar's sister.

Then I remembered Volar's fury when he'd pulled me from the river.

Galen yanked on my hand, his message clear: *Don't tell him!*

"I saw them with the tailor," I said slowly. "I saw them set the boy down."

"How did you see this?"

Galen did not give me the chance to answer. "Many watched from the gates."

"Is this the truth, Hillock?"

"Yes," I whispered.

Volar tilted his head. "I would say that sounds like a lie, if I did not know you."

I sat blinking back tears.

Finally, Volar sighed. "Your voices are small. Perhaps I do not hear your hearts so well as I thought."

Galen jumped to his feet, pulling me up beside him. "We must go, Volar. We must be back to Reggen before dawn."

"Yes," said the giant. He must hear how my heart raced, how my breath caught in my throat. "It is good to know there are *liten* worthy of trust. You are true as stone."

I thought the guilt would strangle me.

Galen spoke for us both. "I wish you well, Volar."

The giant nodded. "It will not be safe for you to return. They will be suspicious if I leave a third night."

Galen tugged me toward the Kriva, then stopped and looked back at Volar. "I have one more question."

"What do you wish to know?"

"Do you have stories of a giant . . . an *uten* with a deathless heart?"

"An *ute* . . . ," Volar corrected, then he folded his arms and dropped his head. He reminded me of Galen, deep in thought.

"There are stories, from a different age, of a king. An abomination. He tore his heart from his body and hid it in a safe place. He could not be killed until a warrior found his heart." Volar shook his head. "It is a child's tale, one you must put from your mind. How would it be done, king's cousin? You know it could not be done."

"Thank you," said Galen. "Fare you well, Volar."

"And you," said the giant.

Galen pulled me into the water and we swam to the far bank. The moment I stood dripping on the cliffside of the Kriva, Galen turned on me.

"What were you thinking, mentioning the scouts like that? Have you lost your *mind*?"

I'd never seen Galen so angry. There was no silence, no stillness in it this time. It was infuriating—and I couldn't even shout back at him because the giants were just across the Kriva.

"He needed to know other giants might listen to him! He needed to know the lies he hears in the duke's voice are real. Now he doubts himself even more!"

"He nearly guessed that you were the champion. How could you be so reckless?"

I jabbed a finger at him. "You knew this would be danger-ous, Galen Verras!"

He took me by the shoulders. "What would I have done if you'd been hurt?"

My retort died when I saw his face. He wasn't talking about a tailor for Reggen, about keeping the city content. He was talking about me. He didn't know what he'd do if he lost *me*.

Sky above.

Galen was just as surprised as I was—he blinked as if some-thing bright had flashed before him. We faced each other, still as stone, his hands warm on my shoulders.

That day the duke visited the court, when Galen had pleaded with the king to act, I'd wondered what it would be like to have someone look at me with that much hope, that much confidence. Now I knew. I *knew*, and I could feel myself begin to unravel.

If I wasn't careful, I'd lose myself to Galen Verras and never find myself again when he married his falcon bride. So I

258

pretended that I hadn't seen a thing, and buried the part of me that had been glad to see it.

"If I'd been hurt?" I echoed. "If something had happened to me, you could put some lad on the palace balcony and have *him* wave to the people!"

It flew out as fast as a bolt from a crossbow. And struck as hard.

Galen dropped his hands and stepped back, scowling at me in the moonlight. Before I could speak, he marched off toward the cave.

I stared after him, not knowing whether I was relieved or miserable to have him move away. Finally, I silently followed him, telling myself the entire league and a half that my legs trembled only from swimming so long.

By the time we neared the foundation stones, the world seemed gray, the cave's opening back to Reggen, a dark smudge in the predawn.

Galen found our lanterns and handed one to me without meeting my eye.

"I'm sorry," I whispered. "You never treated me like a pawn. Not once."

It was a hurried darning—an attempt to stitch the ragged edges of the conversation back together.

He finally looked at me, and I wished he hadn't. He was so serious, so guarded. "Let's just get back." He lit his lantern with a single strike. "Leymonn will send men into the caves at dawn to clear the tunnel to the cliffs."

I waited for an explanation.

 259

"I had to send for help. I couldn't clear it alone. You were—"

I'd been grieving the Tailor and sneaking out of Reggen.

The lantern threw bruiselike shadows over Galen's face. "I still don't know if I made the right decision, so I'm going to be there when Leymonn's men arrive."

I lit my lantern. "Let's go, then."

It felt good to have a purpose. Leymonn's arrival gave us something to talk about. Tomorrow, I'd act as though I'd never thought of kissing Galen Verras. He'd forget how worried he'd been for me. Tomorrow, we'd be as we had before—or at least, we'd pretend we were.

Galen followed the strips of homespun, and I followed him. The way seemed darker just knowing Leymonn would soon be in these caves.

Galen stopped so suddenly I almost walked into his back. "I haven't seen a strip for a while."

I squeezed beside him, peering up the path. No homespun.

I swung the lantern to look back the way we had come. Nothing.

"Does anything look familiar?"

I tried to get my bearings. "We should have passed through the second rockfall by now. I should have tied the strips around the stone. And when I slipped on the way down . . ."

". . . it cleared the path." Galen nodded slowly. "And I just kept walking. I don't know how long it's been since I saw a marker."

I sat and started ripping at the cuffs of my pants. "I'm not moving until we can keep track of where we are."

"I don't think this is a dead end. Look."

I saw the white paint on the stone.

Galen inspected the marking. "Like the ones I follow to go from one room in the castle to another."

He turned to me. It was almost a conversation, both of us weighing whether we should retrace our path or continue on.

"You should be there when Leymonn sends his men into the caves I'll be right behind you."

We stopped every few strides to tie a strip around the stone. Galen grew quiet, his shoulders hunched as he followed the markings.

Then he stopped again, suddenly, and this time, I did bump into him. He reached behind for me, to keep me from falling. "It's daylight. Look."

I saw a pale glow ahead.

"It's near the wall, in the old part of Reggen . . . I don't like this."

"Daylight?" I asked.

"*You* in daylight." He held the lantern up, studying me. "Pull your hair back."

"But people will see the birthmark."

"Your hair looks too much like a girl's right now. It curled in the water." He reached toward my face as if he would tuck it back. Just as quickly, he pulled his hand away.

I pretended I didn't notice, running my fingers through

my hair to smooth it, then tying it at the nape of my neck with a bit of homespun.

"Better?" I asked.

"Yes. Much." He nodded. "Now flip your collar up. It'll hide the birthmark."

I did, then glanced up for approval.

Another nod, and in the morning light, I saw something like sadness in his eyes. No, it was loneliness.

We were both of us alone again.

I pushed past Galen and ran into the daylight.

Chapter 32

The moment I reached the street, I felt as if no disguise was good enough. I slid to a stop and waited for Galen to join me.

"Let's go."

We hurried up one street and then another. Galen led us within a street of the Tailor's shop. The road was clogged with people. Had something happened to the shop? I hopped up on a crate to get a better look.

A crowd was gathered around the narrow little door. It looked as though they'd been there all night waiting for help that would not come.

Galen motioned to me. "Come on, Saville. We need to hurry."

I hopped down and landed wrong, sending the crate clattering away. We traveled two paces before the first shout.

"The tailor! He's come."

Galen's hand caught my back and propelled me forward. "Move, Saville!"

The crowd followed us, and the shouting grew closer. Galen pushed me behind him and turned to face them, hands raised. "I am not the tailor! It isn't me!"

I ducked my head and scurried away while he drew their attention.

"He's too dark to be the tailor."

"Too old! The tailor was just a lad!"

Then someone grabbed my arm. "Tailor? Is it you?" It was a scared, skinny man. I tried to pull free, but he held tight and shouted, "I see it! Fate's Kiss!" He tried to touch the birthmark, as if it would bring him good fortune.

I wrenched away, but he kept hold of my shirt. I felt my sleeve tear.

"It's the champion! Behind the other one."

Hands grasped at me from all sides, the crowd separating me from Galen.

"Please, lad, tell us your plan for routing the giants. Let us help you."

"You have to save us from the deathless duke."

"My little ones, they're too young to be eaten by giants."

It was like drowning, the crowd pressing closer and closer, reaching for me. I didn't speak, afraid my voice would give me away.

"Say something, lad!"

I tried to squirm away, but they took hold of my clothing, anything to keep me with them. I heard another rip, and then another.

"I've a bit of his shirt!" cried a woman, waving it like a flag. "It'll protect me from the giants!"

Another rip, and I felt the morning breeze on my shoulder.

"I'll hold it while I pray for you, lad!"

Where was Galen?

And then I was drowning, the current pulling me under, beating me against buildings, and all the while I kept my arms wrapped around my middle and told myself not to scream, not to speak. It would be over soon.

It was—in a heartbeat, in a breath.

The people who had pressed against me stepped back, eyes wide, mouths slack. My shirt was torn to tatters, strips of it hanging from my waist. My still-wet trousers clung to me, revealing hips more rounded than the softest lad could boast. The binding around my chest remained, still looped over one shoulder, but with no shirt to cover it. . . . I wrapped my arms more tightly around myself.

"A *girl?*" a voice cried, and the word echoed back through the crowd. Shock changed to anger. Hands clenched. Eyes narrowed.

"Please," I shouted. "I didn't mean to—"

My words were lost in the howls of outrage. One face stood out: a woman, her eyes wide with fear as she realized that there was no one to save her and her babies. She shook her head, then turned away.

Fists and stones rained down on me. I put my hands over my head to protect myself, but it did little good. The world had grown so loud I couldn't make out individual sounds. *Just don't fall down,* I thought. *Don't fall. They can kick you if you fall.*

Finally, one sound—my name—rose over the crowd. I saw Galen, sitting above everyone else. He sat on a horse that he must have plundered from a cart. And he was reaching toward me.

"Saville!"

I tensed my body, and the moment I felt a give in the press around me, I lunged. He caught my arm, tugging me up, and swinging me in front of him.

He shouted something as we pushed through the crowd. But hands still caught at us, and something rough struck the side of my head. The horse began to move faster, yet I couldn't hear the sound of its hoofbeats, and the shouts grew faint.

Galen leaned over me, as if I wasn't giving him enough room. I didn't mind. It felt good to lie over the horse. I'd have slept right there if it weren't for the rocks hitting my shoulders and arms.

"Saville!" Galen's arm looped around my waist. I felt the dampness of his shirt against my back. "Sit up! I can't protect you if you don't sit up."

Then there wasn't anything striking me because he was there. I wondered if the stones were hitting him. The horse moved into a canter, its hooves ringing against the cobblestones. My head hurt, hurt, hurt, but I made myself sit up. Galen's arm tightened around my waist. I was sure, somehow, that he was the only thing holding me together.

He was angry. I heard him curse as we tore toward the

castle, and I felt the roughness of his cheek against the side of my head that didn't ache.

Then a shadow fell over us.

"Close the gates!" he shouted. "Close the gates!"

I knew when he slid off the horse—I felt the wind across my shoulders and back.

"Come on, Saville." He helped me down, keeping an arm around my waist as he walked me toward the small, dark door, just as he had the first day he'd brought me to the palace.

"They know," I whispered. "They know that I'm the champion. The whole city knows."

"Yes. They do."

"I'm sorry," I said as he led me into his room, but he didn't hear. He was shouting down the hall about a doctor. He sat me in my favorite chair, the one with the patchwork, and knelt in front of me.

I shivered all over, even though I wasn't cold.

He shook me very gently. "Saville, look at me."

I did, but he didn't notice; he was checking me, my arms especially. They were covered in scratches, and bruises were beginning to darken my skin, even though I couldn't yet feel them.

I couldn't feel anything. But I could tell Galen was scared, though we'd left the crowd far behind.

"Don't worry." The words were so hard to find. "We're safe now, both of us. Why are you worried?"

He looked at me and whispered, "You silly, silly girl." And

then he turned my chin and looked at the right side of my head, the side that hurt.

"Sky above." He shook his sleeve down over his hand, then began to wipe at my neck and cheek. His sleeve came back scarlet. He dabbed at it again, then gently pushed my hair back so he could see the cut better.

I bit my lip, though I was grateful for the pain. The room was sharper now, more focused. I looked down at my hands in my lap. My shirt had been completely torn away, but the lower half of one sleeve remained, gathered around my wrist.

"The cut's bleeding too much for me to see," said Galen.

I pulled the cuff off and handed it to him.

"That will help." He pressed it against the side of my head, wincing when I flinched. "The doctors will be here soon."

"I can't stop shaking. Why can't I stop shaking?"

"It will pass."

"Good." The word chattered out. My body didn't seem to belong to me. "I hate this."

"So do I."

I leaned forward and rested my head in my hands. The face of that one woman swam before me—the one who had been so scared, so disappointed. I felt her gaze on me, even in that room.

And I couldn't stop shaking.

"Here." Galen moved my hand to cover the cloth. "Hold this."

I heard him go to the door and speak to someone. He

returned and stood over me. Nothing happened.

Something featherlight and warm touched my shoulder, then the base of my neck: his fingertips. I looked up at him.

"You have bruises there, too," he said, his mouth set.

"I don't feel them."

He nodded, then dropped something warm across my shoulders. "It's a guard's coat."

"I'm not cold," I said, but I settled back into it.

He knelt in front of me again and pulled the coat tight under my chin. "I don't care."

The door swung open. A doctor walked straight to me and lifted the scrap of shirt I held to my head.

He kept his eyes on me, but spoke to Galen. "Leymonn demands your presence, Lord Verras. The city . . ." He shook his head. "You can hear the mob from the courtyard."

"You'll see to her?"

"Of course. I'll report to you as soon as I've examined her."

Galen stood by the door, still wet from the Kriva, one cuff red with my blood. But he didn't leave. He just looked at me, and I was too tired to do anything but look back.

I didn't feel the cold until after he'd left.

Chapter 33

The physician's draught made sleep easy, but it couldn't stop the dreams: the scouts' heads in the duke's wagon, blinking their sightless eyes . . . the shouts of a mob that never appeared . . . Volar's low voice threading the chaos . . . Galen whispering, *Silly girl, silly girl.*

I woke, scared of the foreign room's darkness. I'd been moved. A physician bent over me. "Look at me, Saville. Follow the candle's light."

I tried, but, oh, how my head hurt! The pain had only been biding its time.

"Your head?"

"Everything." I stretched my legs beneath the blankets. "No. My legs don't hurt."

"Good."

"What time is it?" I asked.

"Barely noon. Go back to sleep."

I tried, but the dreams were too close. I smelled blood when I saw the giants' heads. I felt stones when I heard the mob.

Another memory surfaced: Galen's arm around my waist, the barrage of stones stopping when he pulled me against him.

Tomorrow, I would be embarrassed that he'd held me so close, that I'd worn only my binding, that I'd felt his warmth against my skin. I would be embarrassed tomorrow, but not now. I slipped beneath the memories like a cloak against the cold. I fell asleep remembering the roughness of his cheek against mine.

"Saville? Saville?"

I blinked up at the physician.

"Lord Verras wishes to see you. Do you feel well enough to go to him?"

"Yes."

"Sit first on the side of the bed."

I sat slowly, but the right side of my head throbbed nonetheless. I put a hand to it and felt a bandage.

"You've a nice cut there," said the physician. "Dizzy?"

I shook my head. "Just sore."

"There are clean clothes on the chair. I'll step out for a moment."

I dressed slowly, moving as if I were underwater. My arms were scratched and bruised. My shoulders ached. But I'd live. I smiled. It was a trite expression, but true. I'd live, and there had been moments when I thought I wouldn't.

The dress was similar to the one I'd worn as the princess's errand girl: simple, but made of good, soft fabric. When I opened the door, a guard waited for me.

I followed him, but he did not lead me to Galen's room. Something was wrong. Galen should be in his room, trying to find a solution to this mess.

Sky above. *Mess* didn't begin to describe what must be happening now that Reggen knew it had no champion. Had the duke discovered the truth? I followed the guard up several flights of stairs, through silent halls.

No servants scurried to or from errands. An entire hallway was dark. Something was dreadfully wrong.

The guard finally stopped outside the king's suite. The last time I'd stood outside these doors, I was Avi, meeting the king for a fitting.

What would King Eldin do now that Reggen knew my secret? Would he be swayed by Leymonn and have me killed? Would he hand me over to the duke?

Surely, Galen wouldn't summon me to my death.

I was still staring at the doors when Lord Cinnan, the king's old advisor, joined me, holding a sheaf of parchment.

"Good evening, Miss Gramton." His lips twitched into a smile. "It is a pleasure to meet the lady behind the tailor's apprentice."

I could only gape at him, wondering why Leymonn had let him back into the castle.

Lord Cinnan held the door open for me. "After you, Miss Gramton."

The room was nearly empty, the only light coming from a lantern on the king's desk. Galen stood alone, studying the papers spread across its surface.

"I've returned from the archives," announced Lord Cinnan. "With company."

Galen straightened when he saw me. "Saville!"

A moment later, he was at my side, his gaze moving over my face, shoulders, arms. He knew where the bruises were, even the ones my dress now covered. "How are you?"

I glanced at Lord Cinnan, who sat at the large table, sorting through the parchment, and tucked my questions away.

"I'm well. Just sore." I remembered how I'd stopped feeling the stones when Galen pulled me close. His shoulders must be as bruised as mine. "And you?"

His smile didn't reach his eyes. "Nothing that needed bandaging."

His mouth was tight with worry, and—there was fear in his eyes.

"What's *happened*?" I whispered. "What's wrong?"

He tipped my chin to the side to see the bandage. I felt the touch all the way to my toes.

"Does it hurt?" He was stalling.

I brushed his hand away. "What happened?" I asked again.

He straightened his shoulders. "King Eldin and Lissa left. Leymonn cleared the tunnel to the top of the cliffs while you slept. . . ."

I shook my head, unwilling to believe it.

"Half the guard went with them. Leymonn says they're going for help, to find allies."

King Eldin had deserted Reggen.

"They took Will with them."

I drew in a shaky breath. "I suppose he'll be safe, then."

Galen nodded. "I hope so."

I looked around the room, trying to make sense of the king's decision. "What about Reggen? Did the king leave instructions for the city?"

There it was, whatever had been troubling Galen. I looked over at Lord Cinnan for some clue, but he resolutely shuffled through the parchment.

Galen took a moment to collect himself before answering. "He named me regent in his stead. It makes sense that someone from his household sit on the throne."

"He's never listened to you before. What does he expect you to do? Negotiate with the duke? Fight?"

Galen just looked at me.

"No," I said, shaking my head. *"No."*

The king expected Galen to die.

The duke would take Reggen, one way or another. After King Eldin's attack, he would show no mercy. He'd kill whoever sat on Reggen's throne.

"I can see only two options," Galen said. "One is to hold the duke off for as long as possible. But I don't think Eldin will be able to recruit aid and return to Reggen in time. The duke may be so enraged that he levels the city. Or"—he didn't even pause—"I can surrender. I can give the throne and the crown to the duke. Perhaps he'll show mercy."

"He'll kill you."

"Saville." Galen waited until I was looking into his eyes,

until I could see that his determination ran deeper than his fear. "He'll kill me anyway. I have to think about Reggen, and . . . I don't know how to keep the city safe."

I couldn't answer.

"That's what I do," he said. "I look, and I watch, and I see the things that others don't. But I don't see anything, Saville. Not a thing."

I wanted to take him by the hand and drag him someplace safe. We could follow the king. We could hide in the caves. We—

"Please," he whispered. "Help me save Reggen. I see more clearly when I'm with you."

Galen was asking *me* for help, when I wasn't sure I could even stand.

There was a scrape as Lord Cinnan pushed back his chair. "I've found something, though I don't know how it will help us."

Galen pulled in a great breath. I watched him put his fear aside. He had a task to complete.

And I would help him.

Chapter 34

Lord Cinnan pointed at the stained parchment before him. "Tales written by one of the first merchants in the north. He cut the trails that our wagons follow, even today. These are the stories he heard on his journeys through the Steeps."

"Stories about giants?" asked Galen.

Lord Cinnan scratched his chin. "I wish we had such fortune. I found no stories of giants, but there is a tale of a knight who could not be killed."

I thought of Volar's story about the king who had hidden his heart away.

"The language is simple enough," said Lord Cinnan, "but the parchment is spotted in places:

We did not wish to attempt the Belmor Mountains so close to winter. Already, the frosts had crushed what little life still persisted in the Steeps. My men and I stayed one night in a village a good week's ride from the manor of the Steeps' lord."

Lord Cinnan looked up. "There was no Duke of the Western Steeps then. This was written before the emperor ever conquered Reggen.

The villagers were a ragged crew, unwilling to break the ice

in the troughs until they saw we were prepared to barter. They would have none of our coin—where would they spend it?—but demanded spices and dried meat in exchange for a place to stay. Once payment was made, they saw to our horses, then led us into the largest hut to pass the night. It was vile food and viler company, save the stories they told around a low-burning fire.

"Stories such as I'd never heard: A groom pulled from the bridal chamber and cut to pieces by a vengeful wizard, his limbs scattered to the far corners of the Steeps. Yet the faithful bride would seek the many pieces of her husband, and once she had found them all—did I not tell you this was a gruesome tale?—she had only to sprinkle the water of life to find him restored and whole. My men discovered versions of the tale in which she did not gather all of her bridegroom. You can imagine how those stories ended.

"The villagers saved the tale of the knight who could not be killed till after dark, when the fire fell to embers.

"The knight feared nothing on earth, save death. One night, as he lay beneath the stars, a wolf came to his side and told the knight what he must do to live forever. When the knight awoke, the wolf was gone, but the solution remained, eating at his mind like disease consumes a limb. The seasons passed as the knight crafted a chest from wood hard as stone and forged great chains to wrap around it. He coated the inside of the chest with pitch so that water could not creep inside. Then he carved another, smaller chest.

"Finally, he lay under the stars again, and this time he did

277

not need the wolf to know what he must do. He took up a knife sharper than thought, bared his breast, and cut his still-beating heart from his body. The wolf had said this would be the most difficult part, for few possessed the will to commit such an act or had the strength to move once it was done.

"But as the knight placed his heart in the smaller chest, he felt stronger. And when he placed the small chest into the great, pitch-covered chest, he felt stronger still. He wrapped the outer chest in chains and threw it into one of the fathomless lakes near the Belmor Mountains. And walked away, deathless.

"He became the scourge of the Steeps. Champion after champion challenged the knight, and champion after champion fell to him. He grew in power, untouched by pity for those he ruled, until a farmer's son, a worthy lad, discovered the knight's secret and destroyed his heart.

"Only a people who scratch out their living in the rock near these mountains would tell such a story, I think."

Lord Cinnan set the parchment down. "That's all. Perhaps the knight was like the duke, and his insanity gave him strength. We must—"

"What if it's true?" Galen's voice was soft, yet certain.

"What do you mean?" asked Lord Cinnan. "That the duke really is the emperor's descendant?"

Galen sat back in his chair, seeing something we couldn't. He reminded me of a hunting dog that had caught scent of its quarry. "This knight, who cut out his heart. The abomination who Volar spoke of . . . What if the stories are true?"

"They're just tales told from knee to knee," I answered.

Galen looked at me, head tilted, just like Volar. He was more certain now. "We would have said the same about giants a year ago."

"A month ago," murmured Lord Cinnan.

I was certain something awful crouched at the end of this conversation. "Don't stop there," I snapped. "Let's consider the stories of dragons and princesses locked in towers and kings welcoming back the children they banished. . . ." *And sweet-tempered servant girls who marry the prince, despite the betrothed waiting for him . . .*

I looked away.

Galen tapped the table with a finger. "*These* stories—of a human and a giant king who could outwit death—both come from the same place. The Belmor Mountains rise out of the Steeps. What if . . . what if the duke cut out his heart and hid it?"

"Ridiculous," Lord Cinnan answered weakly.

"Nearly two years passed from the time the duke was ousted from the counsel and when he reclaimed his castle. There is no record of him during that time, but at least one merchant heard rumors that the duke wandered the Steeps. What if he cut his heart out then—in the land where those stories sprang up?"

"Galen . . . ," protested Lord Cinnan.

Galen slapped the table. "You cannot say it was *insanity* that allowed the duke to pull a crossbow bolt out of his heart!

I saw it with my own eyes. Volar said the duke fought a giant warrior and *did not die.* We've all seen how easy it is for a giant to kill a human. Surely, at least one tried to crush the duke when he marched into the Belmor!

"No. What we witnessed yesterday wasn't insanity. It was ghoulish immortality."

He stopped, giving us time to think, to see how much sense it made. Neither Lord Cinnan nor I wanted to believe this tale of a deathless duke, and yet we couldn't deny it.

Galen leaned closer. "If these stories are true, if the duke has cut out his heart, what do we do?"

Lord Cinnan scowled, then looked at us from under his eyebrows. "We find it. And we kill him."

"Saville?"

I slowly shook my head, the way I had when Mama died and I hadn't been ready to believe it. "Of all the stories," I whispered, "why do these have to be the ones that are true?"

"You've argued all along that there was a reason the giants followed the duke," said Galen. "You were right: he used his strength to make them think he was their high king. But the duke's authority will be shattered once the giants see that he's mortal. We must find his heart if we're going to stop this war."

"It could be anywhere!" I said. "He could have thrown it into a lake in the Steeps."

"We're lost if he hid his heart in the Steeps," said Lord Cinnan, "but we have no reason to assume he left it there. You tell me he's given himself the title of Holder of the Eternal Heart. Have you gathered any other clues?"

"Nothing else from his titles," said Galen.

I rubbed my forehead, trying to remember what the duke had said as he stood by the heads of the giant scouts. "When I asked about *Oma*, the duke told me he'd scold the princess about letting me leave her side. He said she shouldn't let her treasure get away. He—what was it?—didn't like treasure kept at a distance." I looked up. "The duke's heart is his *only* treasure. He'll keep it close."

"In his tent?" asked Lord Cinnan.

"He had guards around the southwest corner of his tent," said Galen. "I assumed it was to guard the place he slept, but . . ."

"He has no need to protect himself," said Lord Cinnan. "Nothing can kill him. But his heart? That's another matter. Are you sure we can't sneak into camp?"

"I'm sure," I said. "The giants will hear us. But there's another way. The duke said he'd be willing to meet with the champion."

"No, he said the champion could challenge one of the giants," corrected Galen. "I won't let you go."

I tried to smile. "You're just jealous that you weren't invited."

Lord Cinnan watched me. "The duke may still agree to a meeting. He might prefer the champion after the king's attack."

"That's ridiculous!" snapped Galen. "You'd never reach the duke's heart."

"Ridiculous? You think—"

A guard burst in, unable to hide his fear. "Lord Verras, you're needed at the city gates."

Galen slowly stood. "What is it?"

The guard swallowed. "It's the Duke of the Western Steeps. He has King Eldin."

Chapter 35

The sun rose as Galen and I walked along the ramparts to the gates, our shadows thrown to the side as if even they wanted to escape. Over and over, I imagined the duke commanding his giants to wring the necks of the king and princess while I watched, unable to save them.

"What are we going to do?" I asked.

"I'm going to use what he wants to keep Eldin and Lissa safe."

"He wants Reggen," I snapped. "He wants the crown. He wants Lissa."

"No. He wants to be treated as a king. He doesn't want to be seen as a usurper even if he wrenches the throne away."

We took stairs to the lower level of the gatehouse. It was as deep as the wall itself, with two gates: a small one on the city side and a larger one built of timber, which faced the Kriva. Any army that attacked Reggen would have to pass through both gates, and all the defenses used by the soldiers were positioned on the wall above.

Soldiers slammed their fists against their chests in salute as we passed. As the regent passed. Whatever decisions had to be made, Galen would make them.

 283

And he would bear the consequences.

One of the soldiers opened a small door beside the gates, the one I'd run through to reach Will when the giant scouts had hold of him. Galen walked through but stopped me when I tried to follow. He pressed his spyglass into my hands. "Please, Saville. Be my eyes."

So I stood in the doorway and watched.

The willow the Deathless had thrown was still there, its leaves yellowed and dry. Beyond it, on the far end of the bridge, stood the duke. And Lissa, King Eldin, and . . . Will! I released a ragged sigh. They were safe.

For now.

I raised the spyglass to see their faces. The princess and king stood beside the duke, their hands chained. King Eldin had been stripped of his coat. Everyone could see his narrow, sloping shoulders, his pudgy belly.

Will was balanced on crutches, and as I watched, the duke dropped a hand to ruffle Will's hair like he was a puppy. Will scowled for a moment, then looked up at the duke, grinning. He was still playing the spy.

I could only see the back of Galen's head and one shoulder. He stood so tall, so straight, as if he—like the city's foundation—were rooted in the stone beneath the Kriva. The duke might push all he wished, but Galen wouldn't yield.

"Ah!" shouted the duke. "There you are! The city's regent come to salvage the ruin that King Eldin abandoned."

I fiddled with the spyglass until I could see clearly. King

Eldin's face burned, but he remained quiet. Lissa was pale beside the man who viewed her as part of his prize.

Galen ignored the insult. "What do you want?"

"I told you when I arrived with my bride-gift: I expect you to give me Reggen at midnight. I could simply take the city, but it would be so tiresome to rebuild everything."

Tiresome. The king had used that word so often. I swung the spyglass to him. Never had a man looked less regal. I quickly scanned the camp for Volar. I thought for a moment that I saw him near the pens, but I couldn't find him again.

And still Galen did not reply to the duke's taunt.

The duke grew impatient. "Answer me, Regent!"

"I trust you'll keep the king and his company safe until then, as any honorable man would? Only a usurper murders his way to the throne."

The duke's face contorted with rage, but he mastered it a moment later, and laughed, an empty, echoing sound that lasted far too long. "Perhaps. The king's advisor did not survive the trip here, I'm afraid."

Then he caught King Eldin by the arm and tugged him forward. "Killing? There's no talk of killing. The king is quite safe, as you see."

Galen looked back, right at me, and I saw the decision in his eyes. He was going to go to the duke now.

No. Not like this. I didn't even say good-bye.

"Tell him, Little King." The duke gripped Eldin's shoulder. "Tell your regent to join me this evening. Tell him to

 285

open the gates to me tomorrow morning."

King Eldin stood silent, hanging his head. Perhaps he was too frightened to speak.

"Nothing? You are *tiresome,* Little King! I spent years dreaming of conquering your brother. And all I have is you."

King Eldin raised his head and looked at Galen.

"Tell him!" bellowed the duke.

The king hunched his shoulders, as if preparing for a blow . . . and shook his head.

I nearly dropped the spyglass.

The duke half smiled. "I can't hear you, Little King."

"No," said the king, his face set. For once, he appeared deserving of his title.

I was not the only one who noticed. Surprise washed over the duke, and he struck out, a blur in the morning sunlight. The king stumbled and fell.

"Eldin!" Galen began running.

"Regent Verras," the king shouted from the ground, "I command you to stay!"

Galen stopped, uncertain.

The duke yanked King Eldin to his feet. "Command the regent, Little King!"

King Eldin's chest heaved and, once more, I saw the narrowed eyes, the braced shoulders.

"Regent Verras," he shouted, "I *command* you to hold the city! You will not surren—"

The duke struck King Eldin again. Again, the king fell. He

286

raised a hand to his face and panted as he looked up with wide, disbelieving eyes.

I realized the king was shocked not by the duke's violence, but by his own courage.

He smiled. "Remember that summer, Galen? When you and Tor wanted to see the cave?"

Galen, halfway across the bridge, nodded.

"I don't want to see you at midnight!" called the king.

"Take him away!" screamed the duke. He quickly composed his features. "Yes, stay, Regent!" he called across the bridge. "Stay behind the walls for this last day. I have found something to keep me from growing bored. But remember: if you wish to save this city, you *will* come to me at midnight."

The duke turned, and the giant guards herded the king and Lissa back to the camp. The king moved slowly, but I thought I saw a shadow of a smile on his face.

Galen's pounding footfalls brought my attention back to Reggen. As he passed through the gates, he told the captain of the guard, "No one goes through these gates. You will hold them, Captain."

"What did he mean about the cave?" I asked as we started back over the ramparts.

Galen glanced at me. "It was one of those summers I told you about. We were swimming in the Kriva—Eldin, Tor, and I. Tor wanted to explore a cave upstream but Eldin was scared."

"What happened?"

 287

"He said he wouldn't go and Tor tried to make him. Tor twisted Eldin's wrist badly, tried to drag him along over the rocks, but Eldin wouldn't give in. Tor, for all his strength, couldn't budge him. He said that the only thing Eldin excelled at was being stubborn."

I turned the story over in my mind, trying to make sense of it. "That was his message to you? He could be stubborn?"

Galen stopped, and his shoulders sagged. "I hope so."

Then I knew why the king's expression had reminded me of our first meeting, when he blocked Lord Cinnan's insistence that he read Galen's report at every turn. King Eldin had shown that same doggedness on the bridge.

"I think the king will do it," I said. "He realized he could, I saw it."

"What do you mean?"

Galen didn't have the spyglass. He hadn't seen. "Did you hear the frustration in the duke's voice? King Eldin is stronger than we thought. He's stronger than *he* thought. His brother was right: King Eldin is stubborn. And he's buying us time."

Galen took me by the shoulders, "Do you think so, Saville?"

"I know it."

Chapter 36

We spent that long day researching the midnight meeting between Reggen's rulers and the emperor so many years before. Lord Cinnan read that Reggen gifted the emperor with gold and amber found at Gantaras, a great inland sea a week's ride from Reggen. So Galen took gold and Gantaran amber from the castle's treasury and placed them in a small ivory chest.

He grimaced as he locked it. "I hate to give the duke anything."

"Perhaps it will please him enough that he doesn't watch you closely," said Lord Cinnan. "Let's hope he stores it with his other treasures and you'll see where he keeps his heart."

The emperor had walked into Reggen shortly after dawn. If the duke copied the emperor, Galen had six hours to find the duke's heart and destroy it. None of us believed he would keep Galen alive after he claimed the city in the morning.

Lord Cinnan looked at Galen, and I could see him struggling with all he wanted to tell his protégé. Finally, he put a hand on Galen's shoulder. "I'll see you at dawn."

Galen and I walked along the ramparts in silence, looking out over the giant camp smudged with fires. I thought of how he'd pulled Will to safety, how he'd stood beside me when we told the king my secret. I'd never felt so safe as when he'd pulled me from the mob and tucked me close.

I wanted to tell him a thousand things—and couldn't find words for even one.

We reached the gatehouse just before midnight—a small, cramped room with spears lining one side of the wall and a table tucked into a corner. Galen silently placed the chest on the table. Then we went to the arrow slit and peered out over the Kriva, waiting for the duke to appear.

Galen stood so close that I could see the stitching of his coat in the candlelight. He was regent, yet he still wore a simple wool coat.

Fine Coat.

I put my hand on his shoulder, smoothing the fabric.

Galen jumped at my touch, and I yanked my hand away, grateful for the dark that hid my blush. But he stepped closer, peering down at me in the gloom. I hardly dared to breathe, but didn't look away, hoping he'd be able to see everything I couldn't speak.

Gently—so gently!—he captured my hand and placed it over his heart, pressing it to him until I could feel his heartbeat against my palm. It was like flying and finding solid ground all at once, the one place I was safe.

We stood there, his heart racing beneath my hand, and

then even that distance was too great. I moved closer, my arms around his waist, and he held me tightly, as if he couldn't pull me close enough. His hand swept long, slow circles on my back as my breath fell into time with his.

"Did you know I was jealous of Lynden that day we walked to Reggen?" He sighed and rested his chin on my head. "I'd been thinking about giants all morning, but I did everything I could to eavesdrop on your conversation. *That* was why I knew I'd seen you the day you saved Will."

I squeezed my eyes shut and told myself that the sound rising over the Kriva wasn't the duke approaching. "I thought I was just some girl," I whispered.

It was clearer now, the stamp of giants. They were here. But Galen pressed me closer, and I felt him chuckle. "Some girl indeed, waving that ridiculous candlestick like a sword—"

A trumpet rang out. Galen flinched.

And then we were standing apart, and all I could think was that I'd left some piece of me with him. I felt hollow and feather-light, like I could blow away at any moment. Galen gathered up the duke's chest and we walked out onto the gates.

The duke stood on the other side of the Kriva, his torch throwing a jagged shadow across his face. "I am the Duke of the Western Steeps, Heir to the Ancient Emperor's Crown, Holder of the Eternal Heart, Bearer of Halvor's Spirit! I demand an audience with the regent!"

Galen straightened his shoulders, but I held him back, my hand around his wrist.

 291

He looked at my hand, then up at me and smiled. "You're just jealous you weren't invited."

It wasn't fair, his using my words against me.

"It's time, Saville," he whispered. "Let me go."

"I don't think I can."

He twisted his wrist, forcing me to loosen my grip. "You can."

Then he looked at me in that way I loved. He looked at me like I was velvet. "If I could have that morning over, I'd walk with you."

Before I could answer, he walked away, his dark coat fading into the night.

In stories and songs, something always happened before that awful moment.

That night, there was no reprieve.

Stories weren't always true. Sometimes home was left beyond the horizon and lost there. Sometimes fathers died without speaking their love, without even wanting to.

Sometimes heroes died.

"Galen will find a way," I whispered. I hoped I spoke the truth, the way I'd hoped the giant army would never come to Reggen. But I didn't believe our plan would defeat the duke.

I knew it wouldn't.

What had we missed? *Think. Think!* I closed my eyes, mind traveling back to the duke standing by the bridge . . . *Holder of the Eternal Heart, Bearer of Halvor's Spirit.* He'd added another title. Bearer of Halvor's Spirit.

Halvor. Where had I heard that name? For a moment, the gates and the bridge faded, even the image of Galen walking away.

Halvor.

And then I remembered other tales—tales the duke and Volar had told us—and I knew in my bones that those stories held truth. I scrambled up the stairs to the ramparts, looking out over the giant camp for a moment. Then I raced back to the castle, back to the caves.

I had to find Volar.

The duke had used the giants' tale of Halvor the high king to lead his army into battle. He'd used his immortality and his ability to see through human cunning to convince the *uten* that he was their high king. He'd used my deception to strengthen his hold over the giants. But he wasn't the only one who could hear truth from lies. Just because the duke had twisted the tales didn't mean they weren't true.

I reached Galen's room, ran to the tapestry, and slipped into the caves.

The *uten* really did have a high king: a mountain-breaker who heard truth in rock—and in human voices. He was everything the duke pretended to be. And he didn't know.

Chapter 37

The air was choked with late-summer damp when I pulled myself onto the island a few hours later. I'd tugged off my petticoats before swimming across the Kriva, but I must have wrung half the river out of my wretched skirt once I stood on the bank. I'd almost changed before the journey, but whatever happened, whatever was required of me, I wanted to do it as myself. As Saville.

"Volar!" I called. "I need to see you!"

There was no answering splash from the far bank. Nothing.

If I walked into the camp, the giants might kill me before I could find Volar. If I waited for him to come to me, Galen might die.

I waded back into the Kriva and swam for the duke's camp.

The sun had not yet risen and the whole world was painted in gray and black. To the north, I saw the dull flash of lightning buried deep in a tangle of thunderheads.

Yet I still saw the giant approaching, a dark tower against the thin line of gray on the eastern horizon. As he neared, I saw he didn't wear the bone collar of the Deathless. Nor did he carry any weapons. Not that he needed to. One stomp would be enough.

I silently held my hands up to show I meant no harm. The duke had taught the giants to fear a human's voice.

I had taught them to fear a human's voice.

The giant didn't slow as he neared me, the ground trembling with each step. I stumbled back and raised my hands higher. Finally, he stopped, looking down at me through the predawn gloom, head cocked. *Could he hear how my heart raced?* His brow furrowed—I was close enough to see that. Perhaps he didn't like the duke's order to kill humans on sight, either.

"Please," I whispered. "Don't hurt me."

His eyes widened as if I'd shouted at him and he raised his foot. I threw myself to the side, arms covering my head.

"Volar!" I shouted as if he were nearby, as if he could save me.

Perhaps he did. Nothing happened.

The sole of the giant's boot, as wide and long as a banquet table, hovered above me. I scurried out from under it before the giant could change his mind.

"You ask for Volar?"

I backed away and spoke softly, desperate not to frighten him. "I do. Volar, son of Kelnas, the mountain-breaker."

"How do you know him?"

"I met him earlier." I didn't know how much to say. "By the river."

The giant's eyes widened. He knelt down, just as Volar's nephew had. It didn't frighten me as much, but my breath still caught.

"Please," I repeated. "Tell Volar that Hillock is looking for him."

The giant's face creased in surprise, then he looked over his shoulder—more giants raced toward us. He snatched me into the air and turned to face them. I rested my hands on the edge of the finger that wrapped around me. His eyes flicked to me; he'd felt my hands.

"Thank you," I said.

He dipped his head in a quick nod as seven or eight giants gathered around us. I strained to see their faces in the predawn light, but none of them was Volar.

"A *lita!*" shouted one, his hand stretching toward me.

I arced through the air as my captor swung me away from the new giant's reach.

"It knows Volar," he told the others.

They fell silent and he brought me close so they could see me. I nodded to them, not daring to speak.

The giants looked—and listened—their fill.

"It has such a tiny breath."

"Can you hear its heart?"

Finally, an older giant with a weather-beaten face straightened. "You will be punished if you do not kill it, Iden."

"I will not kill something that knows Volar. He is near the other *liten.* Tell him I have Hillock, and to come quickly."

"Hillock?" The giant looked at me.

I bobbed up and down as Iden shrugged. "It said that is what Volar calls it."

"It lies!" said the giant. "They all lie!"

The other giants nodded, and even Iden seemed to hesitate. I needed them to trust me—or at least not fear me.

"Volar said he did not fear my voice," I murmured. "But I will stay in your hands, under your power, until he comes. Please. Please, tell him Hillock must speak with him."

The giants looked among themselves.

At last, Iden rumbled, "How would it know to pick such a name, Hylag? No. I will not kill it until Volar comes. I am not the duke's *kadyr.*"

Kadyr. What did that mean? *Slave?* Whatever it was, it seemed to sway the group.

"I will go," said one carrying a massive scythe. He disappeared into the camp.

I sighed in relief. In just a few minutes, I would see Volar. I looked up at Iden as he peered toward the camp. He winced as another giant approached.

It wasn't Volar.

After a moment, I could see the collar of bones, a pale smudge in the darkness.

"Be careful, Iden," said Hylag, gripping his spear. "Here is a Deathless." He looked down at me. "So much trouble for a *lita.* Was it worth our lives?"

Iden's hand around me tightened.

No. Not this. I looked toward the camp, but I still did not see Volar.

The Deathless had reached us. His long hair was plaited back, and he wore some sort of paint on his face. He pointed to me. "Kill it."

Iden pulled me back, out of reach.

The Deathless bared his teeth. "Wring its neck, farmer, or I'll kill you myself and scatter your pieces in the sea." He tilted his head as if imagining something that pleased him. "I like that: the fish eating what is left of you and *srati* you out on your precious kelp."

Iden hesitated.

Would he risk his life for a lita?

He transferred me to his left hand, and I choked back a shriek. He was going to wring my neck just as the Deathless had commanded. But his hand swung past my head—toward his belt.

Iden pulled a knife from its sheath.

I looked to Hylag, half expecting him to swat me from Iden's hand.

He and the other giants drew weapons as well.

Hylag brandished something like a spear with a great, hooked head on it. "I've hunted whales three times your size, Ynnix."

"Your whales did not carry swords." Ynnix drew a huge blade with a forked tip from its scabbard, and raised it above his head.

It was a signal. He must be calling the other Deathless.

We needed more time for Volar to reach us.

I looked at Volar's friends with their weapons: knives, the spear, a pick. Nothing a soldier would carry. They'd have little chance against the Deathless. I looked up at Iden and saw the worry in his eyes. He was protecting me because of Volar.

Once more, I saw the heads of the scouts in the wagons. Once more, I heard Volar telling me not to hurt his friends. *These* friends, the giants. No more *uten* would die because of me.

It was time to speak.

"The duke will not be pleased that you have deprived him of his prey," I shouted. Ynnix jumped at the sound. I waited until I had his full attention, until he leaned toward me, eyes narrowed. "I am the champion of Reggen. The duke will want to see me himself."

Iden's hand trembled, but he did not squeeze me to death, though he must have wanted to. Tears burned the back of my eyes.

Ynnix laughed. It sounded like something being twisted in on itself, like the willow the Deathless had ripped from the earth at the duke's command.

"You lie," said Ynnix, "like all *liten*! The champion of Reggen was not a she."

"The champion *is* a woman," I said. "Why do you think Reggen has thrown me out?"

I could tell the lie made sense to him. "Why should I believe you, *lita*? If you do speak truth, why would the duke want you?"

"I'm not asking you to free me. And I did not say the duke

 299

wanted me. Only that he would want to be the one who kills me. Would you deprive him of that opportunity?"

Volar's friends must have sensed Ynnix's hesitation.

"It would not be so great a mistake to kill it, Ynnix," taunted one off to my right. "The duke would only remove you from the Deathless. It would not be so bad to return home and work the forge."

Ynnix was a blacksmith?

Ynnix snarled, then spun on his heel. "Follow me! I will take our captive to the duke."

Our, he said. I covered my mouth with my hand to cover the catch in my breath. He wouldn't kill me now. At least, not until the duke gave the order.

Iden's grip on me loosened as we began to walk. In thanks, I patted his hand like a child bringing her palms down against a tabletop. Iden barely nodded. His brows were drawn low over his eyes, his mouth set. Shame, thick as summer heat, smothered what little courage I had. In minutes, Volar would look the same. He'd never call me Hillock again.

Did the *uten* have a word for *traitor*?

Ynnix led us deeper into the camp. It was near sunrise, and I could see more and more in the pale, gray light, despite the clot of dark clouds to the north. Every few strides, we passed Deathless shouting orders to other giants. Giants moved purposefully, stamping out fires, rolling up blankets the size of small lakes, and sky above . . . readying weapons. They were preparing for war. Even the sounds in the camp were bigger:

the roar of campfires as large as huts, the crash of supplies being collected.

And still, no Volar. We were getting closer and closer to the duke's crimson tent. How could I explain everything to Volar if the duke was there? He'd kill me first.

I caught a hint of the song I'd heard when I stood on the walls with Galen, the one that made me think of hearth fires. I closed my eyes, trying to remember it, gathering the melody note by note. When the song grew clear, I began to hum. Maybe Volar would hear me.

Iden's hand jerked when he heard my humming. I patted his hand again. This time, he nodded. A moment later, Hylag began to sing. I'd heard snatches of the giants' songs on the walls, but this was like wind or water—it washed over and through me. Every tune I'd heard until then was only a husk of sound.

Ynnix turned back to glare at us, but a shout claimed his attention. More giants were jogging toward us: more Deathless. He strode forward to meet them, and they saluted, right fists over their hearts.

"The farmer says he has the champion of Reggen. I take it to the high king."

The Deathless looked at me and laughed, but I didn't care. I held Hylag's song inside me. For a little while, it had pushed the fear aside.

"The dull farmer carries it?"

"Perhaps the champion will speak and kill them, too."

"If they do not die of lack-wit first!"

A Deathless stepped close to peer at me. "Its voice could not be big enough to kill."

Ynnix shrugged. "The voice is like a bird's: thin, no heart. Perhaps it only touches weak minds."

I remembered what Volar had told Galen and me: how the other giants had not been able to hear anything else in a human voice. He truly was unique among the *uten. I was right, I told myself. He really is*—

The Deathless laughed again. "The farmers are in great danger, then!"

"What is this?" The question rolled out like thunder, stopping their laughter.

"Volar!" My heart rose just to see him.

Iden held me up, though I noticed he was careful to keep me out of the reach of the Deathless. "It said it knew you."

"I have to talk to you, Volar," I murmured, hoping I spoke low enough that only he would hear.

He cocked his head. "Hillock?"

"You know this *lita*?" Ynnix snorted. "You have grown soft, mountain-breaker, sleeping next to the pens. We know you guard them."

"I guard the *uten*," corrected Volar. "I guard us from the disgrace of acting like animals."

Ynnix laughed. "You don't know how good they taste. But you will! The whale flesh is nearly gone." He captured Iden's wrist and yanked the hand that held me close. "I may feed you this one. For your first."

His breath smelled like a slaughterhouse. The bones strung around his neck weren't even clean; clots of browning tissue clung to them. I cringed, bile rising in my throat.

Volar's hand came down on Ynnix's shoulder, the tendons in his forearm rigid as he squeezed. Ynnix ignored the mountain-breaker's hold at first, then gasped as it tightened.

"You will let her go." Volar's voice was like an avalanche.

Ynnix staggered back.

Iden swung me away out of reach, and I patted his hand again to let him know I was safe.

"Sir!" piped a voice from below. "Sir!"

Will was on his crutches, thumping among the giants' feet like a three-legged puppy.

My heart lurched when I saw him down there. "Be careful!"

Ynnix, face still burning, raised a boot over the boy.

I screamed and clawed, desperate to reach Will. The world tipped as Iden flinched. From the corner of my eye, I saw a blur as Volar swept his foot under Ynnix's. Will tumbled aside a moment before Ynnix's foot fell.

Ynnix snarled to see Will still alive, then lunged toward Volar. But one of the Deathless stopped him with a hand on his shoulder—the shoulder that Volar had gripped. Ynnix winced and shrugged away.

"Not yet," said the Deathless, nodding toward Will. "It is the duke's *kadyr*. Leave it in peace."

Ynnix shoved Volar back. "I will not forget this, mountain-breaker."

 303

Will, still treacherously close to Ynnix, gathered his crutches.

"We will take the *lita* to the duke now." barked Ynnix. "I am ashamed it has lived this long."

Iden handed me to Volar, who caught me up gently.

"Please," I whispered. "May I see the boy?"

Volar scooped Will up and held him close to me as we followed Ynnix. "You know the duke's *kadyr*?"

"Kadyr?" I asked.

"Small animal. Pet."

I nodded and pressed a hand to Will's cheek, wanting to be sure of him myself. "Yes, I know him." Then to Will, I said, "Are you well?"

He nodded, all business. "I like this bandage, Sir. It keeps my foot from hurting."

"Have you seen Lord Verras?" I asked.

"He's been with the duke all night. But they hurt the king. The duke wanted to show them that a human couldn't squeeze a rock. What are you going to do?"

Couldn't squeeze a rock? What did that mean? But we didn't have time. And Galen hadn't found the heart.

I took Will's face in both my hands. "Listen to me," I whispered, so soft I hoped the Deathless would not hear me over the noise of the camp. "We know why the duke doesn't die. He's cut his heart out and hidden it." Will didn't even blink at the outrageous news. "We can't stop him until we destroy it."

"And you need me to find it," said Will.

"You believe me, just like that?" I exclaimed.

"I saw the duke, that day on the wall. I'll find it, Sir."

I hesitated, then brushed the hair out of his eyes, the way his mother used to. "I love you, do you hear me?"

"Don't say it like that!" Will scowled. "That's how Papa said good-bye. I'll see you again, Sir. I promise." Then he tugged on Volar's sleeve. "Put me down, please."

Volar tilted his head to me, asking if he should.

"Yes," I whispered.

In one swift movement, Volar set Will down. He glanced at the giant with the scythe. "Watch him, Ober."

I leaned over Volar's fingers to better see Will. He waved at me, then hobbled off.

"Did you hear what I told Will?" I asked.

He nodded. "It was a story that I told you and the king's cousin, Hillock. A child's tale."

"It's more than a child's tale, Volar."

He grunted and glanced down at me. "You should not have come, Hillock. I do not think this will end peaceably."

Nor did I. Volar would hate me once I told him. I remembered how his voice had carried: *Two of our scouts were killed because of your city. Two good* uten *dead because of the lies of your champion.*

"I have to tell you something important, Volar."

He cocked his head. "*That* is why you came?"

We were moving fast, the giant's strides eating up the short distance to the crimson tent. There was so little time.

 305

"Volar, do you remember the night you found me? How you could hear what I felt? And how you are the only one of the *uten* who can?"

He shook his head. "Hillock, I do not hear you so well as I thought. I learned that when last we spoke. I was too proud."

"No, you weren't. You heard the truth."

He didn't respond. More Deathless joined Ynnix, flanking us. Volar pulled his great pick from the sling on his back and held it in his other hand. He was worried.

Tell him. Just say it.

The giants stopped in front of the duke's tent. The outer layer was brocade, not the usual weatherproof canvas. It was already darkened with spots of mold and rot.

Ynnix knelt before it. *No time left . . .*

I clutched the top of Volar's finger. "I'm the champ—"

Ynnix's voice rolled over my small one. "High King! I bring you a tribute. The *lita* claims to be the champion of Reggen."

I felt the shock travel through Volar. He trembled and I did not have the courage to look up and see if it was in surprise or rage.

Chapter 38

"What is this, Hillock?" murmured Volar. "I do not believe it."

I did not have time to answer. The flaps of the crimson tent opened and the duke stepped out. From my vantage point in the air, he looked so small, so human, one footfall away from death. Yet this entire army revered him. And no wonder. He stood as if he were a giant, gazing up at the *uten* surrounding him.

"She's come, has she?" called the duke calmly. Too calmly. "Put her down."

How did he know about me? It must have been King Eldin. I'd been mistaken to think he could remain strong.

I dropped through the air as Volar knelt to place me down. For the first time since Iden had taken hold of me outside camp, my feet touched earth. They tingled and burned, but I hardly noticed. All I knew was that Volar kept his hand wrapped around me. It was warmth against the morning chill. It was armor.

"Release her," commanded the duke.

Volar remained kneeling, his left hand around me.

 307

The duke glared up at him. After a moment, he turned his attention to me. "Why have you come?"

"I did not come to see *you*, Your Grace."

"I'm sure you didn't. But here you are, Reggen's champion, just minutes before I claim the city. You are mistaken if you think I will let you drift away."

A human arm pushed aside the tent flap . . . and Lord Leymonn walked out, holding a crossbow and—

"Galen!"

I stumbled back against Volar's palm. I didn't know where to look: at the duke who made me feel hunted, even with Volar's hand around me; at Leymonn, who was supposed to be dead; or at Galen, his hands chained together.

"What are you *doing* here, Saville?"

"I realized something. Other stories might be true, too. I—"

"Are you *mad*?" Galen whispered through clenched teeth. He was furious.

Leymonn yanked Galen back savagely. "Lord Verras was so cooperative when he visited the duke last night. Too cooperative. Even you—" He smiled slowly as he corrected himself. "No. *Especially* you know that he is always thinking, always turning a situation to his advantage. The duke did not want to chain Lord Verras, but I thought it wise."

Galen met my gaze and almost imperceptibly shook his head. He hadn't been able to find the duke's heart.

Leymonn laughed. "You look crestfallen, Miss Saville—"

The duke pushed Leymonn back. "And you talk too

much, Lord Leymonn. I have little time before I take Reggen. Remember who let you live."

Leymonn's face darkened, but the duke didn't notice. He stepped toward me, eyes narrowed. "I know you!" he exclaimed. "You were the maid to my future wife. You asked about Oma. . . ." I felt Volar's hand spasm. "And you didn't think much of the champion. Yet, here you are, maid and champion! Oh yes, you *will* talk to me."

The duke stepped closer. Once again, I saw madness glowing behind his green and blue eyes. When had he first looked at his reflection and decided he would reclaim all that the old emperor had lost? His eyes roved over me as the Tailor's had, seeking weakness, imperfection.

I'd learned long ago how to weather such a gaze. I folded my arms and stared back at him, silent.

"I have no time to play with you. Today, I claim what is due me. You will tell me why you are here or . . ." His gaze flicked to Galen and he smiled. ". . . or I will make you watch the regent's execution."

"You won't kill him if I tell you?" I asked.

"Oh, Champion!" The duke laughed. "How did you manage to outwit my scouts? I will still execute the regent. I just won't make you watch."

I looked at Galen, then up to Volar, who still kept his hand around me. "Volar, I—"

"Talk to me, Champion! To me!" barked the duke. He smiled when I turned back to face him. "You have until the sun rises."

 309

I looked toward the east. Half an hour to convince Volar that he was high king. To save Galen. I rested my hands on Volar's fingers and looked at the giants gathered around us—the Deathless scowling down at me, Volar's friends with their cautious, curious gazes. It was like standing in the clearing of a moving, breathing forest.

And then I knew what to do. It was like remembering the next verse in a song that I hadn't sung in a while, when I couldn't find the words ahead of time. Yet when I opened my mouth to sing them, they'd be there—and not a second before.

I nodded to the duke. "Your Grace, I came to speak to a friend."

The duke glanced at Galen. "Did you now? What did you want to tell him?"

I pressed my palms against Volar's hand. I needed him to listen. "I wanted to tell him that he was right. He heard anger and sadness in my voice. And he caught me in a lie—"

Volar's fingers tightened around me.

The duke threw back his head and laughed. Then he held his arms wide as he shouted up to the giants, "Did I not tell you? They lie! You heard it from her own mouth! That is why I command you to kill them before they can speak, before they cause death with their words!"

He turned again to face me as if it were part of some savage dance. "I am not afraid of you, Champion, and so these giants are safe. Speak on!"

I paused, knowing I stood on the edge of a cliff. "As I said,

Your Grace, I lied. I wanted him to know it. He was not wrong to suspect me."

I patted Volar's hand. *You were right. You heard the truth.*

"Stop it, Saville," muttered Galen. "That's enough!"

The duke chuckled. "You're not bringing him much comfort before he dies, Champion."

I swallowed back the fear. "I didn't want him to doubt himself."

Leymonn scowled. "Your Grace, something is—"

Volar interrupted him. "You *are* the champion?"

He didn't call me Hillock. My heart dropped away. One last time, I claimed the title I had never wanted.

"Yes," I said, looking at the duke, but speaking to Volar. "I am the champion of Reggen."

Volar's hand around me loosened. A rumble of disgust swept the giants. Several of the Deathless drew their swords, the ragged tips flicking near me.

"Shut up, Saville!" Galen shouted. "She's confused, Volar! She isn't the champion."

Leymonn yanked him back. When Galen stumbled, Leymonn kicked him in the back of his knee and he toppled. Before he could rise again, Leymonn lowered his crossbow to Galen's chest. "You'll stay there, Verras."

Galen glared up at Leymonn, and I saw his anger gather itself. But it melted away when he looked at me, his eyes worried, so worried. He shook his head: *Don't do this.*

I smiled so he wouldn't see how scared I was. *I have to.*

 311

"Don't let the regent's outburst stop you, Champion. Continue."

I gripped Volar's hand. I needed the strength he provided, even if he despised me. "I was dressed as a lad, Your Grace, when I met the scouts. . . ." My voice faltered and I prayed Volar believed the grief he heard in my voice. "I expected monsters, witless beasts. They weren't. But they had a boy. . . ." Suddenly, I knew how to tell Galen that Will was searching for the duke's heart. "A street brat with the unfortunate skill of discovering hidden secrets."

Galen's eyes widened and I saw the question in them: *Will knows?*

I nodded, a quick tuck of my chin, and looked at the duke. "Still, I didn't want the boy to die, so I challenged the giants to a game of strength. I tricked them into believing that I could squeeze water from a rock and throw a stone so high it would never fall back to earth."

Volar murmured something, a mix of bewilderment and, finally, belief. He released me, and the morning air touched my wet gown. I wrapped my arms around myself, but I knew I wasn't trembling from the cold.

"Two good *uten* dead," he rumbled. "My sister-son dead. Because the champion lied. Because *you* lied. What does it matter if you tell the truth now?"

His anger had won. I was defenseless.

It was easier to speak after that, in the emptiness on the other side of heartbreak. The worst was over. Volar believed me, believed me and hated me. All I had to do was make him believe the rest.

"I didn't know," I said. It wouldn't make a difference now, but I needed to say it all the same. "I didn't know they'd be killed. I'm so sorry. . . ."

The duke raised an eyebrow. "You're boring me, Champion. And you have not yet told me why you came to my camp."

I wiped my cheeks and stood straighter. "I came to beg the high king, bearer of Halvor's spirit, to stop this war."

The duke clapped his hands. "There's a request I didn't expect! I thought you'd ask for the king's life. Or the regent's. As bearer of Halvor's spirit, I say . . . *No.*" He whirled toward me with a flourish, as if it were my turn to dance. "Now what do *you* say?"

It was time to step off the cliff. "I told you before, Your Grace: I didn't come here to speak with *you.*"

I turned to face Volar. "It's true." He wouldn't look at me, but I saw the tilt of his head as he listened. "I'm the champion. But you . . . you heard truth in my voice. You heard it the first day. You heard my lie. Volar, *you* are the high king. Please, stop this war!"

Volar's eyes widened. The Deathless stood as though they'd been turned to stone, but Volar's friends glanced among themselves. Iden even lifted a hand to touch Volar, as if he almost believed me.

"She lies!" shouted the duke. "She's trying to trick you all. Silence her!"

I called to the giants, "You don't need the duke to know if a *lité* is lying! Ask Volar!"

"Silence!" The duke's fist caught me on my left cheek.

I never saw him move. There was only the explosion of light as I fell backward.

I heard Galen shouting and the clang of his chains. When I opened my eyes, he was still in the dirt, struggling against the foot Leymonn had planted on his chest. Leymonn leaned onto his boot, twisting his heel until Galen cried out and grew still.

"That's better. His Grace was trying to speak." Leymonn chuckled and gave his heel another savage twist. "I never thought I'd say this, but I like having you underfoot."

"Do you see what she's done?" the duke cried. "She's been here minutes and has already deceived Volar! I, alone, can hear the truth in a human's voice. As the bearer of Halvor's spirit, I tell you: she lies! Every word has been a lie!" He looked around and I detected a desperate note in his voice. "She's not even the champion!"

"You say now she is not the champion?" asked Volar. "But you called her by that name."

"She is not! It was a game, an insult." The duke could not hide the tremor in his voice. "Every word she speaks is a lie. I hear it."

I wished I wasn't the champion. I wished I had had no part in the deaths of the giant scouts. . . . Then I laughed. I could prove to the *uten* that Volar wasn't deceived. I could prove I was the champion.

I struggled to my feet. How had King Eldin done it, making it look so simple to stand after being struck?

"I *am* the tailor who met your scouts," I shouted, the words heavy as stones in my mouth. "I talked to them! One was young. He had blue eyes, blue as the sky. The older one had a beard and brown eyes."

The giants shifted their weight uncomfortably.

"The entire city saw their heads!" screamed the duke. "That means nothing!"

He struck out again. I saw it coming and twisted so his blow wouldn't land as hard. My vision danced nonetheless.

"Their eyes were pecked by the time the duke drove them through Reggen!" I shouted up at the giants. "No human but the champion could know about their eyes. Volar is right: I'm telling the truth. He could *hear* it. It's the duke who lies! He's done nothing but lie to you."

I stood in the center of the giants, turning in a slow circle to see their faces. The giants shifted as another joined them: Ober, the farmer Volar had told to watch Will.

Will. He'd reached the tent. I remembered the boy holding a lock of my hair in his hand, telling me he liked to find things.

I'd give him the time he needed to find one last secret.

The duke drew a dagger, but I backed away and shouted, "The duke's strength comes from an abomination, not from Halvor's spirit! He's cut his heart out, and he keeps it hidden. *Holder of the Eternal Heart*, that's what it means. *That's* why he's so strong. You can't kill him until you find—"

The duke struck me again and the world became a roar of noise and light. I wished that, just once, I could faint. But I'd said all I needed to say.

"Saville! Saville, do you hear me?" Galen's voice came from a distance. "Get up, *get up*!"

I forced my eyes open. The duke loomed over me, dagger raised.

Fingers took the duke by his coat, plucked him off me, and dangled him above the ground. I pushed myself up on my elbows, blinking to clear my vision.

Volar held the duke in the air, watching him as he flailed.

He spoke two words: "You lie."

He looked at the gathered giants and bellowed, "He lies!"

A whisper like the wind before a storm rolled through the giants, but they didn't move. Volar himself looked stunned. He'd done more than simply challenge the duke. He'd claimed to be the high king. When I looked up at Volar's face, I realized he believed it.

He knew who he was.

Chapter 39

The duke thrashed against Volar's hold. His clothing ripped and he fell to the ground. When he stood, his shirt hung open. A net of scars covered his chest like a purple-edged spiderweb.

Galen and I had bet our lives that the duke had followed in the footsteps of the deathless knight, but I still gasped to see the proof. He'd cut his heart from his body.

Galen lay under Leymonn's boot, gaping.

For a moment, I thought the duke would run. I thought the Deathless would leave him. Then he stood and calmly straightened his ripped clothes. He acted like he'd had a tussle with boys, but now the fun was over and he needed to go back to his business.

The duke shouted up to Ynnix, "Fetch the humans."

Ynnix saluted and signaled two Deathless to carry out the command. The duke turned to me, still sprawled on the ground. I scrabbled back.

Volar pushed the toe of his boot in front of me. The duke might have been immortal, but he was not stupid.

The battle for the *uten* wasn't about the champion of Reggen anymore. It was between Volar and the duke. He turned away, as if I wasn't worth considering, and looked around at the giants who were murmuring like a storm gathering on the plains.

"Quiet now," said the duke softly, and it carried far more menace than his shouts. "I will have silence when I speak."

And there was silence. The still before the storm.

I glanced at the rotting, crimson tent, flapping in the breeze, and hoped Will was inside. *Let the duke be as foolish as I was. Let him hide his heart where Will can find it.*

I stood up slowly, making sure that my legs could hold me. The dizziness passed, but I rested a hand against Volar's leg. He nodded but did not take his eyes from the duke.

"See how they listen?" the duke said. "They recognize Halvor's spirit. I don't have to grope after it. You are no king. Your mind is weak. It has been twisted by this tiny *lita*." He chided Volar as if he were a wayward child. "I will forget your insolence. I will forgive that you laid hands on me. I only ask that you leave." His bicolored gaze flicked to me. "You may even take this human you have chosen to protect. I will grant you both safe passage."

Before Volar could answer, the ranks of the giants behind the duke rippled and broke as the Deathless brought King Eldin and Lissa forward. Princess Lissa's arm was wrapped around her brother's waist and he leaned against her for support. His hands . . . Sky above, his hands. What had Will said? *The duke wanted to show them that a human couldn't squeeze a rock.*

The king's hands were mangled, crushed. He held them up in front of him, away from his body. They appeared broken in a hundred different places.

"You must sit," the princess told her brother.

"No." He shook his head. "I will stand."

The duke clapped him on the shoulder. "You grow more and more brave, Little King." He laughed when Eldin flinched, then shouted up at Volar. "I will even let you take the king, though he should be put to death for his attack on me." The duke tilted his head, as if considering something new. "Yes! If you leave, you may take the little king *and* the champion. If you do not, then . . ." He flipped his dagger in the air again.

I thought I saw movement inside the duke's tent.

Will?

Galen must have suspected the same thing. He nodded once. A moment later, when Leymonn looked toward the tent, Galen shifted his weight, recapturing his attention.

Leymonn dug in his heel again. "Verras, will you never *learn*? Be still!"

Galen grunted, hands twitching toward Leymonn's boot, but he did not move. His mouth curved into a smile.

Please. Find it, Will!

"Well, mountain-breaker? Will you accept my offer? It's more than generous."

Every soul—human and *uten*—looked at Volar. I almost believed that the sun would stay below the horizon until he spoke.

"You lie." Volar looked down at the duke, eyes narrowed. "I hear it. You do not forgive me, and you will not grant anyone safe passage."

Not a sound, not a breath from the giants. For the first time, the duke looked small among them.

"Ah," he said, "there you go, trying to sound like a king again. You cannot kill me, and yet you claim to be heir to the high king?"

"I do."

A roar of surprise from the giants so loud I jumped.

Volar raised his right hand for silence. It was given.

"I did not seek this," said Volar. "But I will not let you disgrace the throne."

"You will not *let* me?" The duke laughed. "What authority do you have? Can you depose me? One word from me and the Deathless will kill you."

Volar's hand tightened around his pick. "They can try."

The duke laughed again, as if he really were king, as though it were only chance that he was small enough to walk around Volar's feet.

"I will show you the power of life and death! Since you value his life so little"—the duke pointed at Eldin, crouched over his shattered hands—"Ynnix, the little king!"

Ynnix raised his sword over the king and Lissa, and swept it down.

Volar's pick arced through the air, and Ynnix toppled back like a felled tree. His boot twitched once and then he grew still.

The duke laughed—laughed as if he'd never heard so great a joke.

"Well done! But you cannot kill *me*. How, then, do you claim to be high king?"

"You cannot be killed because you are an abomination. The *uten* should not be led into war by one who bleeds but cannot die."

The duke stopped smiling. "If it's blood you want . . . take him!"

The Deathless stepped forward, but so did Volar's friends. I saw Hylag with his spear and Ober with his scythe. Somehow, as they stood beside Volar, I believed they *could* match the Deathless. Perhaps it was because they believed it themselves.

The Deathless did not move.

"Take him, I say!" The duke was so preoccupied with the giants before him that he did not see the tent flap move.

He did not see Will peek out, cautious as a turtle emerging from its shell. The boy watched, and when he saw that no one but me would notice, he eased out of the tent.

He held a small box of stained wood wrapped with metal bands. It was too heavy for Will to hold with one hand, and yet he needed both to maneuver his crutches. I edged toward him.

Galen saw, and slowly raised his hands, positioning them so that the chain connecting his manacles slid over the toe of Leymonn's boot. All the while, Galen's gaze flashed between

Will and Leymonn, tracking the boy's progress, watching to see if Leymonn noticed.

I took a step toward Will . . . and another . . . keeping a hand on Volar's boots as I crept behind him. He needed to know where I was.

Almost there. I circled behind Volar and stood by his right heel. There were only ten strides to Will—all of them in the open. I paused, glancing at the duke to be sure he was still preoccupied with Volar and the Deathless.

When I looked back, Will smiled triumphantly. But when he tried to move toward me, one of his crutches caught on a tent peg and he tumbled to the ground, still holding the box. He didn't cry out, but everyone turned at the clatter of his crutches.

The duke paled when he saw the box in Will's hands. "Get him!"

The world dissolved into motion. Galen grabbed Leymonn's boot and rolled beneath the advisor, wrenching his leg from beneath him. Leymonn toppled and dropped his crossbow as I darted toward Will.

I scooped him up and he dropped the heavy box. Leymonn was back on his feet, but so was Galen, the fury he'd suppressed for so long released. He charged the advisor, driving him back. Leymonn fell on his back and kicked Galen away as he reached for the crossbow.

The bolt swung toward Will and I twisted to protect him, to take the brunt of the blow.

There was a rush of wind—

A great boot caught Leymonn and flung him back. He tumbled through the air, until his body slammed against a Deathless's leg. He crumpled to the ground, eyes lifeless, his neck at an odd angle.

"What . . . ?" I looked up.

Ober. Volar had commanded him to guard Will.

Will squirmed in my arms. "Let me go, Sir! The box!"

Galen was already there. He picked up the box, turning it over and over, trying to find a way to open it, fumbling because of his chains. "Saville! I don't see how to open it. . . ."

"Kill him!" the duke screamed. "I must have the box!"

One of the Deathless raised his boot over us. I darted back, dragging Will with me, but Galen didn't move. He looked up at the boot, watched it begin to fall—

At the last moment, he dropped the box—right underneath the giant's massive boot—and rolled away.

Galen looked at the boot, then at me, eyes wide. Surely, nothing could survive a giant's footfall. How fitting that the duke should be killed by one of his own Deathless!

We watched the duke, wondering how he would die.

He didn't even stumble. "Stand away, Nulaq!"

The giant lifted his boot and stepped back, revealing the unbroken box. Galen darted forward and pried it from the earth.

The duke did not care that Galen held it. That scared me more than anything. I pressed Will closer to me.

"I carry Halvor's spirit and his strength," announced the duke. "I can extend that strength wherever I wish. Even to a box." He laughed as Galen clutched it to him. "Ironwood and blood, boy. *My* blood. You won't break that. It's too strong. I'm too strong."

"I thought all we had to do was find it, Sir," whimpered Will. "It was under, just like important things always are . . ."

"Shhhhh," I whispered against his hair, my mind humming to make sense of it.

Ironwood and blood. I didn't remember anything like that in the story of the deathless knight. The merchant had only written that a young man had found the box and destroyed it.

The duke stalked toward Galen. "No one is stronger than the high king, boy."

I set Will down, and motioned him to stay near Volar as I crept closer.

"I'm not a boy," said Galen, stepping back. "And you're not the high king."

"Does it matter? I *am* the mightiest one here. Now give me what is mine!"

Galen shook his head.

No one is stronger than the high king. No one—

I looked up at Volar, at the high king.

Sometimes the stories are true. I knew it in my marrow. "Throw it to Volar, Galen!"

"To me, king's cousin!" shouted Volar.

The duke's smile faltered. "I'll have that now, Regent, or you will not live the day!"

It was Galen's turn to smile. "I never expected to."

Galen lowered the box toward the ground and flung it up to Volar.

"*No!*" screamed the duke.

He wasn't fast enough to seize the box, but he was still able to reach Galen. I saw it all as I ran to him: the flash of the duke's dagger, the surprise on Galen's face.

The duke raised the dagger again, but the second blow never fell. He reared up, back arched, screaming like the wolves I'd heard on our journey to Reggen.

I dropped to my knees, my hands fluttering over the crimson stain spreading across Galen's tunic.

"No," I whispered. "It's not supposed to end this way . . . not like this."

The duke shrieked something up at Volar, who had closed his fist around the box.

The duke was too close. He might strike again. I turned back to Galen. He looked up at me, eyes wider, each breath shuddering though him.

I put a hand to his cheek. "I'm going to move you, and it's going to hurt."

He gripped my wrist, insistent, and I leaned closer.

"I love you," he whispered.

It was a lightning strike: white fire and thunder and heartbreak. I knew, suddenly, how Will had felt earlier.

"Don't you dare try to tell me good-bye, Galen Verras. Don't you dare!" I hooked my hands under his arms and pulled back with all my strength, dragging him away to safety.

Then I knelt beside him again, pressing a handful of my skirt against his side. My hands shook so badly I could hardly manage the simple task.

"Will!" I called. "Come here!"

Will thumped over just as the duke screamed again.

One of the Deathless lunged toward Volar, but Ober met him and wrestled him aside. Volar was absorbed with his task, his hand tightening around the box, his knuckles white.

"He's not strong enough," sang the duke in a childish voice. "No one is strong enough. I'm safe. I'm safe."

Two more Deathless attacked Volar and, once again, they were driven back. Volar's entire being seemed focused on the box. His arm began to tremble, but his face remained calm. After a moment, he cocked his head and smiled as if he'd heard something lovely. The sunlight grew stronger and lit his face.

He looked like the Guardians.

He looked like the high king.

His hand gripped tighter one last time. The box shattered.

The duke didn't have time to scream. He fell forward, the life gone from his limbs before he hit the ground.

A gasp rose from the giants, followed by a roar from the Deathless. Volar raised his fist. "To me, true *uten*. To me!" He turned to Iden, who stood beside him. "The *liten*—"

The remaining Deathless threw themselves at Volar and the giants flanking him. It was like sitting on a forest floor while the trees pulled their roots from the ground. I tugged Will close and flung myself over Galen.

A shadow fell over us, and I was plucked into the sky. I flailed against the hand holding me until I heard Iden's voice. "Peace, Hillock."

Iden handed me to another giant, then stooped to pick up Galen and Will. A third giant swept up the king and princess. Then Iden led the giants carrying us away from the fray.

"Will he be safe?" I asked the giant carrying me.

"Volar crushed ironwood with his hand. I have never seen the like in all my years. Worry for the others, not him."

The giant carrying the king and princess agreed. "Few *uten* were devoted to the duke. Only the Deathless and those who wished to join the Deathless. The battle will be short."

The giants took us close to the Kriva, not far from the island, and set us down.

Princess Lissa found a soft stretch of ground for the king.

Iden had carried Galen like he was an infant, cradled in the crook of his arm. He set him down, then nodded to me. "I am too big to help him, Hillock."

"His chains," I said. "Can you break them?"

Iden nodded and, with his fingertips, snapped the chain between Galen's manacles.

I bent over Galen. His gaze was strong, his breath steadier than it had been.

Will hopped beside me, his crutches lost in the chaos.

"Sit!" I told him. "I won't have you hurting your foot again." Then I turned back to Galen. "I have to look . . ."

He nodded.

I pushed his coat back. His shirt was soaked. "I can't see—"

I quickly removed Galen's cravat and unbuttoned the collar of his shirt. I pulled it back and gasped. The cut began at the collarbone and traveled across his ribs.

"You must have twisted at the last minute. I don't think it's touched the lung."

I rested my hand on Galen's chest, felt the rise and fall. He was breathing around the pain, to be sure, but still, he was breathing.

"He didn't hit anything vital, Saville. We just need to stop the blood."

I looked down at my skirt. "I don't—there isn't much you haven't bled on already."

"Here, Sir." Will handed me his coat.

I folded it so that it was the length of Galen's wound. "Ready?" I asked him.

He nodded, and I laid the coat over his wound, then pressed down, using both hands.

"Your eyes are closed," said Galen.

I opened them, checking to see if I'd misplaced Will's coat.

"It's fine," said Galen. "I just think it's funny that you closed your eyes."

I shook my head. "You have the oddest sense of humor."

His hand came up to cover mine. "We won. I should be happy."

And he smiled up at me as if I were the sun coming up

over the horizon, as if he already knew my face by memory, by heart. I let him look his fill, and I looked right back and thought how I would hold this moment to me, even when his falcon bride came to Reggen. I had earned that much.

His fingertips brushed my left cheek. "He hit you *hard*."

"I thought it would balance out the bandage on the other side."

Galen laughed, a quick jump of breath that made him wince. But his fingers traced ever so lightly the side of my face.

"The champion of Reggen," he whispered. "The valiant tailor . . ."

I thought he was going to say that he loved me again. And I hoped I'd have the courage to say it back. Instead, I watched the words fall back inside him like a leaf sinking beneath water. He'd told me he loved me because he thought we were going to die. There'd been a terrible safety in that.

We'd lived, and I knew he wouldn't say it again.

I kept my hands pressed against his bandage, and smiled at him as if every fiber of me hadn't ached to hear him say those words, as if these past few days had been enough.

We used one of Princess Lissa's petticoats to bind Will's coat to Galen's side. I'd just finished knotting the bandage when Volar strode up to our ragged group. "It is done."

He knelt next to me. "Will they live, the king and his cousin?"

"Yes. But we must take them to the castle."

Volar nodded. "We will carry you."

"Lord Cinnan will be anxious to know we're safe. He'll be waiting at the gates," said Galen.

Volar saluted King Eldin, making a fist and holding it over his heart. "We have caused your city much pain, but we will seek to make amends."

King Eldin held his ruined hands in front of him, but his voice was steady. "I owe you a great debt. You have saved us."

Volar shook his head. "You defied the duke, while many of the *uten* gave way to him. You are a brave *lité*. Strong of heart."

King Eldin flushed and his eyes filled. "I don't think so."

"I know it. I hear it in your voice," Volar said. "Come, we will take you to your city."

Chapter 40

Volar led the giants carrying us to the bridge, skirting the camp and the aftermath of the battle. I should have felt triumphant as Iden bore Will and me along, but I'd look down at my bloody skirt and every good feeling would fly from me: Galen was wounded; Will's father was still missing.

And what would I do? I couldn't go back to the garret room or be Lissa's errand girl.

War with the giants had been averted. Life in Reggen had been set to rights. But I did not know if there was a place for me in it.

"Sir!" yipped Will. "You're squeezing me too tight!"

I loosened my grip and began to hum "Brightwater," the song from Mama's music box. As we neared the bridge, Iden began to hum the tune, and it was like the earth singing it back to me.

"I like that song," murmured Will.

When the giants reached the bridge, Volar hailed the city. Galen had told him who he should ask for—and that he should declare his position among his people.

Volar flushed, then announced, "I am Volar, king of the

uten, the giants. I ask to speak to Lord Cinnan."

I saw a flurry of activity behind the gates. The small door opened and Lord Cinnan stepped out and around the willow still lying across the bridge.

"Lord Cinnan, I have your king and his kin, and I ask safe passage so that my uten may bring them into your city."

"I greet you Volar, king of the gi—*uten*, in the name of Reggen." He spoke boldly, but I imagined him trying to see if a giant really was holding the king—and if he was safe.

"Cinnan!" King Eldin called. "We must reach the castle quickly. Galen is hurt."

The advisor still seemed uncertain.

"I will only send as many *uten* as are needed to carry your king and his people to the castle," said Volar. "I ask that my people be allowed to return to camp afterward."

I bit back a laugh. As if anything in Reggen could keep a giant who did not wish to be held.

"I thank you," said Lord Cinnan. "Please, bring them."

Volar motioned his friends toward the bridge. "Only one *ute* at a time," he said. "I do not think the bridge will bear more than one."

Ober carried King Eldin and Lissa across the bridge first. Nearing the gate, he kicked the willow aside, rolling it into the Kriva. He waited before the gates a moment until the two great doors swung out. They reached only Ober's chest.

"What would you have him do?" called Volar. "Your king is wounded and my *ute* can bring him to your castle quickly.

Though if you wish it, we will let you take him."

Lord Cinnan peered up at Ober and must have seen a signal from the king. "I would be honored if your *ute* would take them."

Ober nodded, then bent double and shuffled through the gates. When he stood again, I could see the top of his head rising above the wall. Then Hylag, cradling Galen like an infant, carefully ducked under Reggen's gates. His head bobbed after Ober's until it was lost beyond the buildings.

When it was our turn to cross, Volar stopped Iden with a hand on his shoulder.

"I will not come into your city today, Hillock. Your king and his cousin must be cared for, and I must see to the *uten*. There is much to be done now that the duke is dead."

I couldn't speak for a moment. "It's good to hear you call me Hillock," I said finally. "I didn't think you would ever again—and I wouldn't have blamed you."

"Ah." Volar tilted his head and gusted a great sigh. "I do not know what to tell you, except that it was right to meet you. It was established, I think."

"There would have been war if you hadn't helped us."

He lowered his head. "I know what would have happened to the *uten* if the duke still lived. It would have been a rot in the heart of every one of us." He looked up and smiled. "You spoke the truth, but you were cunning also. Perhaps Hillock is not the right name for you. You are closer to a mountain, I think."

Before I could answer, he motioned Iden forward. Will and I were carried across the bridge, and then we were in the city. The crowd filling the streets gaped as the giants strode by. Some shouted and threw stones, but when the giants didn't respond, they fell into silence.

"Sir." Will tugged my arm. "I want to get down."

"Why? There's nothing to be afraid of."

He looked up at Iden. "Are they letting the people out of the pens?"

Iden stood up on his toes and looked over the wall. "They are, little one."

Will nodded, satisfied. "Then please put me down here."

I looked down . . . and saw the fountain.

"I wasn't able to go by the pens, Sir. They wouldn't let me. But I have to know. Pa might be there. I'll get to the castle. Don't you worry. . . ."

I looked down at Will's dirty face, pinched with worry and hope, and smiled as if my heart hadn't been hollowed out. Will was mine, at least for a little while longer.

"Please put us down at the fountain. Will is looking for someone."

Iden's face crinkled. "Volar said I should take you to the castle."

"And you will. But please set us down first."

Iden nodded. "As you wish."

He knelt and I slipped off his arm, then caught Will, careful of his foot. I half carried Will to the fountain and had him sit on the edge, his leg stretched out in front of him. One of the castle guard approached, hand on the hilt of his sword, gaze twitching up at Iden.

"What's this?" he asked.

"We wish to see the captives. Iden will take us to the castle afterward."

"Iden, miss?"

I gestured toward the giant. "Iden."

Iden nodded gravely.

The guard shifted his weight. "And you are?"

Lord Cinnan, who had been listening, joined us. "She is the tailor. The champion."

The soldier saluted, but I looked down, uncomfortable with the title.

"I must go now, Saville. Come as soon as you can," Lord Cinnan said. He looked up at Iden. "Do you mind waiting? I can order my men to escort them to the castle."

Iden shook his head. "Volar said to take them. I will."

Lord Cinnan raised his eyebrows. "Very well, then."

Will struggled to his feet as soon as Lord Cinnan turned away.

I grabbed at him. "Sit down, Will!"

"They're coming! How will he see me if I'm sitting?"

I thought of how I'd looked for Mama after she died; I'd turn a corner and expect her to be there waiting.

I braced myself against one of the fountain's statues. "Lean against me, then. Don't put any weight on your foot."

 335

Will nodded, his face pale and intent as if the force of his hope could bring his father to him. He nestled into my side, his wiry arm wrapped around my waist, a handful of my skirt gripped in his fist.

Let his father be here. Please, let his father be here. The captives began to straggle through the gates, casting fearful glances at Iden. Guards, instructed by Lord Cinnan, shepherded them toward wagons waiting to take them to the castle.

They were filthy and unwashed, faces burnt from exposure to the summer sun. They smelled like animals, like cattle. Bile burned the back of my throat. They'd been nothing more than cattle to the duke and his Deathless. If Volar had not slept outside their pens these last few nights, there would have been even fewer survivors. But how many had been lost before he stood guard? I pulled Will closer to me.

Most of the captives wandered through the gate with empty stares as if they couldn't yet believe they'd been released. None looked toward the fountain.

Except for one man. He stopped, jostling the others around him to get a closer look. When he saw Will, he elbowed his way toward us.

I felt Will suck in a breath, his entire body rigid. "Papa?"

The man was in front of us now, his face so dirty I wondered how Will knew him. He looked up at Will with eyes that crinkled around the edges. Concerned eyes.

"Will?" he asked.

Will shook his head. "You're not Papa."

The man's hands hung limp at his side. "No, I'm not. But he told me about you. He wanted me to find you."

I wrapped my arm around Will's shoulders. I wanted to cover his ears and drag him up to the castle, away from this man with the wild hair and kind eyes.

"Where is he?" asked Will.

The man just shook his head.

Will's legs buckled. I clutched at him to keep him from falling. He curled around himself, head between his knees, just as he had been that day in the street. I pulled him against me. He didn't notice at first, his sharp, barking sobs driving his shoulders against my ribs.

Then his arms went around me and I pressed his face into the hollow of my shoulder, whispering into his hair that I was sorry, so very sorry.

Chapter 41

"Hillock?"

I looked up, glad for the breeze that cooled my wet cheeks. "Yes, Iden?"

"The others have already returned from the castle. I must go soon."

"You can take us now."

The man sent by Will's father had left earlier, whispering his name to me so that I could find him later at the castle. Somehow, Iden managed to pick Will and me up at the same time. We rode to the castle cradled in the crook of his arm.

He did not try to pass under the castle's gate. Instead, he reached over the castle wall, and set us down in the courtyard. Castle guard surrounded us in a moment, escorting us to Will's old room. Will had stopped crying, but stared blankly ahead.

His dirty face was tear streaked. The bandage around his foot had grown damp and lost its stiffness. Worst of all, his entire front was smeared with blood from my skirt.

I knelt in front of him. "The doctor needs to look at your foot. And you need to change into clean clothes. I have to do the same. But I'll be back, do you hear me?"

He nodded. I tugged him to me one more time, pressing a kiss against his dirty forehead.

I closed his door behind me and leaned back against the wall, grateful for the support. Covering my face with my hands, I tried to tell myself it would be better soon.

The left side of my face throbbed. I looked down at my bloody hands and the great red stains on my skirts and felt the dampness on my shoulder where Will had wept until he had no more tears.

How was I going to walk down the hall? I could barely stand.

"Miss Gramton?"

A nurse stood before me. "Come with me, dear."

She put an arm around my shoulder and led me to a new room, where she helped me undress and bathed me like a child. When she'd finished fastening my soft, loose gown, she called for the doctor. Once he was sure my jaw hadn't been broken by the duke's fist, he gave me a draught for the pain. As he turned to leave, I put a hand on his arm.

"Please," I said. "How is Lord Verras?"

"He's sleeping."

That wasn't enough. "I saw the cut. I didn't think it was deep, but now I'm not sure—"

"It wasn't deep, though it did cut into muscle. The only concern now is infection." The doctor smiled. "You did a fine job, stopping the blood. I'm not worried for him." He gestured toward the bed. "You should sleep as well."

"I have to see Will."

"I'll walk you there." He held out his arm as if I were a fine lady. By the time we reached Will's room, I could barely stand.

Will lay huddled on his bed, clean, with new bandages on his foot. His cheeks were wet.

I sat beside him and he curled into me, his head on my belly. I swept his hair back from his forehead, the way his mother had, until he fell asleep.

The last thing I remembered was a nurse tucking a pillow behind me and covering me with a blanket.

"King Eldin wishes to see you if you're able, Miss Gramton."

The nurse helped me slip from beneath Will, who stirred but settled back into sleep.

As soon as we were in the corridor, I asked, "What time is it?"

"Past dark," she said. "You slept most of the day."

"And the king? How is he?"

"I've never seen anything like his hands. The doctors were able to set the right one, but I don't know about the left."

She led me to the king's private chambers. King Eldin lay in bed, resting against a bank of pillows. His bandaged hands lay on top of the blankets, and blood stained the bandage on his left hand. Lord Cinnan stood beside the bed, while a doctor and a nurse sat in the corner.

I curtsied. "Your Majesty."

The king looked chagrined, then tilted his head toward Lord Cinnan, who drew a chair beside the bed for me. "I'm afraid I am much too small for my title."

King Eldin looked very different from the first time I had seen him. There were deep circles under his eyes and he seemed a little feverish. Yet there was a steadiness to his gaze that I hadn't seen before.

"I think, *Your Majesty,* that your title fits you better than it ever did."

"Don't flatter me!" There was a touch of the old petulance in his voice, and I sat straighter in my seat. "I don't know what to do with myself, you see." He leaned forward. "What if I ruin things all over again?"

"I saw you stand strong before the duke, Your Majesty. I saw you refuse to give in. You acted like a true king. You can do it again and again and again."

He smiled, just a little.

Lord Cinnan drew near. "King Eldin wished to know how we should reward the champion of Reggen."

I sighed. "I feel I am much too small for that title."

The king laughed.

"As champion," said Lord Cinnan, "you were promised the princess's hand in marriage."

"If I had a younger brother—" began the king.

"Perhaps you would like to be appointed the royal tailor?" suggested Lord Cinnan.

"I've been told that such an arrangement was indelicate."

King Eldin shrugged. "I have seen my person, Miss Gramton." He studied his hands for a moment, his face sober. "I do not believe I would be a source of temptation."

In a heartbeat, I remembered Galen, and the flash of humor in his eyes when he told me not to discuss whether I'd ever been tempted.

Lord Cinnan's voice pulled me back to the present. "Lord Verras told us that you are—without family. The champion of Reggen should not be left destitute."

"Your Majesty, I hate sewing."

King Eldin was surprised. "But you have such talent."

"My father loved sewing more than anything in the world. He loved *his* sewing, more than anything in the world. Why would I love my competition?"

"Ah," said King Eldin, and I saw that he understood. I wondered what sort of man his brother had been. "We shall see you married, then, to a nobleman worthy of your courage. If Galen were not already betrothed, I would have you marry him."

I nearly cried.

"If it is mine to ask, Your Majesty, I would like to have a place in the castle, and to come and go as I please. I should like to be given to *myself,* and not handed off to some nobleman."

King Eldin's eyes grew wide.

"For at least a year, couldn't I have a little corner somewhere? I might become so cheerful that I don't mind picking up a needle and thread again."

Lord Cinnan stood. "Thank you, Miss Gramton. The king will reward you soon. Now you should rest."

He walked me to the door.

I had to ask. "How is Lord Verras? The last time I saw him—"

"Why don't you see for yourself?" Lord Cinnan motioned to a guard. "Take the champion to Lord Verras's room. If he is awake, she may see him."

I followed, almost dizzy with the worry and hope of seeing Galen again. The guard knocked quietly, then leaned in to speak to someone inside. He held the door open.

Galen was propped up in his bed, his head resting back against the wall. He smiled and I released the breath I didn't even know I'd been holding.

"Saville." His voice was strong and steady. "Come, sit."

His shirt was open at the throat and I could see the bandages across his chest and shoulder underneath. They were mostly white, but I thought I saw spots of red bleeding through.

"Even you would have approved of the doctor's work. He put in a row of even stitches." He pulled back the left side of his shirt, revealing the bandages underneath.

I was right: there was blood.

"Saville."

He'd bled all over my gown and I'd hardly blinked, but somehow seeing the blood on those bandages—

"Saville!"

I finally met his gaze.

 343

"You've gone pale."

I wanted to rest my head on his uninjured shoulder and feel his arm steal around me. If I couldn't do that, I wanted to act as though I didn't mind that his falcon bride would come soon.

I could do neither.

I thought of how I must look to him: a girl with hair that barely reached her shoulders, eyes red from crying, face swollen and bruised. A girl who blushed and grew pale and blushed again.

"Saville?"

And then I was talking, just to say anything. "Will's father is dead. I waited with Will at the fountain as the captives came into the city."

"That doesn't mean—"

I shook my head. "A man came to us. . . . Will's father sent him."

Galen closed his eyes. "How is he?"

"He's asleep. I stayed with him."

"You need to rest, too."

"You can't tell me what to do anymore!" It sounded defiant, but how it hurt to say. I didn't mind Galen telling me what to do. At least, I didn't mind fighting about it. And I knew I was being unreasonable and childish.

Galen held my gaze, even though he was confused and weary and more than a little angry. Finally, he said, "I never could tell you what to do. Why would I start now?"

For one moment, I understood why the duke had hidden his heart.

344

I looked down at Galen, saw the curve of his neck disappearing into the bandages, noticed how still he lay. I'd seen illness press the Tailor into bed the same way.

It gave me just enough safety to risk everything. Because, once you do it, you can keep doing it again and again and again.

"I love that you let me ask questions, but still tell me to be quiet when you're thinking."

The sudden change startled him, but I saw something spring to life behind his eyes. I leaned forward and gestured toward the bedside table, already messy. "I love that you don't care whether your desk is covered with papers or books. I love that you were the only person brave enough to carry Will inside the gates, and that you stood between us and the crowd. I love that you would still swim in the Kriva. I love that you didn't know what to do when I thanked you that first day in your rooms."

Galen looked completely bewildered. I leaned even closer, and dropped a featherlight kiss on the corner of his eye, the place that crinkled when he smiled.

He grew still, so still.

"I love the way you look at me, Galen Verras."

I put my hand to his face. His jaw fit perfectly in my palm. I kissed him again, ever so lightly, on his mouth, and pulled away so that he could see me, swollen face and overflowing eyes.

Crying shows your soft spot, that piece of your heart the armor can't cover.

Just this once, I wouldn't hide it.

 345

I looked Galen full in the face, and found the courage I needed. "I love you."

His hand closed around my wrist. Then he turned his head to press a kiss against my palm. But he was sad, so very sad. "I—"

I shook my head. "It's my turn. You said it earlier, and I won't let you be the only one. I love you. I know that you'll be going to your falcon lady or that she'll be coming here, and it makes me wish there was still a war with the giants so I could just . . . hit something. I wish I could have fought with you tonight and walked away after it." I swallowed. "But that would have been too easy."

Then I twisted my wrist in his grasp, just as he and done to me. He was weak enough that he had to let me go. I stood and stepped away from the bed.

"Saville." Galen looked at me like I was velvet and silk all in one, like he never wanted to stop looking. "I wish . . . "

I took another step back. "You are the finest man I've ever known. You are the story that was true, even if you aren't mine. I wanted you to know. I wanted you to hear me say it."

I turned and left, knowing he wouldn't be able to follow.

Chapter 42

Still, I listened for Galen as I walked to Will's room. I listened for his footsteps. For his voice.

I didn't hear a thing.

"The boy kept asking for you," the nurse told me when I reached Will's room. "The doctor gave him another draught, so he'll sleep a while yet."

I sat on the bed beside him. He stirred and turned toward me. His mouth was half-open, and he snored softly.

The nurse blew out one of the candles and reached for the other.

"Please leave it," I told her. If Will woke, I wanted there to be some light.

The dim was comforting and Will's presence was comforting, so when the tears started, I didn't try to stop them.

I'd thought Galen would come after me. I didn't know it until then.

I told myself I was glad I'd told him everything. And I was.

I told myself he was doing the honorable thing. And he was.

 347

I still felt as if I'd been broken open. I fell asleep clinging to the memory of his jaw against my palm, his lips under mine.

How different it was to walk through the castle the next day! Servants I didn't know nodded to me. Those who spoke to me called me Miss Gramton, and whispers followed me like the train of a gown.

I found Lord Cinnan in the corridor outside the king's suite.

"How is the king?" I asked.

"He insisted on meeting with me this morning. He dictated messages for his allies, explaining all that had happened. I have already given them to riders. I'm proud of him." He paused as if weighing something. "He asked to see you."

I waited, knowing he hadn't said everything he intended.

After a moment, Lord Cinnan whispered, "The doctors are worried. . . ."

"Can I see him?"

Lord Cinnan nodded and opened the door. "Your Majesty, Miss Gramton is here."

"Good! I would like to talk to her about a coat. . . ."

I glanced at Lord Cinnan, who shook his head. Princess Lissa sat beside her brother's bed. She nodded at me as I joined her, her face drawn.

King Eldin was flushed. His eyes shone with fever and looked all the brighter for the shadows that hollowed his cheeks.

He squinted up at me. "I forgot, Miss Gramton. You don't sew anymore, do you?"

Sky above. "I might make an exception for you, Your Majesty."

"What do you suggest? And why didn't you bring your fabric?"

I looked down at the bed, uncertain, and saw the king's left hand. The stained bandages smelled like meat that had been left too long in the sun.

I looked at Princess Lissa, horrified.

"Don't feel bad, Miss Gramton," said King Eldin. "I forgive the mistake. Just bring the fabric next time." For a moment, his eyes cleared, and he whispered. "I'm glad you came."

"I am, too." I forgot to keep my voice even. "Don't worry about the coat, Your Majesty. I'll begin right away."

"The doctors will have to take his hand," said Lord Cinnan, once we'd left the king. "They're preparing right now. If they can catch it fast enough . . ."

I nodded.

"Lord Verras is healing well, though," said Lord Cinnan. "He's still sleeping and shows no sign of fever."

I wondered how much he knew.

"I need to leave the castle for a little. I want to see Volar."

He raised his eyebrows. "You shouldn't walk alone in the city. You might be mobbed yet. But . . . you may walk along the

 349

ramparts with Princess Lissa and me this afternoon. She must give Volar a message from the king."

"Thank you," I breathed.

"You are easily pleased," he said. "The king mentioned you this morning as he dictated orders. His fever was not so strong then. There's a set of rooms on the east side of the castle. You can see the Kriva and the East Guardian from its balcony. You'll be moved there today."

"And Will? He shouldn't be alone right now."

"He can move to a small room adjoining yours."

"Thank you. It's very kind of the king."

"Don't be silly. It would be exhausting to calculate what is owed right now. That sort of arithmetic would break the mind of the best mathematician."

Two hours later, Lord Cinnan, the princess, and I stood on the ramparts over the gates. The soldiers shifted uneasily. But the sadness I'd felt in the castle rolled from me.

I loved the wind up on the wall, the way it tugged at my hair and my skirt. It was like a child begging to be noticed. And what a world to be noticed! The Kriva, with its throaty murmur, swept along below us, and the giant camp no longer terrified me.

I leaned against the wall, hands on the rough stone, and studied the camp. The duke's tent had been removed, as had the pens. But something else had changed. I supposed it was

the way the giants moved. There was no tension, no readi-
ness to leap into a fight. The giants walked between rows of
tents the way people walked down the streets of Reggen, arms
swinging, stopping to talk with friends.

And there was singing. I couldn't understand the words,
but the melody reminded me of the land Volar had described:
mountains rising out of the ocean, stately halls carved into
mountainsides, silver in the moonlight.

At Lord Cinnan's signal, one of the guards blew a com-
plex series of notes on a horn. Soon, Volar strode toward us and
stopped at the gates. We were level with his forehead.

Princess Lissa curtsied. "I greet you, King Volar, in the
name of King Eldin. My brother wished to come himself, but
he is not well enough."

Volar nodded solemnly. I walked away so that they could
speak in private. I didn't mind. It gave me time to listen to the
giants' song. It had changed, and I would have sworn by the
ebb and rush of the melody that it was about the sea.

I was so engrossed that Lord Cinnan had to call me back.

"I was listening to the song," I explained. "It's lovely. Is it
about the sea, Volar?"

He nodded. "The ships that travel the sea, yes. How did
you know?"

"I could hear it." I leaned over the edge of the wall.

Volar thought a moment. "Would you like to hear more? I
will take you to them."

"I'm not sure that would be wise, Miss Gramton," said

Lord Cinnan. "If anything should happen . . . The city is still distrustful."

I glanced at Volar. "Then perhaps it will help the city to see the champion in the camp."

Lord Cinnan scowled. "I can't guarantee your safety."

"I can," said Volar. "I will."

I leaned over the wall. "I'll be down in a minute."

"Why?" he asked, raising his hands level with the wall.

I grinned at Lord Cinnan.

"No. Absolutely not, Miss Gramton!"

But I was already hoisting myself up. Lord Cinnan had no choice but to lend me a steadying hand. I let the wind tangle itself in my hair as I listened to the giants' song.

Then I looked back over my shoulder. Princess Lissa stood straight and tall, the wind pulling at her skirts, her eyes hungry. I remembered how much she'd wanted to join Galen and me on the ramparts. "Come with me."

She stood even straighter, as if she couldn't even consider something so irresponsible. Then she smiled slowly, gathered her skirts, and joined me on the wall's edge.

Volar's hands caught us up, and he carried us across the Kriva.

I visited the giant camp many times over the next week. They were joyous trips in an otherwise dark time. King Eldin's fever lingered even after the doctors removed his hand. The castle halls grew quiet, and subdued servants whispered as they went about their duties.

One afternoon, I sat beside King Eldin and sang the songs I'd learned from the giants. They had a wildness to them. I hoped the melodies reminded the king of sunshine and wind and the sound of water.

But he remained quiet in his bed.

"I think it helps him," said the princess. She'd been busy attending to the affairs of Reggen, yet she still sat with her brother every day.

"It helps *me*."

The princess slid a slender finger into her book to mark the page. "Galen left his sickroom today."

My breath knotted in my throat. "Oh?"

She made an impatient sound and tossed her book onto a nearby table. "Did you really think I hadn't noticed? Or that I'd scold you? At least Galen trusts me enough to ask about you."

"He does?"

She smiled, and was kind enough not to make me ask. "I told him you were well. That you play with Will. You read to me. You're sewing a coat for Eldin. . . ." Her voice faltered as she looked down at her brother. "That surprised him."

I turned back to the work in my hands. "I thought it would be easier, this past week, not seeing him. I thought I'd grow used to it."

Lissa waited.

"How is he?" I asked.

"About the same, I think. He's spoken with Lord Cinnan every day. There's a great deal of work waiting for him." She paused, and I knew the words pained her. "And, Saville, there's Lady Farriday waiting for him, too. That hasn't changed."

I didn't even try to hide the hurt. "I didn't think it would."

I saw Galen almost every day the next week, often from a distance. He was recovering well, though he favored his left side and walked a little slower.

Every time I saw him, I felt again how deeply I missed our time together. I missed his silences, when he was lost to his thoughts. I missed our arguments—I'd never had a better or kinder opponent. I even missed the patchwork chair in his room.

Speaking with him was even worse. The few conferences in which I reported all that happened in the giant camp, a chance meeting in a corridor, or visiting the king when Galen was there—it was like leaving his room all over again.

Every time I felt the grief rise, I reminded myself that I hadn't told him how I felt so that he'd choose me. I couldn't hate him because he was betrothed.

I couldn't hate him anyway.

Chapter 43

We were certain of King Eldin's improving health two weeks after the duke's death. Volar had announced that the giants would soon be returning to their home, but the king's recovery meant that we would have a true celebration. For days, humans and giants alike worked to raise a pavilion where the duke's tent had once stood.

Uten and humans would not be able to mingle much—Lord Cinnan had wisely pointed out that we couldn't have people wandering through the giant camp. If a giant didn't look where he stepped, the results would be disastrous. But there would be opportunities for the city to meet the giants. Though much had changed since the *uten* first arrived, the people of Reggen still feared the giants, and some giants still flinched when they heard a human voice.

Already, some of King Eldin's riders had returned. Many were accompanied by representatives who wished to see the giants for themselves.

Will told me the night before the celebration that King Eldin had hired troubadours to tell the tale, from my meeting with the giant scouts to the duke's overthrow. "Do you think they'll have an actor for me, too?"

I looked up from the king's new coat. "Who told you this?"

"Lord Verras. Just that troubadours would tell the story. He didn't say who would play me." Will stopped, and by the set of his mouth I knew he was thinking about the pens. "I don't think I want to see all of it."

I began another buttonhole. "Neither do I."

I couldn't imagine anything more horrifying than seeing my role in the story played out before me. How could they explain why I had dressed as a lad? No one would understand why I ran out to the scouts if they did not know Will.

And the giants! Sky above, the giants. The citizens of Reggen would cheer when the tailor outwitted the scouts. But what would the *uten* think, knowing the scouts would return to the duke and their deaths?

"Lord Verras said not to worry. I like him. Sometimes I sit in his rooms and tell him all the things that Pa could fix."

Will picked up a tool he'd collected from somewhere in the castle and turned it over in his hands. "Do you miss him?" he whispered.

I froze, the needle inches above the fabric. Of course Will would guess the truth.

He looked up. "Do you miss the Tailor? Because I miss Pa."

"Oh, Will . . . the Tailor wasn't like your pa. You know that," I said.

But Will peered up at me expectantly.

I set the coat down in my lap. "When I was little, I used to imagine the Tailor acting like your pa." *He'd compliment the seam I sewed. He'd hug me close. He'd just . . . look at me.* "And that's what I miss: everything I wish he had done."

The things the Tailor hadn't done were an emptiness inside me that oceans couldn't fill. And what was I supposed to do with that? Grieve it? I had, since childhood. Fight it? There was no one left to fight.

The Tailor's ugliest piece of handiwork could not be undone.

That night, I waited until I heard Will's whiffling snore through the closed door. I changed into a simple, dark gray dress that would not draw attention when I went for a walk.

The guards knew me and let me pass, and I took the stairs up to the wall. The East Guardian rose above me, and the Kriva stretched out in the moonlight. I could see part of the giant camp and the fires that burned like red stars in the plain.

I closed my eyes and concentrated on the wind that brushed my hair against my cheek. Galen—Lord Verras—wouldn't let the king commission inferior storytellers. That wasn't his way. He saw so much. He wouldn't let them tell the story in a way that would shame the *uten*.

Or me.

I rubbed my fingertips together, feeling the callouses from the sewing I'd vowed to give up. But it had seemed right to sew the new coat for King Eldin, and I knew, somehow, that

I would sew more. The skill was another inheritance from the Tailor that I could not ignore. That's what he'd left me: a few velvets, the skill to sew a straight seam, and a list of all I wished my father had done.

I thought of Mama, and how the Tailor had dashed her hopes, too. But it hadn't stopped her from making a life for me. From loving me.

I would claim that love as part of my inheritance, too.

I pulled in an unsteady breath and began to sing a tune the giants had taught me about sailing a ship in a storm when the waves are as high as mountains and the stars are hidden. I sang it until my breath came easily and the notes did not break.

The pageant day was clear, with a noon no longer blunted by summer heat. Volar, and the twenty *uten* he had chosen to attend him, stood at one end of the pavilion. The king, princess, Lord Verras, Will, and I sat opposite them, joined by some of the leaders who had returned with King Eldin's riders.

The other two sides were filled with people from Reggen who had chosen seats there at dawn when the gates opened.

The ceremony began when King Eldin presented the high king with fist-sized portions of Gantaran amber. He hoped it would be new to the mountain-breaker. He also gave the giants a great herd of cattle—food for their long journey home now that the whale meat was gone.

All the while, I could feel myself pulled tight as a bow-string. Finally, the moment arrived.

"Ladies and gentlemen, *uten*!" called the first of the singers, a man dressed in black. "We present the story of the tailor of Reggen and the high king of Belmor."

I waited for the actors in bright clothes, the troubadours with their instruments—people who would take the story and twist it into something simple and easy to understand.

Instead, Hylag stepped forward and sat cross-legged beside the man. He began to sing of the home the *uten* had left behind. Of mountains and seas and truth in stone. The tempo changed, and he sang of the duke's arrival, how he challenged their warriors and survived.

When he stopped, his human companion picked up the tale. He sang about me and of the Tailor's illness. I didn't mind hearing my story in his mouth. He didn't try to make the tale anything that it was not.

So the story shifted back and forth between the man and Hylag, and as I listened, I saw the wisdom in it. Reggen needed to know that they hadn't routed an army of monsters, though there had been monsters. And perhaps the *uten* could better understand why I had done what I had. It was not easy to hear the story, but it would have been far more painful had it been altered.

When the song was finished, there was a great, slow silence. Many were crying, even some of the *uten*. Then applause began among the humans and *uten* alike. The giants cheered and stamped their feet until the ground danced beneath ours, and Volar had to tell them to stop.

When King Eldin stepped into the center of the pavilion, silence spread once again. The left cuff of his new coat was pinned up, and I felt a rush of pride that he hadn't tried to hide what had happened. He bowed low to Volar before speaking.

"I could speak of the past, how our people worked to build this city, and how their own selfishness caused them to part ways. But I want to praise what has happened. There could have been more deaths, more loss. I am grateful that this war was stopped."

Volar bowed in return.

King Eldin continued, "We know you must return home soon. We send you with our best wishes and hopes that our ambassadors may join you in the spring."

The crowd cheered.

The king went on to outline what little provision he and Reggen's allies could provide for the *uten's* trip. Then he said, "When the duke's messenger arrived, I acted like a frightened boy. I promised my sister to a champion who could defeat the giants. And when I heard shouts from the street that someone *had* defeated the giants, I didn't try to confirm the rumors. I wasted no time. I declared that person champion and awarded him my sister's hand in marriage."

The king looked around. "It was the most fortunate mistake of my life. I cannot take any credit for what followed."

He extended a hand toward me. Galen pushed me to my feet and made me stand. The humans applauded. The giants stamped their approval until both the king and I could hardly stand.

"The champion of Reggen—"

"—and the *uten*," added Volar.

"—and the *uten*," continued the king, "requested a small corner of the castle as a reward. But it does not seem enough."

The king looked toward me and smiled. Grinned, actually. Galen was shaking his head, trying to say something, but King Eldin continued. "I could not give Saville my sister's hand in marriage, but it seemed only fitting that she should marry close."

I turned to Princess Lissa, who looked at me, eyes blazing with—I couldn't place it. And then Galen was waving his hands, telling the king to stop.

But the king did not. "It is my pleasure to give Saville my cousin Galen Verras."

I dropped back to my seat, amid roars of approval, wondering what horrible mistake the king had made. Sky above, Galen had been trying to tell the king to stop, and now—

Galen bent over me, eyes frantic, trying to tell me something. But I couldn't hear him over the roar. I buried my face in my hands and waited for the furor to stop.

"*Hylag!*" I could barely make out Galen's bellow, but Hylag's hearing was far better than mine. The next moment, he'd plucked Galen and me into the air. It took him a while to pick his way through the human crowd, but once he had cleared it, he strode out along the Kriva until all that could be heard was a low hum. Then he set us down and walked a few steps away. He stood with his back to us, arms crossed, as if guarding our privacy.

We stood there, Galen and I, only a few feet from each other. I forced myself to look at him. He seemed miserable. And I could barely hold all the pieces of me together. Was this how the king had felt with his broken hands? That any touch, no matter how light, would undo him?

Galen straightened his shoulders. "Saville, I'm sor—"

"Don't apologize to me, Galen Verras! Don't you dare."

He shook his head. "Let me—"

"And I don't want you to explain. You don't have to. I already know he's a genius at bungling wedding announcements. Please." I stepped away, backing toward the trees. "Have Hylag take you back and tell the king—"

"You want me to tell Eldin *no*?"

I shook my head. "I want you to fix this!"

Galen closed the distance between us before I could finish. He took me by the shoulders. "Saville, I *told* Eldin to—"

"You told him?" I asked.

He nodded.

I jerked away and slapped him. Slapped him so hard my fingers tingled. "I told you I loved you weeks ago! I cried— *cried*—every night. Do you know what it's been like to walk through the castle with a hurt I can't hide? To know that people

362

are talking about me? Everyone talking except the one person I wanted to speak to most of all? For weeks! And then you *finally* decide to do something about it? In front of everyone?"

He just stood there while I shouted at him, my tears making my voice crack. He was angry: mouth thin, eyes hard.

"Twenty days."

I wiped at my wet cheek with the back of my hand. "What?"

"Twenty days. You told me you loved me twenty days ago, and twenty days ago, I asked the king to release me from my betrothal. Eldin wrote Lord Farriday the next morning."

I pointed, like an idiot, toward the distant crowd, toward the princess who had looked at me so strangely. "But Lissa said—"

"She was right. Lord Farriday replied by his fastest messenger. And refused. He made clear that the other noble families were committed to enforcing the betrothal by force, if necessary."

My heart dropped. "Then why did the king . . . Why did you—?"

"It was Lissa. She replied on Eldin's behalf, when he was so sick. Not even Lord Cinnan knew. She wrote that since an army of giants considered me an ally, it would be unwise for Lord Farriday to attack. And she suggested an exchange."

I stared at Galen, too bewildered to speak.

"The princess of Reggen instead of a third son. To any young noble they chose."

They never ask me. . . .

 363

I tasted salt on my lips, but I didn't bother to wipe my eyes.

"She told Eldin and me this morning, when the messengers arrived with Farriday's consent. She said it was her choice. That her mother would have been pleased with the match. And that yours would have been, too. I thought—*hoped* . . ."

His voice trailed off and he grimaced, so embarrassed that I almost smiled.

He blew out a breath and pushed on. "I told Eldin not to say a word, that I'd hardly talked to you these last weeks. He was supposed to let me tell you. Ask you, I mean." He waved a hand toward the crowd, still not daring to meet my eyes. "But he didn't, of course! I could strangle him! I don't care if he's been ill. It would make it that . . . much . . . easier . . ."

He shook his head and looked down. "I didn't plan for it to be this way."

I put my hand gently to Galen's face, wincing to see how it fit over the red mark I'd left there. He finally met my eyes, wary at first, as if I'd order him away. But I didn't.

I couldn't.

Galen held my gaze one moment . . . and another. Then he smiled at me, the way he'd smiled on the ramparts, the way he'd smiled in the caves. He turned his head, just a little, and kissed my palm.

"Will you have me?" he whispered.

I had imagined Galen asking me so many times. But I'd never expected it. Not once. And certainly not *here*, in the real world, in the sunlight, with Hylag standing behind us, and Galen looking like home and laughter and—

"I love you," he said. "Please, say you'll have me."

I swallowed. "But you told the king to stop. You—"

He laughed and slipped an arm around me, pulling me close. When I looked up at him, he dropped a kiss on my nose.

"You silly"—he kissed the corner of my eye, right where I had kissed him—*he did remember*—"silly"—on my cheek, right by my ear—"girl."

He leaned back to see me, as if he couldn't look enough. "I wanted to ask you first, not ambush you in front of everyone."

"Yes."

"Yes?"

"Ye—" He kissed me before I could finish the word. Kissed me as if he'd been waiting as long as I had, maybe longer. He was as insistent as the wind on the castle walls, as fierce as the melody of a giant's song. He kissed me until the ground danced beneath my feet and I stumbled. Galen just pulled me closer and murmured, "Hylag!"

I looked up. Hylag continued to stomp, beating the ground a few more times. Galen shook his head. Then a small earthquake reached us.

Hylag looked at us over his shoulder. "Volar is happy."

Galen laughed, then sat down against a tree and tugged me down to his side, wincing only a little. "Just in case there's more stomping."

I was tucked close to him, my head resting on his chest. "I could hardly see straight after the draught they'd given me. But the moment you closed the door, I got out of bed," Galen said.

"I didn't hear you."

He grinned. "You were listening?"

I rolled my eyes. "It was an awful night when you didn't come."

"I went to Eldin. Stumbled in the door—the doctors were happy about that, of course. I told him that if he wanted me to stay in Reggen, he'd better act like a proper king and arrange things. It was horrible to just wait for news. I wanted to go to you a thousand times."

"And then Lissa set everything right," I whispered.

Galen pressed a kiss into my hair, and I rubbed my cheek against his coat. Velvet.

Please, I thought, *let him be a good man, whoever they choose.*

"Eldin wants to make me ambassador," Galen said.

"Really?" I craned my head to look at him. "To one of the other River Cities?"

He shook his head, a smile pulling the corners of his mouth. I kissed the corner nearest me, just because I could.

Galen's smile widened, and he kissed me back, not on the corner of my mouth.

"I'm to be ambassador to the *uten.* We could go to Belmor in the spring. Would you like that?"

366

I thought of the halls under the mountains, the great ships that sailed the sea. "You *did* say that you see better with me."

He chuckled. "It only makes sense that the champion of Reggen should be the first to visit the high king in his hall."

"I'm not the champion."

"The tailor, then?" I heard the smile in his voice.

"Just Saville," I whispered.

My second day in the castle, Princess Lissa told the king she didn't want to marry the duke. She said she didn't want giants to dance at her wedding.

Neither of us could have known that they would dance at mine.

The day I married Galen, giants danced until the ground shook and the willows by the Kriva swayed. Only a dance that wild and strong could match our joy. In a week, they would take Galen and me back to Belmor. We would greet the high king, and he would call me Hillock the way he always had. We would walk the halls beneath the mountains, hear the truth in stone, and see stars over rough seas. Will, who walked with only a slight limp, would come with us.

Reggen still sings the songs about the champion, the brave tailor—though I can't help laughing to hear such words describe me. I was not so brave, and there were other champions that summer morning. Perhaps, time will wear away our names until we are as blurry as the Guardians and no one can remember where we came from. But for those who wish to know, this is everything that happened.

This is the story that is true.

Acknowledgments

Everyone in these pages deserves thank-you *books*, and all I have are sentences. But just because I can't thank everyone properly doesn't mean I shouldn't try. So, thank you to . . .

My rock-star agent, Tracey Adams. What a fierce advocate and comfort you've been!

All the wonderful people at Egmont Publishing, who made me and *Valiant* look better than I ever could have on my own.

My editor, Alison Weiss. Thank you for answering all my questions, and asking the perfect ones in return. Your insights and encouragement made *Valiant* the story I always hoped it would be.

My amazing Slushbuster critique group—Stephanie, Michelle, Joan, Alison, Lisa, and Bridget. You ladies raised me as a writer these past nine years. The Turbo Monkeys crit group—Amy, Kristen, Hazel, Julie, Marilyn, Ellen, and Craig. Your feedback and support meant so much. And where would I be without my LYLP ladies, who listened to my silliness and walked me through the long days of writing and selling a novel?

The 2010–11 Nevada SCBWI Mentor Program, run by Ellen Hopkins and Suzanne Williams and hosted by the wonderful Nevada writing community. Harold Underdown, who chose me as one of his mentees! I took everything I learned about mushy middles and used it in *Valiant*. Thank you.

Patti Gauch, for teaching me how important it is to go far enough, and how I must always listen for my story's heartbeat. The people at Highlights, whose support and scholarships made my Patti workshops possible.

Thank you to all the agents and editors and authors at all the writing conferences who spent time with the tall, horribly nervous attendee. Thank you, bloggers (I'm looking at you, Janet Reid!), who made the industry less intimidating.

The WAHS teachers and administrators, who have been so ridiculously encouraging. And my students! (*All* of you—even the ones who think I'm not talking about them.) You make me laugh and work and think like no other job would. I'm lucky to be your teacher.

My dear ones in Brezik, thank you for your hospitality and strong coffee and never minding how badly I spoke Bosnian! I missed those afternoons swimming in the Krivaja so much that I had to put a river in *Valiant*.

My family, blood and otherwise. My characters get their best qualities and their funniest moments from you. Thank you for letting me ramble about people who (technically) never existed, for proofreading my manuscripts, and for never once doubting I could do this. I love you.

And in all this, there is God, who has swept me up into an amazing love, a timeless story.